Avenue of
Eternal Peace

Avenue of Eternal Peace

A NOVEL BY

NICHOLAS JOSE

A WILLIAM ABRAHAMS BOOK

DUTTON

DUTTON
Published by the Penguin Group
Penguin Books USA Inc., 375 Hudson Street,
New York, New York 10014, U.S.A.
Penguin Books Ltd, 27 Wrights Lane,
London W8 5TZ, England
Penguin Books Australia Ltd, Ringwood,
Victoria, Australia
Penguin Books Canada Ltd, 2801 John Street,
Markham, Ontario, Canada L3R 1B4
Penguin Books (N.Z.) Ltd, 182–190 Wairau Road,
Auckland 10, New Zealand

Penguin Books Ltd, Registered Offices:
Harmondsworth, Middlesex, England

Published by Dutton, an imprint of New American Library, a division of
Penguin Books USA Inc. Previously published by Penguin Australia Ltd.
Distributed in Canada by McClelland & Stewart Inc.

First Dutton Printing, March, 1991
10 9 8 7 6 5 4 3 2 1

 REGISTERED TRADEMARK—MARCA REGISTRADA

LIBRARY OF CONGRESS CATALOGING-IN-PUBLICATION DATA:
Jose, Nicholas, 1952-
   Avenue of eternal peace : a novel / Nicholas Jose.
      p. cm.
   "A William Abrahams book."
   I. Title.
   PR9619.3.J73A93   1991
   823—dc20

Printed in the United States of America   R00864 99067
Set in Garamond Light
Designed by Eve L. Kirch

PUBLISHER'S NOTE
This is a work of fiction. Names, characters, places, and incidents either are the
products of the author's imagination or are used fictitiously, and any resemblance
to actual persons, living or dead, events, or locales is entirely coincidental.

For some Chinese friends

Contents

Not that there are no ghosts
But that their influence becomes propitious
In the sound existence of a living man;
There is no difference between the quick and the dead,
They are one channel of vitality.

—LAO TZU

. . . a country so strange that not even the air had anything in common with his native air, where one might die of strangeness, and yet whose enchantment was such that one could only go on and lose oneself forever.

—FRANZ KAFKA

Perhaps I should tell the children
A tale.

—YANG LIAN

Avenue of
Eternal Peace

CHAPTER ONE

Crackers

1

The map under glass made no sense. Wally Frith fingered the wad of notes that Mrs. Gu had given him.

She had been all befuddled, bespectacled smiles at the airport, as they lugged his baggage through the frozen night in search of the car. Now, in the overheated room to which she had delivered him, she presented a different face. Perched uncompromisingly on the arm of a chair, she explained the forms that the Foreign Affairs Office required him to complete.

"Just tell me what to do," Wally obliged.

"No, no," she protested, as if it were unthinkable to tell anyone what to do. "I need eight passport photographs. Meanwhile you will be welcome to a banquet next week. Professor Doctor Frith, thank you."

She was gone before daylight broke, leaving him to study the map under glass on the table in front of him, his neck rucking the antimacassar of the sofa on which his body longed to doze. So this is China, he thought, reaching for the bottle of duty-free scotch and, on inspection of the bathroom, splashing his face with icy water that was unfit to drink. The mission for Day One was to procure eight passport photographs. As morning lightened he was lovingly lacing the old polished walking boots that in younger days had taken him over mountains in three continents. He opened the door, trekked carefully downstairs and stepped outside into a chilly draft of icy dust and soot that tickled his nostrils. There was no green thing in sight, only the gray sky suffused with silver brightness, liverish bricks and tiles, and slashes of scarlet woodwork on the old rooftops. The buildings of Peking Union Medical College, for three-quarters of a century China's leading teaching and research hospital, were moored like a fleet of galleons in the pale and frozen world. Wally pulled down the fur hat his White Russian colleague had bequeathed him, "from the old days," and marched forward.

When Mrs. Gu came next day he was able to supply her with eight photographs of a face-the-future foreigner in a greatcoat, against a painted backdrop of the Eiffel Tower insisted on by the photographer. It was a favorite choice of newlyweds.

"Why don't you sit down, Mrs. Gu?" said Wally warmly. "Would you like a cup of coffee?"

She waved her hands dismissively, perched as before, scribbling characters.

"I'd like to have a talk with you about what you people expect of a visiting professor at the Peking Union Medical College. I mean, I've got my research interests, and as you know there are some specialists in your institute I need to meet, but if there's anything extra you people would like of me . . ."

"You must help us," announced Mrs. Gu solemnly. "We want your advice. Our techniques are sometimes a little . . . backward. We will study you."

"Well I'm flattered, naturally. But I'm ready to make a more active contribution."

2

"We will research you," concluded Mrs. Gu, dealing out an array of ID cards.

He pointed at a calligraphic flurry embossed in gold. "What does this mean?"

"Serve the people!" she exclaimed with a hoot. Chairman Mao had said it. "I must apologize, Professor Doctor Frith, the Director of our Medical College is still in Chicago. Your welcome banquet will be delayed until after Spring Festival. Meanwhile you should get some rest."

Stowing further documents on her person, Mrs. Gu was on her way. As Wally saw her to the door, he reminded her that he hoped, on the auspicious occasion of the banquet, to be introduced to Professor Hsu Chien Lung, whose name he had mentioned in letters. Mrs. Gu gave a little grunt.

2

The days drew in as Chinese New Year approached and Mrs. Gu made no further contact. There was nothing to do but pick his way grumpily across the frozen mud to the canteen three times a day. It had been his own decision to come to China, subject to the College's readiness to issue an invitation, but after the stressful weeks before departure to find himself all of a sudden at a loose end made him uncomfortable. He felt cooped up, his curiosity mounting into restlessness, but at the College there was no one around; the rooms were empty and the doors were locked. He would angrily flick the pages of his Chinese textbooks and his guidebook, then slam them shut and go out exploring.

One evening, in thermal underwear and armed with map, he managed to find his way through a zigzag of alleyways to a recommended restaurant. The outside walls were as liverish as everything else, but through its doors came an irresistible hubbub. Large circular tables were packed with people whose eyes swam and faces flamed in the bliss of food and drink. He knew the mood—from Hong Kong, Boston, Sydney. Packed! He could hardly peel off his greatcoat without demolishing the pyramids of dishes piled to the brink of every table. A table for one, he asked. The waitress scowled. To eat alone on a feast day was a misfortune against nature; the unwieldy foreigner was immediately engulfed.

All about lay the trophies of jubilant and unabashed feasters: duck heads, fish spines, orange shrimp shells and waxy chunks of winter melon. Bottles and glasses clinked. Plates tipped rich fatty juices to the floor. Wally drank beer and his face flushed. Those around him passed little cups of fiery spirits and threw sweets. At the place of honor a bride in traditional jacket of red satin glowed like red wax beside her proud spotty bridegroom. Friends and relations stuffed themselves.

A member of the party placed a huge handful of sweets in front of the outsider, who beamed his thank-yous.

Then the man opposite drew his breath and stuck the tip of a penknife into his throat. When he pulled the knife away, the skin showed the merest dent; the blade had refused to penetrate.

"*Qigong*," he yelled and Wally applauded.

Taking upon himself the role of intermediary, another young man who spoke some English explained the theory and nature of "the breathing power." By exerting the *qi* it was possible to increase the body's resistance at a particular point. Wally asked where the man had learned the technique, and the intermediary translated, "from childhood!" When Wally asked if he would teach him, the man shook his head and laughed. "China's secret," he joked, meaning it. And the intermediary went on to list the feats of *qigong*: causing rain to fall on drought-stricken farmlands, making tumors wither, causing men to fly through the air. His young eyes glowed

4

with enthusiastic irony. When Wally asked his name, the young man said Ying, which means Eagle.

After another round of toasts and fire liquid the diners leaned back in their chairs like the fat pink pigs that symbolize prosperity. One of the fattest lost his balance and sank to the floor, pulling down a couple of dishes. A youth at another table got to his feet and blared a mad speech about Chinese heroes of today who would dare anything. Then he sprayed beer foam across the room onto a woman's bared shoulders and tempers flared into rowdy pitching of half-eaten buns and hurling of soda pop, and the staff joined in, shouting about law and order. It looked set for a brawl as Wally extricated himself. His head was whirling like a pinwheel, and the chaos made him euphoric, since outside was a gray wall, and another wall, and another wall, in mighty order; and a bottle, bouncing against him, smashed in his wake.

The street outside was dark except for a hazy emanation of sky through crisscross boughs. The cold nibbled at Wally's hot face, and he stumbled with a floating sensation, as if he were a pelican about to lift off. The bulky coat, the muffling darkness, the frozen air and the obscure shapes of frames and recesses had an essential Chineseness that he suddenly loved as he was enfolded by the long empty street. He took a few steps, and was fumbling with his clothing behind a tree trunk when the tree spoke.

"Where are you going?"

A pale moon of a face materialized.

"Uh!" sputtered Wally.

"Where are you going, sir? I am Eagle."

"Yes yes. Taking a leak—" No time to explain the idiom. He straightened his coat as Eagle led him by the arm towards a black and massive wall showing left and right through the gloom, lit here and there by dim balls of lamplight.

"The Forbidden City," said Eagle.

Under a stone bridge the moat lifted from its casing a huge ice block studded with frozen apple cores. Rising up in front like a giant overlord was the locked Gate of Divine Pride, as Eagle tugged Wally sideways around the bottom of the Palace wall. A burst of fireworks crazed the musty orange sky. Or were they explosions burning in Wally's head from icy blasts of oxygen? Eagle giggled oddly. Otherwise the silence was massive. The patched-together houses, dwellings of former petitioners to the Emperor, hung over the moat like stalactites. High over their heads a gatehouse bloomed. Nothing was as black as the wall.

Could this nocturnal wasteland really be the northern capital, navel of the universe, seat of Heaven's Mandate? Was it from here that astronomers threw nets across the sky, imperial gardeners produced blood-red peonies with golden stamens, hieratic opera singers electrified the air, women grew contorted for beauty, and men cut off their balls for power? Reverberated the gong to the limits of the four seas? Imperial puppets turned to clay . . . Born again as "Beijing" in the official romanization of New China's standard language, a tongue no one spoke, the city of ghosts had been repossessed by peasants, soldiers and officials rising to the surface of the great Chinese ocean. City of devastation, ring roads, high-rise and infernal dust, trial and error, whims put into praxis, it was a masterwork in the stripping of human dignity. Yet here at its heart was the other masterwork of Time waiting monumentally in shadow. Time's two masterworks, stripping down and building up. Wally peered in alcoholic reverie into the massive stony gloom that he and his companion followed like homunculi, until the silence was broken by the brassy wail of a lone tenor saxophone. A snake of sound crept from a crevice in the wall, growing from strange disharmony into something that he found impossibly familiar. He froze, as in a haunting, and began to moan in a flat baritone accompaniment, until the tune metamorphosed, and he was left mouthing the words

You-izz You-izz while the sax curled into oriental discords and was lost in the night. He welcomed the pressure of Eagle's arm through several layers of clothing. He disliked needless suspicion. Between cramped houses, and the suggestion of voices and moving forms, the path narrowed along the moat, and a few stars peeped through the overhead haze.

"Where are you going?" asked Eagle.

"Where are you taking me? I should be getting home. Do you know where we are?"

They crept like rats along the wall.

"If you want to see a demonstration of real *qigong*, I can take you to the Spring Festival fair."

"Now?"

"Please tell me your address and telephone."

They made a pact to meet again, like errant knights of the Shaolin temple, and, crossing a bridge, emerged abruptly into a lighted street that ran into the megalomaniac thoroughfare of Changan, the Avenue of Eternal Peace, where a taxi lay in wait.

3

Enforced Chinese idleness offered an alternative route to damnation. At home pressure of work, the ceaseless encounters with colleagues, staff and concerned persons, covered over his isolation. Here his only distractions were provided by the Chinese textbooks and the medical papers he had brought for reassessment, some sane, but mostly nutty stuff—excepting those marvelous papers of more than forty years ago by Hsu Chien Lung. To his surprise he found himself taking advantage of the half-price Happy Hour offered by a foreign hotel on New Year's Eve. He was sitting in a corner of the Western-style bar enjoying the raucous talk of a weary, informed group of expatriates when an American woman called to him.

"Hey, stop listening to our conversation. Or else come and join us!"

He moved over and they made room for him without interrupting their argument.

"Power is what it always was," a sharp English voice was saying, "only now they've hired a team of publicity consultants. The modern emperor gets no buzz from tiled pavilions, silk tat, dragon walls. He likes his court nice and modern—revolving restaurants on every skyline, a satellite station in the backyard, the secret police computerized and the nukes in place. It takes a lot of dollars. So the old boy's worked out his cozy charade of openness to keep the foreign payola rolling in. But cut my tongue out."

At which the chesty American woman exclaimed, "You mean you don't believe in the Reforms?" She was Dulcia, a script editor with Central TV. Once she had worked in the provinces educating the peasants with faith and care. She and her husband Cray had been drawn to repressive societies, he to the Soviet Union, she to China. She won out and they came to China as glossy, jogging, all-American specimens. When Cray moved on to Moscow, Dulcia decided to stay. She was like a queen bee in China, Liberty with a sweatband, offering the Chinese personal freedom at the end of her Yellow Brick Road. If she cried, sometimes, for a home, she clung to her belief that the only true home was in that magic land of being yourself.

Stirred by the woman's performance, and her tight cleavage on which, at that moment, he could have laid his head, Wally shouted for a round of drinks. The Englishman, whispering with cherry-red lips, leaned forward to ask what the newcomer was doing in China. Wally explained vaguely that he was on a research project, and the talk quickly turned to health and illnesses round the table.

"I'm not a general practitioner," Wally protested. But people never believed him. He asked the Englishman, Clarence, what he did.

"I am a camera," Clarence blinked. "Agency photographer. Can I have your number?"

"Hey, here's my card," said Dulcia jumping in. "You're new to Peking, hey Doc? I can introduce you to some people. There's a guy from Central TV, he's having an exhibition of his painting. He's doing some powerful stuff. Abstract. Real black. We still don't know whether the authorities will close it down."

The correspondent from *Der Spiegel*, Sabina, pricked up her ears.

"Let me know," said Wally.

"Sure. You should see the other side of Peking."

It was an initiation rite, and Wally let them tell him about China until it was late, and he was kissing people goodbye, shaking their hands, promising to see them again soon; as if he agreed to forget the past, which was not a subject for questions, and share only this disorientating present.

The Medical College was bleak on his return and his bare quarters even bleaker. The room attendant was slumped in front of the New Year's Eve television spectacular.

"It's no good working on New Year's Eve," said Wally, who went and got his duty-free. "Have a Scotch."

"Not allowed, not allowed!" The room attendant waved his hand decisively. Wally poured the boy a full glass and stumbled back to his room without turning the light on, opened the door to the balcony despite the cold, and spread his outsize body on the bed, his thoughts soaring and swooping as he blacked out.

He was woken by the sounds of military attack. In his dream he was darting from trench to trench in a sweat as sheets of light tore across the sky. Grabbing his greatcoat, he made his way to the balcony. The sky was flickering, the ground bubbling with light. In squeals, whistles and rat-a-tat, the New Year had come. Baskets of fireworks hoarded for this midnight were erupting across the city, not to end the world but in a wild celebration of renewal, as everyone exploded their banger, flew their golden phoenix, unfurled their rainbow dragon. The red sky smelled of burning chemicals and paper from repeated onslaughts of flame and sparkle, flak and glittering rain. All across China, for thousands of miles, as for centuries, the people marked a new beginning by waging war on their besetting demons, firing heaven with the flame powder they had invented. *Pao! Pao! Pao!* Wally chuckled like a kid. Tonight each spirit made its own spunky defiance. Nothing so evanescent, so futile, so satisfying—until he was forced to close the door and curtains and insert his earplugs, to regain his world of order and shut his eyes for rest, as the crackers continued.

4

Eagle took him as promised to the temple fair, where he saw a girl lie on a bed of nails while the huge stone slab on her stomach was smashed by her brother's repeated mallet blows; a young man ramming his head into a pile of bricks; the bare-bellied old father twirling like a propeller on a spear tip, flapping his wings like a bird, showing no mark afterwards where the spear end had pressed into naked skin; and other demonstrations of *qigong*. Preceded by invocations of energy, followed by moans and applause, the tricks of self-torture and self-mastery impressed Wally, revealing the long accumulation of body knowledge in those mountain people who came down to the cities to perform. The crowd roared for the toughest trick of all, when a man lies on a bed of nails and a truck drives over his body. It doesn't always work.

That evening he put on his jacket and tie for the welcoming banquet. The holiday was into its last days and a clutch of drowsy dignitaries gathered in the reception room to greet him. They smiled and bowed, and Mrs. Gu sloshed jasmine tea into mugs all round. Ash dropped into unemptied ashtrays, and alongside a calendar of Manhattan, pale in wintry light, wall charts exposed human anatomy. The place of honor beside Wally was held by Director Kang, a shiny-pated shapeless chap who laughed a lot. He was just back from Chicago, in Levi cords, running shoes and a sumptuous blazer, and he spoke with an East Coast drawl. In a speech larded with honorifics he said that the Medical College was a high-pressured place, and that they were all terribly busy and terribly expert. The Dean next to him in a Mao suit nodded furiously. Wally drank his bitter tea. He felt stodgy in his layers of underwear and wore a fixed grin, intrigued by the personal histories of the placid rosy faces around him.

"Well," said the Director, rubbing his hands, "the important business is ahead." Laughing, he led Wally to the banquet table.

Besides Director Kang, the Dean and Mrs. Gu, there was young Dr. Rong with sharp eyes and a high voice, and his wife Dr. Song, an earnest physiologist from Suzhou, China's city of beautiful girls, who was placed on Wally's right, and an old boy who bent his neck and hands to the table like a turtle.

Conversation did not come easily and, despite profligate speechifying, the banquet failed to click.

"We are greatly honored to have Professor Doctor Frith at our College," said the Director. "It is the first time in recent history that so distinguished a practitioner, so distinguished a scholar, has come among us for a whole year, to give so generously of his time and expertise. Professor Doctor Frith is acquainted with the great research institutes of the world. His own contributions in the field of oncology are too many and various to mention. It is our aim to make our own research center here at the Peking Union Medical College the leader in China and an equal everywhere. With Frith's help we will achieve this aim. We have a Chinese saying . . ."

The words slipped down with as much oil as the stir-fried fish. Wally's mind was on the strongman feats he had seen at the fair. He imagined a naked man on a bed of nails, the crowd roaring ambiguously as the wheels ground over him. But he brought himself back to the fish he was squeezing with his chopsticks, and stood to reply.

"In our search for cures, we seek know-how. In our search for know-how, we seek understanding," he said. "China has many secrets, and many of her secrets are the secrets of nature. Now China is opening, perhaps she will open nature to us in a new way, and give us knowledge that so far eludes us. That is what we may achieve in working together."

To talk in riddles was easier than to talk straight. The more his hosts smiled their assent, the more skeptical they probably were.

The old turtle, however, bobbed his head in Wally's direction.

"I'm sorry. I didn't catch your name. You're—" said Wally in a wild leap, "not Professor Hsu, are you?"

"No, no." The man's eyelids lowered behind his glasses in polite demurral. "I am Zhou."

"Been here long?"

"More than forty years."

Wally did his sums to discover that the old boy was in place before Liberation. Probably he had been labelled a Rightist. There was something battered, indomitable, about him. But you never could tell.

"Do you know Professor Hsu? You must have known him."

"There are many people called Hsu."

"Hsu Chien Lung." Wally grabbed a pen to write it.

"That's not how we romanize now. The name would perhaps be Xu Qianlong. I'm not sure."

12

"But you know him?"

"I'm not sure," concluded the turtle, his tongue flickering towards a little glass of wine before his head retreated inside its shell.

Wally looked up, and caught Mrs. Gu watching him, before he turned to the serious Suzhou woman, who immediately asked him a technical question about mensuration. Could he help her? She was experimenting on pigs.

"Of course, of course." As far as he could see, her experiment had inadequate controls. "You don't know a Hsu Chien Lung, do you?" Another stab in the dark.

"Hsu Chien Lung?" The woman's voice rose quizzically, did not descend.

Kang made a last speech, assuring the visitor that his contribution and cooperation would be greatly appreciated, and that if he could arrange solid assistance to be transferred to the College from abroad he would be a true friend. In reciprocity, Kang acknowledged, the visitor's research could only benefit from free and open contact with his colleagues in the College. Wally showered the Director with thanks.

On the way out he also spread some thanks Mrs. Gu's way. "Professor Hsu Chien Lung was unable to make it, I guess. I'm sorry not to meet him. I was counting on him being here. Don't forget, Mrs. Gu, I'm longing to meet him." He pushed his palms forward to press the point.

"Aha, aha," said Mrs. Gu as she led him down the stairs by his sleeve. "We will talk on the telephone."

5

"You better tell me exactly what you want," said Mrs. Gu behind her standard-issue specs. "And you better wear more clothes."

Wally was rugged up like a dumpling already. The clothes,

in any case, didn't stop the flu. He told Mrs. Gu that colds and flu were caused by viruses. His fingers were white and numb as he tried to wiggle them. He was cramped beside the set-up tea table, the spilling ashtray, the slimy spittoon. Mrs. Gu was at least compactly wrapped in knitted long johns and spencers beneath her serge suit. Was she malignant or benign? He could not decide.

"You better tell me exactly what you want"—which he silently footnoted: so you can tell me just what you're refusing.

"I had hoped you would arrange a meeting with Professor Hsu Chien Lung," Wally stated unequivocally.

"We do not know this name."

She had the face of a kindergarten child glowing with the consciousness of power. Power, he was learning, meant the withholding of information.

"Perhaps I'm pronouncing it wrong. Hsu Chien Lung. Xu Qianlong. I'm afraid I don't know the characters or the tones. He's a professor at your College here. An old, old, very distinguished gentleman."

"There must be some mistake."

"Perhaps he is dead," wondered Wally.

But she made no attempt to leap at this offering. "No one of that name is dead."

"You must know who I mean. I've read his papers. I've written to him. He's based in this place."

Mrs. Gu's calm became a shade less congenial. "Please look again, Doctor Frith. There is no such person."

"There is no Professor Hsu?" he repeated incredulously. An accusation was not appropriate. "There is no Professor Hsu," he repeated, his face twisting.

Mrs. Gu laughed, as if the visitor had just confessed to her satisfaction that he did not believe in Santa Claus.

14

CHAPTER TWO

Towards the Not Yet

1

The mirror reflected, undisguised by make-up, the lines etched round Jin Juan's eyes by a cruel climate. Her family name meant "gold," aristocratic descent, her given name meant "graceful." Neither mattered now. Her home was a bare dormitory room that she shared with another woman who, luckily, was seldom there. She turned thirty next year. Perhaps then people would stop their questions and comments, since to conventional wisdom she would be squarely on the shelf. A Chinese can endure because she must, a great strength when there's no choice; but Jin Juan was nearing the point where she could no longer tolerate, ignore, suffer, turn a blind eye. She brushed out her hair, thought better of display, and tied it in a pony-tail. Should she copy her friends and cut it? She untied the ribbon and her hair floated defiantly over her shoulders and curving neck. She used lipstick, her body was perfumed. She stood to slip on her high heels, woolly scarf and essential down jacket. In the small mirror, by the light of the desk lamp, she could not see herself properly. Mirror, make-up, she packed away, leaving only a neat stack of books on the benchtop, the bedroll straightened. She shivered. The room was cold, the window-pane black and uncovered.

Unsteady in her heels, she walked out through dark twisting lanes, pleased to be clean and pretty. She took the middle of the road through thawing black snow. Traffic was thinning as farmers sold off the last of their greens and headed home to manured fields where more seedlings grew. As she reached the crossroads, the New Age sign flashed off in the very moment she noticed it. There had always been a New Age, but nobody could say for sure whether it had passed or was to come. The phrase suggested infinite deferral. Her throat tickled with a laugh. She was drawn forwards to reliable pleasures in which lay enough hope (sheer delusion) to get by on, while knowing better that it was backwards and she should break free. As she walked by on the way to her regular appointment, taking her usual road, past the switched-off neon light, drawn metal blinds and locked doors, behind which people sat on chrome chairs sipping fancy drinks, a cartman passed whispering of home to his horse.

2

The New Age Bar was the first spot in the capital where Chinese with no clout but money could drink cocktails, with foreigners if they wished. The Public Security Bureau nonetheless insisted on a nine o'clock closing time to keep miscegenation under wraps. After nine the blinds went down and, as in Capone's Chicago, clientele came in through a back lavatory where a bouncer, huddled in layers of clothing, had a heavily congested nose to protect himself against the odors of his post. The place was smart inside, or had been when it opened, in a style derided by foreigners as Instant Old. The wallpaper was peeling; the bronze laminate was lifting. The grandiose space was underlit and underheated, and there weren't enough chairs. Like every other establishment in Peking that year, due to overproduction by the No. 1 Food and Beverage Installations Enterprise, the ceiling was festooned with plastic trattoria grapes.

Behind the bar a pale young man with a 1964 Beatles haircut loitered meekly. An employee of the Peking Cake Company that ran the place, he sacrificed his health to long hours in the chilly, dingy chamber. The bar gave purpose to his life. Like an early Christian living for the millennium, Young Bi was dedicated to the day when the New Age Bar would be as smooth and sleek as those in Hollywood movies.

Business was bad tonight. The room echoed with the conversation of two men, vociferous on their third Cuba Libre, who were no older than the polite young barman but comported themselves quite differently: Mr. Foreign Trader and Mr. Party Greenhorn.

"It's getting harder and harder to make ends meet," complained pudgy Foreign Trader in leather jacket and jeans, whose offer of a Marlboro was rejected in favor of one of his friend's own Pandas, the brand smoked by China's paramount leader—impossible to buy.

"Price increases are a necessary adjustment within planned economic growth," responded Party Greenhorn. They had been neck and neck as schoolfriends, until Party Greenhorn went to People's University, the training ground of the new bureaucracy. His father, a high-level PLA man who sold second-rate armaments to the warring Middle East, had decided that the future lay not in the military proper but with the technocrats, and found a place for his son at the appropriate seat of higher learning. Foreign Trader had no such luck; but an uncle settled him into one of the semi-private companies that were mushrooming in the new economic climate and the young man, put to deal with tourist necessities, pretty soon hit on an item which, as Mao might have said, should be stressed as the key link: replicas of tricolor glaze Tang dynasty horses. They appealed to foreigners, tugged at the hearts of patriots, could be exported to overseas Chinese nostalgic for their glorious past, and even had a place in the museum shops of the barbarians. Replica Tang horses were artworks from the world's greatest civilization, and Foreign Trader had struck gold.

"Life's getting impossible," he told his friend. "Taxis, banquets, entertaining customers. I blow a hundred yuan a day."

He was talking like a big-nose, noted Party Greenhorn, who remained curious to hear the monthly income figure his friend was working up to announcing.

"Four thousand a month."

Party Greenhorn got a taste of bile in his mouth, even though current policy held that to be rich was glorious. From fake Tang horses?

Foreign Trader lit up another. Party Greenhorn was accustomed to bragging about his own 300 yuan a month salary, which was high for a new graduate. But there were other benefits to be reckoned up. Originally aiming to study abroad, he had submitted to a hundred North American institutions a research paper entitled "Long-term Perfection or Short-term Gains: The Planned Socialist Economy versus the Unplanned Capitalist Economy." The only reply, from an alleged Head of School in Waco, Texas, had transposed "planned" and "unplanned" with a black felt pen and added a series of queries, exclamations and stars. His father consoled the young man with a job at the Ministry of Foreign Economic Relations and Trade, where his first task was to negotiate a joint-venture contract with a Belgian pharmaceutical company. The idea was that the Belgian side would provide technology transfer for turning Chinese egg whites into a popular proprietary medicine. The Belgians would then buy a quota of the product at reduced price. The deal foundered when the Belgian side refused to buy the egg yolks and egg shells as well. This, Party Greenhorn complained to Foreign Trader, was his first encounter with the pigheadedness, greed and hostility of foreigners.

He liked the job, traveling through China at ministry expense, living like a princeling, with a car at his disposal, the promise of trips abroad and, top of the list, a guarantee of his own flat. He was twenty-four, wore a navy suit and carried a black plastic handbag; had spiky hair and chain-smoked. His childhood worship of Chairman Mao had spread to the whole Party, which would smoothly streamline its methods until triumph was assured and China reclaimed her place as greatest nation on earth. Party Greenhorn saw nothing to contradict his faith—and drained the cocktail.

Smiling more cynically, but equally contented, Foreign Trader emptied his glass in unison. He knew more; keeping his eyes and ears open was his life's blood. He respected the Party and praised the system: the ragged loopy net that gave him 4000 a month. What cared he that across the seas his riches might not amount to much? His mind could not stretch to anything he lacked, which included the satisfaction of winning at a dangerous game. He did not tell Party Greenhorn what else went into the export crates with the fake tricolor Tang horses.

Behind the bar Young Bi heard the figures they mentioned. One earned triple his wage, the other forty times, and Bi already got fifty per cent more than the average worker. Bowing his head, he went forward to ask if they would like another drink. He was invisible to them, a member of the shadow world, as they marched forward in the name of the dictatorship of the proletariat.

In a further recess of the bar sat three foreigners. Chinese thought foreigners looked funny, and foreigners on long-term residence in China lived up to that perception, their hair ill-cropped, their expressions hunted, their eyes sunken, their noses growing longer by the day. Perched like crows, the three in the dark were no exception.

"How far can you go?" giggled the woman, Dulcia, as she signed for the barman's attention. She wanted to put a tape of her own on the sound system. She carried a bag of tapes that she played in taxis to make the environment mellow. "Can you use those shots?" she asked.

"For the file," smiled Clarence, the younger of her two male companions. "It's all material."

"The Empire Strikes Back. Those guys were a mess."

They had come from the hospital where the injured were being treated after a bloody brawl between Chinese and Africans at one of the universities. Clarence was friendly with some of the African aid students who exposed their wounds to his press camera. On the way they had picked up the Doctor to get a professional assessment of the injuries.

Stringy, flaxen-haired Clarence had eyes the pale blue of caustic soda. "I don't see why the Chinese have to take it out on the blacks," he said. He had studied Mandarin at the School of Oriental and African Studies in London, came to Peking for finishing off, and stayed on.

Dulcia had been discussing with him her thwarted project of putting together an aerobics program for Central TV which would make her Jane Fonda to one billion people—the thought made her toes curl. But the project kept coming up against the wall.

"The first thing to learn is not to hope," grinned Clarence.

"I hate your cynicism."

"Cynicism or paranoia. Take your choice," he replied. "Cynicism is the better way. I'll survive you all here."

"You think I'm paranoid?" A fraction of a squint, at close quarters, made her look vampish. "I'll tell you something— I'm paranoid because I'm fighting. We're surrounded by enemies here. I want to free these people."

20

"Liberate the Chinese? Change China? That's the oldest con in the book. Merchants, diplomats, missionaries, generals. They've all tried, all been gobbled up. Now from their citadels of enlightenment come the kids of the 1980s."

"You talk like a book, Clarence."

"I get it from my mother."

Clarence's anger caused the table to brood. Then he started to cough. Peking had given him a permanent cough.

"You should do something about that," put in Wally.

"What the doctor ordered, another of the same!" Dulcia bounced back from the bar with three black cocktails. "Cheers! *Prost! Ganbei!* You gotta keep hoping," she said too loudly.

Dulcia believed—in everything; believed in hard work; believed in making it. She knew her homeland had its faults but believed that on odds it was the best place on earth, offering riches and freedom without which there was no possibility of self-fulfilment. Unlike Clarence, she had clear moral convictions. Wilhelm Reich and Tina Turner stood beside Abe Lincoln in her pantheon. She was an agent of liberation waging a personal campaign to help China.

"You're very quiet, Doc." She turned to the sandy-haired, sandy-faced man whose tall frame seemed to be propped against the chair rather than resting on it. "How are you finding this place?"

"It's okay. I didn't come with high hopes, just to poke around. I'm interested in some of their methods of treatment. But I'd have to admit I'm not finding what I'm looking for."

Wally's explanation was perhaps flimsier than necessary, as if the encounters with Mrs. Gu were sapping his sense of purpose. "I admire the Chinese. The scale is enormous. To have managed even the first few steps on the road to Utopia is an achievement. They've got food. Disease is relatively contained. Things function—more or less."

Dulcia spread her hand on the table. "Look at my fingernails. Even in this light. The place is filthy! We don't blow the trumpet about food and hygiene in our countries," she said. "What's the difference with China?"

"History," said Clarence flatly. "The magnitude of what holds them back."

"For which we are partly to blame," added Wally.

Clarence cocked his eyebrow. "Don't point the finger at me, chum."

But words were only obscure terms for unformulated feelings. Wally hung on to the belief that the present cant of the Reforms expressed some deeper wisdom in the Chinese collective consciousness. Progress was biological, a struggle between mutations; and the Reforms, he hoped, were an organic process leading to health.

"We all love Chinese," acidly concluded Clarence, who was starved for body contact inside his sheath of winter clothing.

"Let's play that one over." Dulcia was tired of fuzzy talk. *Private dancer, a dancer for money*, she sang, clapping her hands above her head as she went to dance in the middle of the space with all her happy American heedlessness. "Hey guys, let's party!"

The barman glanced towards the manager. "Excuse me," he said, coming forward to whisper in the foreign woman's ear.

"What? No dancing! Just try to stop me, honey!"

The manager was next, insisting on the rules . . . their license . . . the Public Security Bureau . . . certain regulations, as Dulcia mocked.

A single person was not allowed to dance alone; that constituted performance. Two persons were not allowed to dance together; that was too romantic. No foreigners and Chinese were allowed to dance together; that was "spiritual pollution."

But according to the regulations, as interpreted by the hand-wringing manager, three foreigners were allowed to dance together. He cordially invited the two men to join Dulcia, who broke up over the regulation—a sly number, three.

"In China it takes three to tango. Come on!"

And Foreign Trader and Party Greenhorn advanced from the shadows to do a crab-like disco on either side of the woman, encircling her with their pincers.

The barman watched with a saintly, lit-up expression, until the sweating manager impulsively pushed the Eject switch and turned on the light. The dancers blinked, began murmurs and protests, then Dulcia screamed. A large fat rat was scurrying (in not too much of a scurry) along the skirting boards.

Earlier in the day the same rat had crossed the room while the hygiene inspector was discussing with the manager catering arrangements for her son's wedding, and a discount was struck.

"Closing time," announced the manager, herding the gang towards the door marked Man Closet Woman Closet.

"It's like those wartime jokes," said Dulcia. "An American, an Englishman and an Australian in a lousy bar in Peking."

"A damn Yankee, a whinging Pom and a gullible Ocker," said Wally. And thought to himself, a sceptic cursed with the need for values.

"Won't you tell us the punchline?" asked Clarence.

"They danced with each other! Nice to see you again, Doc," she called as she threw a leg over her bike.

3

Clarence walked into the cold. At night, disguised like a homecoming worker in cap, scarf and coat, he became a faceless swimmer in the darkness. He loved the night, when his camera was stowed and he could cease looking for shots. He had come to Peking to prevent his mother turning him into a character in one of her novels. She had only the notoriety of literary London to confer. Clarence the child, Clarence the teenager, had been utilized more than once in the Honorable Ann Codrington's heightened fictions. Growing older, he had learned to put himself out of reach, studying a language that could not be quoted on the page, and then moving safely East. His mother's mighty pen had hung over his head through adolescence, forcing private turmoil back on itself to escape expression. He started playing round with the camera then, and photography irresistibly became his medium: art without a voice. What he loved was the accident of the shutter, and his soul remained the amorphous dark against which images formed—tender and witty and lonely, speaking no language, wearing no dress.

He walked past the locked-up bird and fish market where by day fanciers traded rare breeds and curios, past the Kismet spires of the Soviet-built Exhibition Center, and the zoo where the polar bear was bellowing, into the area where itinerants gathered, Mongols and Uigyurs and prostitutes, forming compositions of fur, leather and padding in the steamy glow of the noodle stalls.

Clarence crossed a scrap of park with solid ice puddles on the paths and trees hacked like iron rakes; and entered the unsewered, drafty lavatory where, shuddering and holding his breath, he relieved himself: a little dragon emitting steam. Opposite, the rooftop of a foreign hotel sent out a lethargic light-show of colored stars. He would go to warm himself on free Scotch and gossip from the bar boys; that would do his cold good.

4

Three fates in black tangling their yarns: had they been construing China or themselves, Wally wondered. The shapeless, murky depth of the city had somehow to be placed within a framework of understanding, otherwise you were nowhere, anywhere, at middle life, far from boundaries and bearings, in the Middle Kingdom. He had drunk too much, heard too much, talked too much, and his body was too big for the damned bed, and the damned bed was too big for his damned body. He scratched frantically, pinched the back of his neck as hard as he could, squeezed the acupuncture point between thumb and forefinger that's supposed to induce sleep, and, trying to summon Australian sheep milling realistically through a shearing run, managed only cartoon blobs of wool. On the bedside table lay the photocopies of Hsu Chien Lung's articles. The disappearing man. Wally had flicked through the grayed pages of old-fashioned print and wondered why he admired their elegance so. In one gesture they pointed a mystery and hinted a solution, although the site of that solution had receded. Was his attachment to those old papers purely a road not taken, that he had sentimentally rediscovered as need dictated? He cursed with an insomniac's impotency—and returned on the ferris wheel to the bottom. Where was he? And why?

There had been relics, a black leather-bound Mandarin bible, printed Shanghai 1898, a silver pipe that the children fancied smelled of opium, big black placards with gold characters meaning longevity. There were photographs of the white house with black tiles and turned-up eaves, a woman with a plait in a white pinafore, swarthy converts in tight round caps assembled in a courtyard. There was the brusque memoir, a gathering of stock anecdotes, that Grandpa Frith had awkwardly typed for posterity. There was the fact that Wally's father got cross whenever China was mentioned.

Most beautifully there was The Hut in the hills that family legend whispered had been built by Grandpa in memory of his first wife, Retta. Wally never knew that real grandmother, but he knew The Hut, a cottage of tin and wood and stone where he used to go for holidays as a boy. The soil and climate made exotic things grow there: a Nepali deodar with a cave inside, a spreading lime with leaves of see-through tissue, mountainous rhododendrons, liquidambar, crepe myrtle, peonies, red toadstools with white spots, persistent bamboo.

Viewed from the bottom road the landscape arranged itself in descending terraces and framed The Hut with lofty trees, some European, some native, some oriental, shaded, half-hidden, with an illusion of great distance; revealing, as Grandpa had planned, the Chinese proportions of a roof that yearned upwards with curving iron eaves. It was Grandpa's shrine, or apology, where Wally the child had been happiest, in summer, sitting out on the latticed verandah surrounded by the rattling leaves of the great magnolia whose masses of wide-open flower moons made the air divine ether.

Visits to The Hut were special, planned from afar. His parents had settled interstate out of Grandpa's reach. Then they would drive hundreds of miles to stay with Grandpa and Patsy in The Hut, and everyone always said the time was far too short, until afterwards in the car Wally's father and mother said they could not have stayed a day longer. Patsy was a divorced woman when Grandpa married her, of Scottish stock, staunch, forthright, likeable. She had a daughter from her first husband and a tribe of relatives, and bore two more Frith children. With his high moral tone and medical man's common sense, Grandpa fixed up the mess to his perfect satisfaction by making the second, immediate family the one that absorbed his interest and life. Wally's family was left out.

Family never meant much to Wally. His father's childhood had been broken by Retta's death and ever after his father's relationship with the old man was strained by unexplored resentments and stubborn independence. Jerry, Wally's father, was utterly unsentimental where family was concerned; and Wally's self-sufficient mother was of the same breed.

Against that background, the ritual pilgrimages to visit Grandpa Frith were steeped for Wally in momentous alienness. In the fabulous leafy old world of The Hut the boy found much. Grandpa teased him with oriental mysteries, the white mane shining, gaunt limbs on the chair arms, bones stuck under clothes, eyes darting as the voice croaked its summons for the boy to enter the presence of an ancestral spirit (who was dying, Wally later knew).

He was too young to appreciate old Waldemar Frith's wit, or the sturdy aphorism inscribed in the Mandarin bible that came down to him: *The courage we desire and prize is not to die decently but to live manfully* (Carlyle). But the spirit image stayed in Wally's memory. Jerry had gone gray by the time the day came to fly from Wollongong to Adelaide for the funeral. He didn't say much to the kids afterwards. The clan stopped gathering. That year, when Wally was ten, the year of the last visit to The Hut, summer magnolias stirred riper-than-ever fancies, the Soviets put Sputnik into space and in China Chairman Mao allowed a hundred flowers to bloom before they were quickly scorched. Then came the Great Leap Forward.

5

The snow froze. The road was hard and still, long, empty, unbending. The breath of a puny Mongolian pony pulling the cart home along the usual route formed a little cloud of steam. *Clop-clop, clop-clop*, it moved from city to country with a heavy load of nightsoil. Atop the cart, bundled in great coat and fur cap with earflaps down, the old farmer snoozed, and from his nostrils smoked tiny runnels. If he woke he would growl, but the animal knew without commands to go fast when the road was hard and empty and home approached.

After missing the last bus and taking a roundabout way, Jin Juan came through side streets towards the crossroads. Accursed Peking she knew like her own nervous system. She came home having argued. Her hair was stuffed inside the hood of her down jacket. Probably to the outside she looked no different, but she no longer felt, or cared to feel, clean and pretty. Her perfume annoyed her. She would have to wash it off before class tomorrow. She felt, in fact, strong and savage as her feet hit the iron-hard ground. She had decided; she knew *he* had decided; the matter was communicated in their bodies, though for so long they had played ring-around-the-rosy with hopes and promises, just as her country had gone on waiting and waiting for the Red Dawn so long that no one knew now how to break the circle of chains. If only . . . Jin Juan decided once again that she would win, that her anger and his edginess were but raw materials, and that, rather than exploding, her energy must be used to turn all that recalcitrant matter into well-tempered love. She was tenacious, with a discipline that brought her back from the edge of violent destructiveness to a new deep vein of persistence.

She was conscious first of an intrusion on her thoughts. The animal knocked into her, was trampling over her, and she was down among its hundred-seeming legs. Her body was rolling under the cart. Trotting along the familiar road, the horse could not be expected to take account of a young woman crossing in the dark, and scarcely registered the disturbance, scarcely stopped. The old man snorted and made a lame attempt to pull on the reins. He was not about to apologize. Jin

28

Juan rolled like an acrobat and was on her feet again. "Nothing, nothing," she said, "no harm done." The farmer would only swear at her if she let him. Perhaps her cheeks were grazed by the ice. There was no light to see what state she was in. She shrugged, laughed, turned and made her decisive way before the sleepy farmer abused his puzzled horse into motion once more. She walked away. What guts she had. She sniffed. She did not look vengefully back at the honeycart. Was the stuff all over her? She smelled the perfume, like a film of pollution. She smelled her body, his, their, bodies. She smelled shit. Golden grace spiking ice down the road's black center, Jin Juan walked decisively.

CHAPTER THREE

The Way

1

The driver went through the regular litany of questions as the taxi crawled across Peking. What country are you from? Wally answered faithfully, except sometimes he said Iceland. What are you doing in China? How old are you? Are you married? Yes, he fudged. Children, yes. (Contrary, baffling Jerome, his son.) Home? Car? How much do you earn? By any standards he was comfortable, though his colleagues grumbled, too comfortable. Chinese people too many, Chinese history too long, China too poor. If I go to your country, how much money can I make? What do you make of Chinese people? Wally pronounced the word he had learned to describe them: *lihai*, meaning fierce, a force to be reckoned with, like the hottest Sichuan food.

No one was skittled on the way, though human shapes drifted out in front of the taxi that sailed through the streets like an air-conditioned barge.

Eagle was waiting for him at the Daoist temple, standing at attention against a sunny patch of wall. He wore navy running pants with a white stripe, white running shoes and a bulky sweater knitted with the Armani eagle. Full of energy, he led the Doctor across the swept flagstones to the first courtyard where monks with topknots were pottering about. He tolerated the foreigner's interest in such quaint things, though he had seen too much fakery to regard these Daoists as close to any source. Yesterday's stinking superstition was today's colorful tradition under the Party's magic wand; and the monks, with baggy robes and inturned eyes, performed well.

"If they can't get a better job, it's not a bad living for these guys to be transferred here," he commented.

Wally was thinking philosophically of Lao Tzu. Yet Eagle was the truer Daoist, always taking the path of least resistance. Even the movement of his frame suggested the flow of fish in a stream. Cheeky sarcasm communicated itself in his facial gestures as much as his broken language. He was open and virtuous, while entirely pragmatic, serenely following the accident that had first thrown him together with the foreigner. If the Cultural Revolution had deprived him of education, he had become an alert autodidact, and although he had only a badly paid and boring job in a state office, he seldom proclaimed his grievances. There was more to life than the refrigerator, the video recorder and the foreign passport that his contemporaries worshiped. Wally liked him. He preferred being with Eagle to being with the people from the Medical College who were eager, for their own motives, to act as his guide. With Eagle he felt unconfined and could question frankly. It was necessary to trust someone. When Eagle said he had been a basketball champion in the city, Wally believed him. His height distinguished him, and he had an affable grace that athletic prowess might have conferred. Wally committed himself to the relationship, and would not let Eagle down when the time came. Meanwhile he pestered him with questions, as if Eagle were the representative Chinese who could answer all inquiries about his people.

32

They stepped through bright red and green paintwork into dark lustrous chambers hung with banners and out again into white winter sunlight, accompanied by the monks' babbling wooden music.

"Actually, why did you come to China?" asked Eagle in return.

"You're like the taxi drivers. You ask direct questions and expect direct answers. Why can't you be inscrutable like you're supposed to be?"

"What you say?"

With some exasperation Wally explained that he wanted to learn from China.

"Can you learn from China?" Eagle seriously wondered.

"Like the man said about Everest, it's there."

"You are going to climb Heaven Mountain?"

"Heaven Mountain you call it? I can't climb Heaven Mountain because China has got in the way."

Eagle hung his head in helpless resignation. To be presented with such metaphysical reasons for behavior, to have placed before him the world of Wally, where great actions were undertaken for whimsical motives, where practical considerations were irrelevant or beneath mention, was perplexing.

"Do you believe in religion?"

"Not exactly," said Wally, fluffing it.

"I don't believe," Eagle stated flatly.

2

Wally's grandfather had believed. That, indirectly, provided a reason. But the oblique causation was not easy to explain. New China had begun in 1949, and was already the burdensome past to New Age China of the 1980s. In thinking of his grandfather Wally was harking back to the late Ching dynasty, that perfumed twilight merged already with legend. His grandfather had been a doctor and a Christian in the South at the turn of the century, a craggy old chap whose perdurable Saxon Christian name Wally had inherited. Jerry, Wally's father, had been born in China. On winter weekends in Wollongong, when rain beat down over the ranges, while ma and pa snoozed after lunch, Wally loved to sift through his father's desk. It wasn't snooping; Jerry had nothing to hide, as long as the boy left things as neat as he found them. The father's desk was a model to the boy, of bookkeeping, scrupulosity, and how to get rid of useless clutter. Wally wished for more clutter, though he was scientifically minded and liked to have names on things. He liked best the folder of documents kept in the locked drawer, and his favorite thing there was his father's birth certificate. *Jeremiah Columba Frith*, in browned copperplate, *8th August 1905, Hangchow*. The names and occupations of his grandparents written out in full. *Waldemar Thomas Frith, medical officer. Retta Frith née Glee, nursing sister. Address: The Mission Hospital, Taichow*. In the bottom corner of the yellowed certificate was a vertical row of tiny printed characters, to designate, perhaps, a Chinese manufacturer. The certificate threatened to fall apart along its crease lines from a lifetime's folding and unfolding.

Wally often raised these matters with his father, but Jerry—having long ago ditched the thundering monicker Jeremiah—showed little interest. He had no recollection of China. When the family was shipped from Shanghai to South Australia, Jerry was four. Nor, in later life, was he in touch with his elder brother Lionel, a scapegrace who might have remembered more. Wally's curiosity was kindled but never fanned, not after Grandpa died. The link with China was a stray thread in a life otherwise well-ordered, hard-working and determined. Jerry was a professional soldier, a communications engineer. During the war years, of middling rank and no longer young, he met a woman similarly placed, and when peace came they married. In his forties he entered upon domestic life and a General Post Office job at Wollongong that lasted till retirement. From both his parents Wally got no-nonsense attitudes: do what's best for you; make a good job of things; make the most of what you've got. He was also brainy. In the spirit of his country and the times, the early 1960s, he was encouraged to go for broad horizons and high endeavor. He came top of the class in his final year at Wollongong High; he worked for it. He was offered his first choice, a place in Medicine at Sydney University.

Wally was a straightforward young man, though neither he nor his mates, who read philosophy and literature and talked politics, self-consciously, and involved themselves in campus activities, were typical medical students. Wally was secretary of the Student Socialists, an unfrivolous lot regularly assailed by the more numerous Libertarians, a flamboyant anarchic set who were not politicized until Australian boys died in Vietnam. Wally did not need a stinking post-colonial war to establish his convictions. He was a socialist on scientific principles. He believed in the common good being served by common co-operation. Knowledge as much as wealth was power and neither should be the privilege of a few. His views set him at odds with his brothers in the medical school, who had sharp eyes for money under the blazon of the Hippocratic Oath. Wally's altruism was bullshit, they said, and Wally was a bore. Their attitudes turned him towards a career in medical research rather than lucrative practice. He was superior, even if he didn't come from the North Shore; and he stuck by his thinking mates and kept himself clean.

In the summer holidays he worked on the Wollongong docks, loading ships that took Australian wool and minerals to Japan, and later at the steel smelter, and eventually in the workers' compensation office of Broken Hill Proprietary Company. To put in the twelve weeks each summer he turned down more diverting proposals, again out of pride and a desire to have the stuffing knocked out of him. To the blokes on the job, who wished he was more talkative, he was known as Doc. He sat around with his nose in a book. When he did open up, he was all opinions and hot air.

On weekends, Wally walked in the bush and on the mountains that ran along the central coast. He roamed the Budawangs in drowsy fragrant heat, through stands of eucalypts whose curling boughs created crackling gray-green canopies, through tufty buzzing clearings, into cool gorges dense with wattle, to creeks and pools overhung with willows and wild apples and spiky melaleuca, and up, at high altitude, to outcrops of rock split by ice and heat. To walk the ridge of an elevation was Wally's pleasure, to find the natural trail or swear by the compass and reach a crest where under the purest indigo sky the softened furry mountains, sheer cliffs and spread plateaus rippled into terrain that, however ancient, answered to human contours and desires. To him it was a more seductive sight than the flat shimmering sea stretched to disappearing in the other direction. Once he climbed Pigeonhouse, a mountain topped with a rock that from out to sea had reminded Captain Cook of a dovecote: or perhaps that was Cook's discretion, since the mountain was a huge breast with nipple aroused which, from afar, or if he was standing atop like Gulliver in Brobdingnag, fed Wally's fantasies. On the horizon of the sea, where Cook's ship had sailed, passed the dark shapes of cargo ships heavy with ore, wheat, wool, the vessels of trade going to and from Wollongong, Sydney, Newcastle. On their stained sides, the young man had seen at close quarters, some had Chinese characters. Now Wally's people were creating a blockade of incineration and carnage in Vietnam to stop the Yellow Peril. His mother said she didn't want to break her back in a rice paddy and eat stones for bread. His father said that if the Chinese stood in a line holding hands they would ring the globe.

36

Exhilarated on the summit of Pigeonhouse, he wiped the sweat and grime from his brow. The breeze tugged at his sandy curls. His face was burnt pink with blotches of orange freckles. From his peak in Darien, he considered, the world lay all before him. He was twenty-two, a few days into the New Year 1967. His resolution was to be an explorer of whatever terrain the modern world laid open. A letter had come to inform him of his final results. He had won a scholarship to study overseas. He did not know he would still be out of the country when his father died, and then his mother.

3

In the courtyard, incense smoke arose from a bronze urn over which dragons played. Wally and Eagle followed an elderly monk into a pavilion where the rite was in progress. Amidst hangings of scarlet and yellow silk embroidered with cranes of longevity and pink clouds and flowers and many-splendored butterflies, the monks lined up to chant. They wore black caps over their buns, and over their white stockings and blue smocks they wore scarlet cloaks bordered with black. They were mostly young. "Unemployed youth," whispered Eagle. The chamber was lit like a theater, to make the most of the dusky images and the shiny purple Ching dynasty vessels. The music began, syncopated and percussive, as gongs, bells, copper strips and hollow lumps of wood were struck. The indecipherable grumbling chant commenced, with a moderate amount of ducking and rising, to bring the living and the spirits of the dead together. The spectators watched blankly, too humble to be skeptical, until a plain man in a blue cotton dustcoat came forward, lit a handful of incense, kowtowed, and led forward a frail, shuffling woman, also in a cotton dustcoat, evidently his wife, and placed her on the kneeler. She was blinded by glaucoma, Wally diagnosed. Afterwards, neither husband nor wife having met the eyes of an onlooker, she was led away, lifting her feet high over the raised threshold of an entrance she couldn't see.

In the attached museum Wally studied a Daoist chart of the human body which made the names and relationships of the body's organs and passages into a narrative about spirits and demons.

At the kiosk, buying postcards from a young monk who came of Marxist-Leninist parents in the barren North-East, and who had chosen Daoism because his parents could not feed him, Wally asked what was the aim of the faith.

"Long life," said the monk succinctly, and implied that no other religion laid itself on the line so frankly.

"How is long life achieved?" asked Wally.

With suitable circularity the monk replied, "By training."

4

Wally Frith was an educational product of Sydney University and the two Cambridges, in a process that took sixteen years of his life and sailed him into intellectual and social waters unimaginably far from his boyhood mountaintop.

In Cambridge, England he was a graduate member of Christ's College, a chap with a tawny beard, blue jeans and a shapeless tweed jacket, whose family was the lab where he worked with unflagging discipline as ideas sparked. In the same buildings a few years earlier, the DNA helix had been isolated by Watson and Crick. As a phalanx of researchers marched abreast to realize the implications of its discovery, embryology enjoyed a revolution. Wally went to the wildly hypothetical forefront—gene pathology and its links with cell mutation. The time was the high 1960s, when briefly the prospect of a massive social transformation offered. Wally's former socialist principles were strengthened by his encounter with the nobs and yobs of Old Albion; but unlike others he had no time for full-scale revolutionary theory, not at the expense of embryology. It was with difficulty that he held his own in political debate over a pint. His work demanded, and absorbed and satisfied, as only a vocation can. In May of 1968, when the rallying cry issued from Paris and spring burst in red flags over the Cambridge meadows, Wally was in the lab eighteen hours a day, refining his data on the oncogene: what a colleague nicknamed the human face of the Brave New World.

Next stop was transatlantic, in one of those lateral moves that give a career its curious pattern, whether destiny or drift. He entered further into the white and lonely corridors of a freemasonry whose techniques were, they claimed, humanity's highest mastery. By taking up a post-doc position in the Sidney Farber Cancer Institute of Harvard Medical School, Wally was able to apply theoretical research to clinical medicine. Some genomes were viral. Absorbed into the gene was a virus making the gene "infected," so to speak. From those same genes, after triggering, came the production of cancer cells. Yet between the viral genome and the final cancer was a gulf, an unexplored terrain of indeterminate causation. A gulf too wide and unruly to be charted, many scientists said. To find a way across would be to show, with classical simplicity, that a cancer could be caused by infection; explicable, non-numinous—to show that a cancer was a mundane, therefore curable, disease.

When the plane landed at Boston, Wally had left his beard behind. From the sun of his childhood his eyes were already frayed with lines, though from England his skin was pale. He brought with him a wife and child, and from the first meeting with his immensely distinguished seniors handled things professionally. Pretty soon he was part of the team, and befittingly earnest. Not only his work mattered, but his opinions. "As I see it," he would begin, to give more rather than less definitiveness to his remarks. Still, as an Australian, he had the common touch, luckily, thrust upon him.

He produced a string of major papers, but the gaps remained. Ninety-five per cent remained inexplicable. When the new information, seized upon, was tried out clinically, nothing tangible came of it. If a treatment could be even partially effective, if a disease process could at any stage be retarded or reversed, there might be some pointers to a working explanation. As in the case of Edward Jenner's discovery of the smallpox vaccine, even those who seemed accidentally immune could show the way to the relevant nature of the immunity. But there was a woeful lack of clinical data, and too many different conditions had been lumped together under the name of cancer. No one had thought to record case studies of successful and unsuccessful treatments in sufficient detail. In pre-war medicine a cancer was thought of as an invader of the body, to be removed by surgery; a recurrence was a secondary assault, to be removed again, and so on until there was nothing left of the alien body to be removed, often nothing left of the body itself. The radiation treatment that came into vogue after the war used more advanced weaponry for the same approach. The move to chemotherapy was a partial recognition that the tumor or malignancy existed not in opposition to the body but symbiotically in a shared environment. The more radical treatments that followed—hormones and meditation, for instance—moved closer to a recognition that the cancer was created by the body itself, in response to poisons or triggers or signals of some kind. Wally's basic postulate, that the malformation originated from viruses absorbed into the gene itself, shared such an approach at the most fundamental biochemical level. The cases where a cancer ebbed and flowed, where it metastasized and subsequently went into remission, were of consuming interest to him. Where the body's processes adjusted in such a way as to turn from infirmity back to health, where a route to life was re-achieved,

Wally was particularly concerned with what stimulated the turnaround—but there had been no organized collection of the data.

He often discussed the problem with his boss, Harvey Heilmann, who had been in the field for decades and didn't believe in breakthroughs, despite his being a Nobel laureate for some allegedly revolutionary research. Harvey believed, instead, in steady progress, in the nature of geological change, and he had faith that some day all their work, their conferences, societies, learned journals, scrabbling for funds, feudings, backstabbing, false hopes, follies, errors, despair, would all be justified by humankind's clumsy arrival at Understanding. So he was a great boss, even if his crawling time-scale and drowsy voice sometimes looked like lack of fire to his younger colleagues.

With a shrunken gangling body and an elongated face in which the teeth were too prominent, Harvey Heilmann was a soft, slender-necked, leaf-munching dinosaur. It was over a bowl of lettuce after an afternoon's swimming in the neighborhood pool one summer in the green outskirts of Cambridge, Massachusetts, that Wally once again started to complain about the paucity of case studies that might suggest an overview, a framework of ideas and explanation into which his laboratory experiments could be placed. His heart needed a sense that his work in the clean-air lab was connected with the ignorant, irrepressible life and destruction outside. He needed to feel that his isolated test-tube cells were part of people's stories—not for sentimental reasons, but to grasp at the Whole Thing.

Old Harvey got up and swayed into his study.

"You might take a look at these," he indicated laconically.

Laid out on his desk were three faded copies of the *New England Journal of Medicine*, with the old blue-paper covers, dating from the 1930s.

"There was a chap on a fellowship here when I was starting

41

out. A youngish professor, came over to us from China. As persnickety a gentleman as they come. We tried to get him to join in the work we were doing, which in those days, as you know, was largely directed towards surgical techniques. The Chinese swam against the tide—oh, as politely as you could imagine. He worked on metabolic processes—on what we would now think of as hormone synthesis and deficiency in relation to the failure of the immune system. What we're just moving towards ourselves, thirty years later. He'd trained in Western hospitals in China, but his family was from a rural area in the South, an old official family, I believe. He was with us for nearly ten years—I never got close. He wasn't a Red, but when the Reds won, he went back, for love of the mother-land. I never found out what became of him after that. Read these papers. The assemblage is elegant, the data are there and the conceptual pointers are remarkable."

Wally flicked to the table of contents. "Efficacious Treat-ment of Liver and Other Cancers in Chekiang Province, China: A By-Stander's Records" by Hsu Chien Lung.

5

The blood-red lacquered pillars of the temple challenge the gray flagstones, the frozen pine trees, and a gray sky that dis-guises in haze an industrial chimney oozing filthy smoke over the neighborhood. All around the temple are narrow lanes running between factory compounds, tarred walls hiding fur-naces, assembly lines, packing houses and tubs for chemical conversions; and the chilly, unadorned housing blocks for workers whose lives, even in deep winter, burst on to the balcony where things in daily use are piled up for want of other space: bicycles and empty bottles crammed beside dor-mant potplants and pigeon cages. Wally walks with Eagle through the narrow alleys to the main road. At the corner is a mountain of white Chinese cabbage, brown from frost on the outside, giving off a rotten smell. On a tiny stool sits a woman beside a glass box where she proudly displays her skewers of candied crab apples, her round face the same caramelized red. Eat *tanghulu*, she calls. A toddler in a cape and hood of emerald satin is led along by a limping grandpa whose furry earflaps stick straight out from his hat. A cyclist rings his bell; no one pays attention. On the main road expensive oranges and apples blaze with color as they are lifted from the hawker's scales to the housewife's plastic briefcase. A kid vends roast sweet potatoes from a rusty drum; no one buys. They crowd round the newspaper seller in the gutter whose *Sports News* flies into the air like plucked feathers as soon as she unwraps a bundle.

There are no taxis. They take a bus. Wally's back is nearly broken by the press of people maneuvering for position, all muffled in winter clothing, more skillful and less perceptible in their movements than worms. The buses are like caterpillars too, two buses joined at the middle by a concertina and pulled by one motor. Every society has its own survival of the fittest. Wally, whose body does not bend around bars and boxes and impassive human forms, goes under here. Eagle grins.

6

The farmhouses among the ruins of the Old Summer Palace, what was the Garden of Perfect Brightness before the British and French fired it, had fallen into dereliction and were occupied temporarily by urban fringe-dwellers. Down a lane, across a sluggish, iced-up stream, a cluster of brick shanties edged a field; a narrow path led through a doorway in the carved stone arch to a tiny courtyard with a light in one side.

Dulcia had cycled from the city. She knocked on the window; a voice called out a greeting; bundled inside, she sat by the stove and hot tea was put into her frozen hands.

"This late!" He could smell drink on her breath.

"I got lost on the way," she lied. She had been to his house once before, and her sense of direction was unerring. "Well?"

"So-so." He tossed his long hair out of his eyes. "I've been painting."

The room was cluttered and cramped; a rumpled bed, a coal stove, books, boxes, huge paintings hung or pinned across every available space.

Jumbo was not tall, even for a Chinese. When he unscrolled a painting, holding his arms above his head and standing on tiptoe, the bottom of the scroll bumped on the ground. Brooding, malformed shapes in black ink escaped from the paper like genies from the bottle, straining away from the painter's body, probing at the walls.

His head popped impishly around the side of the broad scroll. Dulcia sat and admired. She liked the cool acerbity of his work; emotion held in restraint, knowing the chains. Too much of what passed for art was sickly-sweet and infantile; Jumbo's use of black, his refusal to specify form, made his different. The haunting of tradition was there: rock, water, mountains, leaves of bamboo; but, as she looked, their definition vanished into a bad dream, black inchoate masses expressive of emptiness and terror at the center, where the individual ceases to exist.

"Drink some tea." He stooped to pour more hot water into their glasses, traditionally solicitous of the guest and surrounded, in his artworks, by the hallucinations of his race and time. His small body was tough as steel wire; his features refined; his hands and face lined prematurely into a mask of carved smiles. The physical definition Dulcia achieved through aerobics had been inflicted on Jumbo by the People's Liber-

44

ation Army where for six years he had trained by treading water for five hours a day in the river in full uniform and greatcoat, holding a rifle over his head. His body became a weapon that could endure everything, even his thoughts. He had killed men. After the Cultural Revolution he got a place at university with other older students from intellectual backgrounds, and was assigned to work at Central TV, where he met the foreign woman who nicknamed him Jumbo because he was "small," she joked, "and mighty." The name he had been given by his long-suffering patriarch father meant "rousing spirit of a great wave." His painting had been criticized for going beyond realism. Few understood, though some admired. The improvised exhibition had not been a success despite Dulcia's talking it up all round Peking. On the third day the authorities had closed it down, and Dulcia had become a crusader on Jumbo's behalf, calling all her journalist friends.

"The artistic environment here is wretched. For a thousand years now there's been this pull backwards down a great drain as we try to get back to our old cultural roots. I don't want the old yellow earth, you understand; I want the mind, myself, my individuality. Here to seek individuality is blasphemy, swimming against the stream of the great state river. Here individuality is the waste product to be washed away by the mighty current of tradition, the Party, the people. But I don't know if what I'm doing is really new. I need to go outside and see for myself."

He talked of leaving the country as if it were stepping outside the family's front door.

"Can you help me? Give me the names of a few art schools in New York. That's all."

She nodded. She wanted to nurture him. But she made no further move.

She thought of Cray, her husband. Theirs had been a college romance, a language lab affair at Berkeley when he was a skinny four-eyes studying Russian (before the contact lenses) and she was the fat girl before the aerobics. They had been flattered to be treated like bionic Californian gods when they arrived in China as teachers. Dulcia competed in the college sports meet and defeated the school's best men and women athletes, including her own husband. The Chinese made a joke of their humiliation, but no foreigner was ever asked to compete again, and the change in Dulcia and Cray's marriage dated from that day. Chinese men could not resist pitting themselves against her physical supremacy. At the end-of-term party she arm-wrestled the chunkiest graduate student, Wildman, and won. Cray decided to move on to Moscow. Behind their tears of farewell at the airport were a skinny boy's sniveling and a fat girl's tremulous exultation. Hooray! She had got outside the body America told her was a problem, and now she could be everything America told her it was her right to be. For the tin men, the straw men, the cowardly lions of China, she had hearts, brains and nerves on offer.

Yet her forthrightness was inhibited by the rites Jumbo imposed. She yawned, and Jumbo asked if she was cold or tired. Was she in love with this fastidious, fine-boned Chinaman, his long oily hair and long fingers draped over crossed legs? Would he fit in her baggage? She speculated as to her motives, and his, and Jumbo sat tight on his stool, breathing smoke and brooding.

Perhaps he scrupled at taking advantage of the woman he called on for assistance. Perhaps modesty held him back, or, more likely, the paralyzing passivity that prefers to maneuver the adversary out on the limb first so that, when both are on the limb and it breaks, its breaking can be blamed on the one who first claimed it was safe.

Outside, on an eroded hilltop, stone columns lay as they had fallen a century ago, great white shapes nuzzling each other under a velvety snow-bearing sky.

7

"Perhaps I did not understand," said Mrs. Gu. "I thought you wanted to see Professor Hsu, but there is no need for that."

In front of her was a copy of one of Hsu's papers that Wally had produced. She had changed key remarkably.

"I thought you were insisting that Professor Hsu was at our College, when he is not, because he has retired."

There was not even a pause for dramatic effect when the professor who did not exist was now declared to be in retirement. But Wally saw nothing to gain from pointing out this miraculous logic.

"I did not understand that it was our work on clinical therapy for liver and other cancers that interested you. You have only to ask, Professor Doctor Frith, to tell me exactly what you want. Now I know what you want, I can help you. That area is the responsibility of Director Kang. Indeed, Director Kang has pioneered that field. He would be honored to have the opportunity to talk with you. But I'm not sure of his program. When would suit you?"

"I'm causing you so much trouble, Mrs. Gu," replied Wally, taking up his mug of cold, floral-tasting tea.

CHAPTER FOUR

April Fool's Day

1

For fifty cents, at the public bathhouse, Eagle could stand under a hot shower for as long as he liked, scrub his body all over, lather his scalp and scrape his beard (a weekly occurrence). Home, one room and tiny attached kitchen in a maze of lanes near the station, had no such washing facilities, nor a lavatory. Winter and summer alike Eagle squatted at the public convenience down the street, freezing his bum or offending his nose according to the season, in the name of the revolution.

Today he cut his shower short. If he was not at the front of the queue the beancurd noodles would be sold out. Flushed from the shower, in his freshly laundered clothes, he stood with his pannikin by the vendor's trolley for forty-five minutes as the cold drew in. He was determined not to hear the old lady croak: "All gone!" The Doctor was coming.

His mother had quizzed him. What did the foreigner want? What kind of person? What was her son's aim? She would not have taken the risk. But because her son wanted it, she devoted herself to the visit.

Mother Lin was old Peking—a squat woman with a dropped shoulder and doubting, jeering eyes. Once, before Liberation, her family had owned a courtyard house. She married out before the house was sequestered and when she walked down the street ten years later she found the neighborhood replaced by a boiler factory. Her father, a very petty bourgeois with no money, had sung Peking opera. She remembered him slipping out the gate at afternoon and returning late, pleased with himself. For all she knew, he might have been a considerable artist. Only in later life had she grown affectionate towards the old opera. As a girl she had been a romantic rebel, sharp as a pin, and harangued her young man, a Communist officer from Canton, about the corrupt ways. She laughed in his face before she married him. Two years later came the Red Dawn. Her husband studied, and on graduating was reclaimed by the army. She went to work in a glass factory and kept the one-room home in Peking to which he returned once a year. The 1950s were prosperous and optimistic; then only optimistic. Eventually her husband was resettled in the city, and two baby sons crowded the house. But her man had grown cautious, punctilious, maintaining ideological correctness and discouraging contact with outsiders. During those empty, flavorless years of the 1960s and 1970s, whatever strength or joy they managed was kept close within the family circle of four. Since Old Lin was wary of milking connections, living conditions did not advance and few favors came their way, until existence was as scant and furtive as a mouse's in a borrowed hole. Out of what surprised his wife as terror, Old Lin permitted not one grumble, even within their walls or under the covers at night. His nature warped; the scholar's ideals became nasty puritanism, disguised as the uprightness of a self-denying Party member and family man. When even the smallest good fortune fell his way, Old Lin distrusted, and when the new season came he was unable to adjust.

Eagle was seventeen then. He stood in Tiananmen Square

with the crowd and cried without knowing why. Beginning from that day the boy found words for trees in leaf, for the tastes of the year between his teeth, for the glint and nudge that go with foul-mouthed jokes. He was quick and fast, and tried out for a place in the district basketball team. After a couple of months of impressive play, he was selected to audition for All-Peking. He had never been a dreamer, he was almost without self-consciousness or aspiration, not even aware of his own naiveté: a lifetime's Mao Thought had done that to him. His elder brother called him a straw dumpling. But his passivity, the stupefying creation of Mao Thought, allowed him to be pliable, to live for the day. On the eve of the basketball trial, as he sat cross-legged on the bed pondering, it seemed that his day might have come. Sport was the route to self-advancement; a successful athlete was the people's hero—and no privilege was out of bounds.

He slept deeply that night, and next day won his place in the squad. But his father was suspicious of the ease with which success had come. Good luck was dangerous. His mother worried that when he moved out to the Sports Institute, he would not be fed properly, her motherly pride unwarmed with joy, as if success was a kind of shame.

Old Lin continued to dote on his elder son, Sunshine, who had found an alternative future hawking foreign cigarettes. Old Lin saw both his sons in jeans and wristwatches: in Sunshine's case he commended enterprise without inquiring too closely; in Eagle's case he became gloomy and disapproving. Against his father's advice, Sunshine made contact with relatives in Canton to whom he was determined to prove his business acumen. Eagle brought money home from the Sports Institute; Sunshine took the money out again.

Then Eagle broke his ankle. He was a good basketballer, but not the best. The teammates were closer to him than brothers, like lovers in their preoccupation with each other. But the determination to win for the sake of China, to drive himself and his teammates on to certain victory in gratitude to the Party, was lacking in Eagle. He had not joined the Communist Youth League. Neither did his family have rank or connections with the coach. There was something detached about the boy. It was decided that the young comrade should be reminded that the talent of the masses could produce ten thousand other basketballers as good. His weak ankle would always make him vulnerable. The Sports Institute could not afford to keep him on.

Eagle came home. His mother hugged him. His father's mistrust was confirmed, and he also blamed the boy for failing. Sunshine, meanwhile, had made himself plausible and a woman had taken him on. As happened when the wife's side brought the greater portion to a match, the man moved in with the woman's family and became subordinate to their operations; so Sunshine moved into a spacious flat provided by his wife in the west of the city and devoted himself to her business interests. And Eagle, the son left at home, was fixed up with a dogsbody job in a state office when his ankle was better. The family's fortunes had not been glorious. Life in Peking opened like a paper flower with changes in the economic policy, but still Mother Lin queued for rationed noodles, Old Lin had to beg for his medicines, when Sunshine called it was to scrounge spending money, and Eagle felt buried alive.

2

April Fool's Day was a day like any other in Peking, but Wally had mentioned the holiday for playing tricks, so Eagle invited him on that day. Where Eagle waited, the setting sun was a ferocious gold lion among the smoggy black clouds over Peking Station.

When the Doctor arrived on his bicycle, Eagle held up his hands.

"No food," he said apologetically, "there's no food!"

Wally was embarrassed. "Here, let me—"

"Not even you foreigners can buy food. Haven't you heard? The city's run out of food!"

Wally frowned, worried, until Eagle squeezed his waist: "You're really hungry, aren't you? April Fool!"

There was enough: tea and sweets, garlic shoots, spinach, meatballs, cabbage, chilli noodles, plate after plate of food. Mother Lin made the two males sit while she prepared more. She would observe what the Doctor ate, then pile up his bowl with more of the same while pronouncing on the fact that he ate this or that.

"Eat! Eat!" she kept saying.

"You eat!" retorted Wally.

Eagle picked gracefully while Wally ate. "There's no beer," he said. "I couldn't find any."

"Is that another joke? The pub with no beer?"

"Impossible to buy. I went everywhere."

So the Peking good life was precarious after all. Chinese historians describe a time when the population was decimated by war and plague as "people few, goods many."

"Will you drink spirits?" asked Eagle.

Wally waved his hands in protest.

"Can he drink?" asked Mother Lin.

"Can he drink!"

But Wally was content with company. Mother Lin sat back to smoke, her old woman's prerogative. Voices and the sound of television came from very near, behind the walls.

Eagle removed the dishes and stacked the table and stools away.

Wally patted his heart and told Mother Lin what a good character her son had.

"He shows his good side," she said wryly. "Isn't your character good too?"

"Average."

She made a great joke of it. "The Doctor's character is average," she called to her son—then to him, "Have you really eaten enough? You need to eat more than we do."

"I've eaten too much. It's all been too delicious."

"Are you used to Peking food?"

"I love it, especially the noodles, the ravioli, the dumplings."

"Dumplings! Dumplings!" She seized on the word. "He eats dumplings. Why didn't I know? He should eat my dumplings, and not the dumplings outside. Tell him to be careful."

"Be careful of dumplings? Why?"

"Haven't you heard?" Eagle stood in the doorway. "In the west of the city the dumplings have human meat in them. They arrested some people last weekend. A man and a woman and the woman's little brother. They'd been luring hawkers from the country up to their flat and killing them and turning them into dumplings. I know someone who lives over there. She said they couldn't catch any more peasants so they were going to eat the brother. He ran for the police. The neighbors found a thighbone in the alley. They thought it belonged to a pig. The local doctor knew better."

"Horrible. Why isn't all Peking talking about it?"

"We are."

"It's not in the press."

"Naturally."

"Those people must have been quite desperate," said Wally with automatic compassion.

"The man was asked why. He said he'd tasted many things in his life but never human flesh. The woman said that the price of pork was ridiculous these days. The dumplings tasted like good pork dumplings."

They snickered and fell silent.

54

Mother Lin added that a famous restaurant during the Sung dynasty had served up babies to the Emperor.

"Probably."

The silence was accepting yet ashamed of the perversities they were capable of, as Chinese, not as human beings. Eagle's way of recounting the incident had flatly placed it among things possible, not in the exotic realm of cannibalism where Wally's culture would have placed it.

"I don't taste like much," joked Wally.

"No, no, no!" Eagle protested too much.

"No taste," quipped Mother Lin.

Wally changed the subject. "Do you want to go abroad?"

Eagle shrugged. "It's not interesting to travel. I've no hope of going abroad. I haven't studied at university. My English level is low. I've got no money, no connections. So it's for the best if I don't want to go. I look after my mother."

Mother Lin was nodding off to sleep beside the stove, her face drawn contentedly.

"If you could have a wish come true," asked Wally, "what would it be?"

"A new flat. For my mother and me, a new flat with electricity and water and no stairs."

3

Eagle's father had had a stroke. For three months he lay partially paralyzed and the family's money drained away on medicines, doctors, hospital visits and special foods. Mostly Old Lin lay staring at the wall, troubled but not speaking. He asked for Sunshine, who came sometimes for meals. He squeezed Sunshine's hand, calling him "Good son, good son," as Sunshine fussed over his invalid father—then was gone. Eagle exercised his father's pet bird, swinging it to and fro in its bamboo cage. He went on buses all over Peking in search of expensive remedies recommended by the latest quack. If his father needed soup of fresh chicken or trout, he would devise ways of procuring live produce. He emptied the pots and twice a week carried his father to the public bathhouse.

No sooner had the patient's condition stabilized, and the little household's routine around it, than a second, lesser stroke came. Time was running out, and Old Lin was dying not at ease with himself. One day as he lay in bed, he quite violently caught hold of Eagle's wrist and, for the first time, said the words he had reserved for Sunshine. "Good son, good son." He made a broken speech. "You are my worthy son. You care for your father and mother. You don't think of yourself. You have strength and spirit. I entrust you with the duty of looking after your mother when I am gone. Your brother looks after himself." The words were less commendation than imperative, a sealed command that transferred status from first son to second son. The resentment at Eagle's success, and the disappointment at his failure, had been overcome, and young Eagle was filled with extraordinary joy to be given the approval denied all his twenty-two years. Such was the burden, offered as blessing, that the dying man placed on the boy. Afterwards Eagle wondered whether his father intended to say more— but he was dead within three days. Eagle and his mother sat alone in the room, as they had lived ever since, waiting for Sunshine, who was late turning up to organize the funeral.

4

Right outside the door came the sound of cold windy rain pelting suddenly, making the inside chilly.

"Aiya!" cried Mother Lin, stirring from her snooze. The

rain was fierce. There were windows to be shut, pans and towels to be put in position.

"What about him?"

"I must go," said Wally. "Doesn't matter if I get a bit wet."

"Stay here!" they shouted.

"Too much trouble! Have you got a raincoat?"

"Going out in the wet is too much trouble! The rain's too heavy. Catching cold!"

Wally argued that he had an important meeting in the morning.

"Then leave in the morning!"

It was settled. Eagle brought a basin of warm water for Wally to wash himself. They lay down for the night, Mother Lin on the sofa, the Doctor and Eagle sharing the bed. Only when saying goodnight did the old woman let her hardbitten humor drop. "Our conditions are poor. Forgive us. Will you be able to sleep?"

The rain kept up, gurgling round the corners of the gutters. Wally curled the quilt round like a cocoon, listening to the noise of the heavens, the grandest April foolery, and Mother Lin's stertorous breathing. Eagle lay on his back staring at the roof.

After a while Eagle said softly, "My grandfather had a big house. His furniture was all blackwood. Antique. He had porcelain too. He was a chief general of the Kuomintang."

It began as a bedtime story.

"Your mother's father?" asked Wally to show that he was listening.

"My father's," Eagle corrected. "We never knew. My father was a strict man. He never talked about useless things like the past. He got angry if we asked. The past was supposed to be dead in New China. But he hated the future as well. One day, it was after I got thrown off the basketball team, when I was in that boring office, I answered a newspaper advertisement for models. Fashion models. There'd never been such a thing before. Part-time work, but the money was good, and it was something interesting. I applied. Lots of people applied. I've always had luck, you know, good luck and bad luck too. So I was chosen. My father really lost his temper, out of fear that his son would be involved with a life of glamor and rottenness that could be dangerous. And the more I succeeded, and was paid, the stronger he demanded I stop. He said it would be used against me later. But we needed that extra money. In the end my mother and I agreed to keep it a secret from him. I kept up the office job, because he had got that for me, and did the modeling work after hours. My mother and I never spoke of it between ourselves either. She still doesn't like to speak of it. But the work paid for his medicines. 'Good son,' he called me at the end. When at last he said those words, he accepted what I was doing.

"A little Party member. When he died we found in one of his pockets a letter written years ago during the anti-Rightist campaign, when my father was still in the army, concerning one of the Kuomintang generals. Mother couldn't explain the letter to me. But in the year of mourning a relation of father's came on a visit and took me aside, assuming I knew or wanting to tell me, I'm not sure. He was father's half-brother, one of two sons of the Kuomintang general's two wives. Father was the son of the concubine, the 'second' wife. Perhaps that had something to do with it. Or perhaps he did have convictions after all. Anyway, when he guessed that the Communists would win, father switched sides. He was a young soldier. By the time the general was executed, father had cut all ties with the Kuomintang and was trying to line up with the Communists in Peking. His half-brother made his peace with the Communists more openly, more abjectly, saving his face and in the long run his property. My uncle's rich today. The separation between our families is complete. My father's whole life was shaped by guilt for betraying his forebears, and fear that the Communists would find out where he'd come from. A counter-

58

revolutionary. The letter must have come just when he thought he'd got away with it, to remind him never to lower his guard. He never even told his wife. She doesn't know all the details even now, doesn't care to know. That's why our family had nothing. He played it by the book. He brought no attention on us. My luck must have seemed like a curse to him. When he called me 'Good son' at the end, he was saying that I could be a completely different person. And so I am. I feel sorry for him. There's more than one kind of casualty. The past walks beside us, even if we don't always understand its language."

He turned his head to one side and his grin was visible. "Tomorrow."

5

When Wally woke, the rain was still falling steadily to thaw the earth. Waterdrops glistened on Mother Lin's silvered hair when she came in from the kitchen, crying out as her muddy feet nearly slipped from under her. Eagle yawned, stretched and hopped up. His mother already had bowls of rice porridge to set on the table.

"Nearly seven-thirty," Eagle scolded the Doctor with a prod. "Up, up, up."

Wally rolled out of a baby's sleep and pulled himself to a sitting position. Rubbing his stubbly chin and matted hair, he stared out into the shining rain and wondered aloud, "My meeting with Director Kang is at eight-thirty. I can't be late."

"Quick. Eat. There's no time to wash." Like a magician, Eagle pulled from a trunk an enormous plastic cape.

The scientist in Wally believed it impossible to keep dry while riding a bicycle through pouring rain. Eagle assured him there would be no problem. Only button up the hood and pedal slowly, keeping your knees under the cape.

Wobbling, disguised, the foreigner flowed out among the bicycles, plastic coverings, mire, umbrellas and frantic bells. He couldn't look up or his hood would fall back. He sliced through sheets of water following—he hoped—the curves of the route planned. The Yellow River of traffic, soaked, spattered, jostled to defeat the elements.

Taller than whomever the raincoat was designed for, Wally was sopping wet from the knees down, and generally bedraggled, when he arrived late at the meeting room trailing the dripping raincoat. Mrs. Gu rushed forward sympathetically as the Doctor bowed his apology. By the time he was settled in the armchair, he had picked up that there was no one in the room besides himself and Mrs. Gu.

"I'm sorry but Director Kang has gone."

"Gone!" Faint-heartedly he looked at his watch.

"He's gone to Chicago."

"That's ridiculous." Wally was only fifteen minutes late.

"Very ridiculous," laughed Mrs. Gu girlishly. "He will be back in ten days. The University of Chicago has awarded him an Honorary Doctorate."

"Good heavens!"

She opened her plastic briefcase and pulled out a swatch of untrimmed photocopies and dog-eared Chinese journals.

"I know you are interested in Director Kang's work, so I make these samples available to you. Unfortunately, not all is in English."

Wally looked glumly at the testimony to Director Kang's distinction. He detected for once a certain unease in Mrs. Gu's manner. By not immediately, enthusiastically, gleefully taking up the bundle she offered, he had upset her strategy—here was the thin edge of the wedge that allowed him to make his move.

"You mentioned last time that Professor Hsu is in retirement. Can he be visited? It would be a delight to talk with him—"

"Hsu? Oh, he's not in Peking."

"Where is he then?"

"He's retired. I don't know."

"You mean he's severed all ties? Can you find out?"

Mrs. Gu pushed the pile of Director Kang's papers across the table to Wally.

"I will contact you." And she broke into her sweet befuddled smile.

"Thank you, Mrs. Gu."

She rang Wally after lunch to say that Professor Hsu was in a rest home on the coast some five hours by train from Peking.

"Couldn't be better," he yelled into the phone. "I've been fancying a trip to the seaside. Can you get his address?"

"You will go alone?"

"Sure!"

6

Wally had the sketchiest idea of how his grandfather Waldemar had stuck China so long. He had seen photographs of a hospital built under his grandfather's supervision, an imposing whitewashed building with neat inset windows and a tiled roof along Chinese lines, with at one end a church incorporated, a steeper slope to the roof, gothic windows and a cross on top. Outside, in rows for the photograph, were the staff: Chinese in traditional dress with round glossy heads; Western women in long full skirts and men in suits with the odd dog-collar, and in the middle (if you used a magnifying glass) sunken-eyed, droopy-moustached Waldemar, beside whom was a small beady birdy woman in a pale blouse with floppy bow—his wife Retta. A ragged, painterly line of Chinese mountains faded into the sky. Behind that scene of the little mission hospital lay, to Wally's eyes, all the capability, vanity and pathos of Victorian imperatives.

Waldemar Frith was the second son of a prosperous Bristol merchant called Zachary, a name and personage to conjure with. The money came in foreign trade (tobacco to be precise), unrelenting hard work, and obsession with every penny. Vigilant, at attention, the righteous burghers of Bristol carried themselves, while their ships carried their goods, every crate accounted for, to the four corners of the empire, and returned laden with tea, spices, wool, silk, sugar, tobacco for warehouses and suppliers throughout the kingdom, every ounce inventoried and profit-bearing. Bristolians grateful for what the bounty of nature provided, along with the natural laws of a free market and their own superior position in the chain of being, were ready to pay tribute to the natural world by promoting Natural Science, Philosophy, Education, Self-Improvement and, once souls were improved, Philanthropy. From the modestly large bluestone houses aggregated on the rises of Clifton were sent outwards goods of a more spiritual kind to ballast the inward traffic. Here too the accountancy was strict in an economy inseparably practical and moral and buoyed up by a generous conception of self-interest. No accountancy was stricter than that on Sunday mornings to one's Maker and profit-bestowing Friend, no one nearer to God than the men of Clifton, assured in their evangelical projects and social reforms. Hence Zachary Frith argued in persuasive pamphlets that the advantage of Bristol, and consequently mankind, lay in the abolition of the slave trade. Zachary saw far enough. As a beginner in business with a run of good luck, he already felt anxious to make some sacrifices to balance the books. His first son would carry on the firm. But his second son was given the second name Thomas for the disciple who took the word east to the heathen. His first name was a reminder of Saxon origins. Waldemar Thomas Frith.

As fate had it, the third child—a daughter—was the stay-at-home whose husband ended up taking over the firm. The first son turned out to be a black sheep and unbeliever who ran off to the colonies, from where he wrote such enticing letters that young Waldemar went racing after him and, at the age of nineteen, stepped ashore at Port Phillip Bay: but something about Melbourne offended him. He worked as a pharmacist's assistant acquiring a certain medical knowledge and broader acquaintance with some soft and some very hard cases. The snobbery, pomp, ignorance, wretchedness of Marvelous Melbourne had an unfamiliar and shocking accent, though perhaps no worse than the same things at Home. He was a free thinker.

In the damp winter of 1891 twenty-year-old Waldemar, who had a weak chest, caught flu that became pneumonia. Matter clogged his lungs. For six months Retta Glee, a Scottish nurse in the hospital, made it her mission to cure him. She was by his bedside at every opportunity to make sure that with her care and prayer he would pull through. Letters came from the anguished mother and pious father in Bristol, always the more affecting for being so far behind current developments, until when Waldemar was at last cured, and delicately, breathlessly walking about in the sunshine, the sternest letter of all came from Zachary, "your loving father." While the mother prayed, the father had made a contract. If the Almighty saw fit to spare His creature on this occasion, the child would devote his life to service: if Waldemar survived the disease, he was to become a missionary. In the febrile condition of his convalescence, Waldemar received the commandment with passive recognition that his life had been saved for a purpose. When Retta saw the letter, she confirmed that it was a matter of duty, less to God than to his earthly father.

Waldemar wished to aim higher than his circumstances in the colony allowed. He cared little for Melbourne, but more for Retta who he feared would not like to leave the dear ones of her family. But he could not go alone. He put it to her: if he pledged his faith, would she pledge hers? When they squeezed hands, kneeling on dusty ground under a lime tree in the Botanic Gardens one blazing afternoon, their destiny became the Mission.

They honeymooned on the voyage back to the Mother Country and on arrival in London embarked in an appropriate institution on a training scheme two parts medical, two parts Christian doctrine and one part Mandarin, and a year later presented themselves at Clifton for uplifting farewells before sailing for the Orient.

Reaching Shanghai, they were put up in the flourishing commercial headquarters of the British and Foreign Bible Society, and a few days later took a transport boat up river to Hankou. They shared the one "first-class" cabin on the boat with two young girls headed for an American Baptist station, and a traveler gentleman who did recitation. The deck was covered with bodies curled against each other. Christian enlightenment had penetrated not far; and the new recruits, savoring their relatively clean and spacious cabin where candles were in good supply, felt already somewhat besieged. Waldemar stood on the deck, hands behind his back, and gazed at the wide river, recording later in a letter the "marvelous contrivance" by which coolies on the bank were able to pull the craft upstream. He never ceased to marvel at China's contrivances; and Retta never ceased to make sure that the drinking water was boiled.

They stayed in Hankou for in-the-field training before they moved out to a small market town on one of the many rivers that make up the network of waterways in southeastern Zhejiang Province, a Chinese heartland of milk and honey, fish and rice; an imperial seat of the Southern Sung dynasty that has continued to produce canny, conservative, entrepreneurial people who speak one of the most difficult of all the Chinese dialects. The Anglican bishop of the diocese, Bishop Mowbray, an empire-builder, recognized an opportunity in Waldemar

Frith, trainee doctor, a young man of vigor and practical knowledge with a spouse to keep him sane and a bedrock Low-Church faith. He would serve to pioneer a new parish in the populous, plenteous east of the province where Nonconformists and Catholics had alike failed to make inroads. The Bishop's aim was for Waldemar and Retta to prove the singular efficacy of Anglican methods.

Ten years later proof was there in the photograph of the substantial white hospital with attached chapel and numerous trainee Chinese and foreign staff lined up outside against a backdrop of mountains. Waldemar's matter-of-fact diary of appointments recorded consultations, operations and a routine of lectures on hygiene and medical science carried out seven days a week for ten years. He recorded the birth of a daughter, May Martha, and two sons, Lionel Aurelian and Jeremiah Columba. He recorded almost daily meetings with local worthies during those periods of hostility against the foreigner when the hospital was closed and the price of keeping the peace rose steeply. Near the end of the record: "Letter asking Mowbray to seek my replacement." Three months later, the last entry: "Your wisdom and mercy are great." They were bound for South Australia. On the ship Lionel and Jerry, the two boys, were photographed standing in bamboo baskets and laughing like clowns at the camera.

How had Waldemar and Retta stuck it? Wally imagined deep reliance on each other, trust, loving-kindness, a universe unto each other to sustain them even against all China. He imagined pressures on the two of them turning to strength, a remarkable achievement about which details were far from clear. Before leaving for Peking he had written to his cousin Hilary, a mango grower near Cairns and his closest link with that mad old boy, Uncle Lionel.

For his early life, into his fifties, Lionel had held down clerical jobs (in between madcap schemes) and supported his family; but once the girls, Wally's cousins, the Dionysiac Hilary and the Unspeakable Penelope, had celebrated their majorities, one in a beach romp, the other in evening dress under a marquee, then Uncle Lionel was off, unfettered, free to squander all his curious, enterprising energies. Operating a lugger in the waters between Cape York and New Guinea, he had some luck with salvage; but it was short-lived. At sixty he fell in love with an Aboriginal woman, half-caste, and set up house with her in an upturned corrugated-iron water tank up north.

The Unspeakable Penelope and Lionel's good-humored wife forgot him, while the Dionysiac Hilary, by now slowing down, made occasional pilgrimages on the fuzzy assumption that she was the living link. The Aboriginal woman died or left; Lionel resisted the authorities' attempts to institutionalize him. When the mood or need took him, he visited Hilary's mango farm; but neither father nor daughter desired permanent cohabitation. He ended up in a shack above a northern beach. Wally spoke to Hilary, and Hilary promised Wally she would get the China stuff out of her old man if she could. No one knew what was there exactly, and Wally assumed that old Uncle Lionel had lost his marbles long ago. But perhaps there would be an illumination, a fragment of story, a missing part of the past.

7

Staff and students gathered round a long table for Wally's first seminar, which turned into an impromptu lecture moving uncomfortably between first-year biochemistry, technical minutiae and remote speculation. The questions asked in public were at a level of remoter speculation. Was the gene pool becoming poisoned, someone asked, and, if so, what measures could be taken?

In private different questions cropped up. Orange soda,

beer, spiced beef and cup cakes were produced at the conclusion and talk broke into whispering conclaves. The Suzhou beauty (M.D. Stanford) cornered Wally. With darkish skin, startled eyes and waving thick hair, Dr. Song beautifully belied her thirty-seven years.

"I and my husband want to invite you to our home. Are you free on Saturday?"

Surprised, charmed, he accepted.

Dr. Song then returned to the question of her experiment. She was trying to implant alien gene material into pig embryos in order to cause tumorous growth instead of normal fetal development. There were difficulties; to get the embryos she had to operate on sows that had newly conceived, and the numbers in each litter were frustratingly unreliable.

"Chinese pigs!" She laughed. It was a variant on the common cry that Chinese pigs were too fatty. Dr. Song went on to explain the difficulties of an experiment with so many variables carried out on a small scale.

"Like cottage industry. We don't have the equipment to carry out this kind of experiment on a large enough scale to produce compelling results."

"That disadvantages you when it comes to convincing the rest of the world of your findings. But I get the idea anyway that you Chinese are resistant to the elaborate testing procedures we go through."

The remark, addressed to a woman of Dr. Song's intelligence and experience, risked causing offense, of accusing the Chinese of skepticism about the processes of inference and deduction and the very existence of ascertainable laws of nature; it might have been taken as an accusation of mere lip-service to the fundamental assumptions of Western science. If you could get results, what need theory, what need tests? Dr. Song smiled as she replied: "We must continue to experiment. But we must not overlook the differences between animals and humans. We are doctors. Our aim is simple and practical—

to heal people. To cause a cancer in a pig is not simple and not practical."

"But you can do it!" Wally added with a swagger.

"I cannot predict it," she said. "Anyway, you will come on Saturday."

8

The gathering took place in a small concrete-floored apartment on the fifth floor (there was no lift). Dr. Song greeted Wally with apologies for the apron under which her tightly cut red dress swelled. She had a rounded face, rounded perm, rolling shoulders and rolypoly middle. She introduced her husband, boyish, bespectacled Dr. Rong.

"I can't call you Dr. Song and Dr. Rong," laughed Wally.

"I have an English name," said the man. "David."

"Fine. And can I just call you Song?" he asked the woman.

David set a cup of tea before Wally and started unfolding the table where they would eat. "Are you accustomed to the life in Peking?"

"Is Peking life accustomed to me? I feel like the proverbial bull most of the time."

"A bull in China?"

"It's an exciting time to be in China, with the Reforms. Do you approve?"

"Life is better now. No one wants to go back."

"That's one question the China watchers are obsessed with. Will the door close again?"

"There are problems. Resentments. Some intellectuals are unhappy about their position, their low pay. But we cannot go back. Of course the open policy is not yet entirely realized.

China must work towards being open, without becoming too humble or too proud."

"In the West we tend to think of freeing things up as going with human nature—individualism, entrepreneurship, market forces—all instinct. Here it's a conscious ideological move, you're saying."

"Those things are natural here too, but the Party must also learn to allow them."

"To let go control?"

"To find new controls. Chinese people are afraid of chaos. That is where you people are so sophisticated."

"With chaos?"

"With narrowly avoiding it."

The man's smile suggested layers of experience of what was so abstractly being discussed.

"Excuse me," David said, "I must prepare food."

There was a knock at the door and both David and Song went to answer it. The woman who entered, of medium height and build, held herself modestly, and stood with hands loosely clasped. She wore a plain dress of rich pine green, and had a fat braid of hair on one shoulder. Her face was long, delicate, suggestive of vulnerability yet also strength and a fierce quickness. She was introduced as Song's schoolfriend, Jin Juan. When she sat down, in brighter light, Wally saw that her skin was not as petal-soft as it looked from the door. There were minute lines, rough patches, and beneath the powdered surface the skin was taut, weathered.

"I have heard you are very distinguished," she said to Wally with incisive, elegantly modulated English.

"Heaven forbid!" He waved his arms in protest. "Are you in medicine too?"

"I am a middle-school teacher," she answered with blank eyes.

"Then we talk no more shop. You're from Suzhou too?"

"No, I'm from Zhejiang. Or do you say Chekiang in English. From Hangzhou."

"Above is heaven, below are Suzhou and Hangzhou," intoned Wally.

"It has that reputation," she added with evident irony.

David came worrying in to move the table to the center of the room. "Please!" He hurried back with dishes, bottles and glasses.

"A model husband," noted Jin Juan.

Meanwhile Song brought from the bedroom their four-year-old daughter, a chubby child who squirmed like a bear cub on her mother's shoulder. The guests ooh'd and ah'd.

"Abu Dhabi, Accra, Amman," began the child, and squawked as she was heaved off to bed.

"That kid has a speciality," said Jin Juan. "She can recite the capital cities of the world in alphabetical order. You should try her some time. Not now! Eat!"

Song asked Wally if he had caught up with the Professor—Hsu Chien Lung, was it?—whom he had expressed interest in meeting.

"I'm working on it. They tell me he's retired to a seaside resort town somewhere. I'm planning a visit. The place is called Beidaihe."

"Why do you want to see Hsu Chien Lung?" asked Song. "He must be old now."

"He's one of the reasons I came to China. Before the war he published some papers in the States that contained some insights into the work I'm doing now. I want to see what further information he has, what conclusions if any, at the end of a lifetime's work."

The others smiled. They seemed to show concern for the foreigner's opinion, and the weird, miraculous fact that, of all things, an old man in a rest home at Beidaihe should be the key link.

"When are you going to Beidaihe?" asked Song. "We are

going there with our little girl for a few days. You will accompany us."

"Really? No, no, no—" For a moment Wally panicked. Was their company another means of thwarting him? He wanted these to be the honest, *simpatico* people they seemed.

"We will go together then," confirmed David. "Jin Juan, you will come?"

She hesitated; a play of self-interrogation crossed her face.

"Can I take a raincheck?"

The idiom was for Wally.

CHAPTER FIVE

All Souls

1

Near the College was a sealed road edged with rubble, pot-holes and pale hard strips of mud. One day a work team came to the street with a water truck, buckets, baskets, hoes. They were mopheaded kids in baggy trousers, jackets, pink singlets, with thin hard arms, or family men in blue cotton caps with faces like pickled dates, who shouted, whistled and sang as they broke up the ground in work that was like making mud pies. At the end a mule-drawn cart came with a load of long thick sticks wrapped in sacking. The workers planted these broom handles and packed the earth around each one. When they piled on to the water truck and the mule cart, they left behind a row of tall sticks standing in the bare mud.

By the first of April there were buds at the tops of the sticks and one or two had produced tiny leaves. On the hard mud was a brush of emerald fur. The days became bright, though the nights were chilly, and after a wind, when the coal dust was blown away, the Western Hills were revealed in craggy purple-jade splendor, yet never near enough to seem part of the flat gray city, rather like memories of China's sighing imperial greatness, a stage-shy presence always nervously in the wings.

2

For Song, David and the child to visit Beidaihe for a weekend was a complicated matter. The College authorities had to clear their absence, buy train tickets and reserve beds in a residence. Obstruction lurked at each of these stages. For Jin Juan to accompany them was more difficult. She knew from experience that her work unit, the humble middle school, owed her no favors. For two days either side of a Sunday she could take sick leave if a medical certificate was provided. Some units were more suspicious than others about sick leave, but malaise was an art form in New Age China, especially among teachers. If David would sign a medical certificate, she could go.

The College, battening on to all available privilege, had booked Wally "soft," while the Chinese got "hard" seat tickets. But Wally was able to swap with a kid who would enjoy the ludicrous perk. "Hard" was a floor show. A girl conductor in cocked hat and epaulettes announced in singsong her pleasure to be serving the travelers, as she came around with the kettle for tea. Intermittent broadcasts urged people to be civilized and polite and extoled, as it flashed by, the glories of reconstructed Tangshan, the city flattened in 1976 by an earthquake that killed a quarter of a million people and presaged the death of Mao. A decade later Tangshan offered a vista of untidy industry and thrown-up housing blocks in a treeless moonscape. When the train reached the more picturesque hills of the peninsula a television program started up from sets above the carriage doors, and attention was drawn to a Soviet contortionist in pink gossamer sheath, filmed through vaseline, who twisted and gyrated to the Song of Joy and did impossible things to the rope between her thighs that suspended her above a roaring crowd. The businessmen looked up from their discussion of prices. The schoolteacher stopped knitting her cardigan. The honeymoon bride awoke from her daydream. The guys in operetta uniforms neglected their poker game. The clip was followed by a multi-racial American jazz ballet from Broadway, and then came China with a series of demure matrons in evening attire who sang of snowflakes, seagulls and willows south of the Yangtze. Attention drifted. The child started to list capitals, "Cairo. Cabinda. Canberra. Caracas. Cayenne." Once again Wally was asked where he came from and how much he earned.

The mild coastal spring was well advanced in the chirpy seaside town. At the Diplomatic Guesthouse, where Wally was obliged to stay while the others went to the cheaper College-approved dormitory, there were lots of petunias in painted pots. There were layers of human hair in the bathroom, and wicker chairs on the pleasant balcony. Alone, Wally slept soundly, lulled by the sea's presence and the sweet clean air after the travails of Peking.

He woke early and found his way to the beach for a dip, just as he would have done on a holiday morning back home. The flat sea of the swimming enclosure between two rocky promontories was ringed with a net. Some old people in blue and gray pajama suits were out exercising, swinging their arms intently and bending vigorously at the knee as prescribed: Beidaihe was a playground for ailing Party leaders whose life had become perpetual vacation. A couple of girls were collecting shellfish and grit in plastic briefcases. There were boats out, sailing towards the radiant misty east. The sea had carried invaders from Korea and Japan; not far from here the Great Wall itself came down to the ocean's edge in an attempt to stop them. The Greatest Gate Under Heaven was there, the

Gate That Controls Inside and Outside. Much further away, thought Wally, the waters of this Pacific Ocean could have carried Chinese voyagers to San Francisco, Tierra del Fuego or Capricornia. It was icy. No sooner had he dived than he wished to be back on shore. The swim shook his senses and after breakfast and a shower, ready for the appointment, he felt alert and frisky; excited, too, about meeting the Professor at last.

Only Jin Juan was at the gate to meet him. David and Song's child had come up with a fever overnight, so they were staying put. Jin Juan would be the Doctor's guide. She was dressed for the beach in big sunglasses and a candy-pink dress with a V-neck and big buttons down the front. But her manner was strained. Wally asked if she had slept well.

"No! Tossed and turned."

They took a bus from the main street to the *Qigong* Rest and Recreation Institute, a glassy construction amid tall pines on an eastern rise. When stopped at the gate they asked for Professor Hsu Chien Lung.

"What unit?" snapped the woman.

"Peking Union Medical College. Retired," answered Jin Juan in kind.

"And you?"

"Same unit."

"Him?"

"Expert at the unit."

"Wait a minute."

A higher official arrived, and they told the story again.

"Wait a minute."

The process was repeated three times as they inched along the chain of command from the gatehouse to the reception desk to a second building out the back, and a third that lacked the modern facade of the block facing the street: it was anti-quated, colorless, medicinal, with light searching its long corridors on this bright morning. There was a sharp scream followed by a drawn-out moan behind one of the doors. It had a familiar unpleasant institutional feel; the condition to which, in China, many buildings aspired.

"Hsu Chien Lung? Hsu? Hsu? Hsu Chien Lung! Professor! Professor? Hsu! Hsu! Shoo-shoo-shoo." The name was shouted, whispered, passed from voice to voice.

"Wait!" commanded a dustcoated chap whose spectacles crowned a bald pate. This time "Wait" was meant seriously; more than half an hour slipped by. Wally and Jin Juan sat staring at the blue sky outside until they were summoned to an office and a desk behind which sat an imposing woman, also in a white dustcoat, with permed black curls and a concerned, almost ardent manner. Wally submitted to the ritual quiz and she quickened at the discovery that he had worked at Harvard. She herself had visited Tufts University in nearby Boston once, and was "well acquainted" with Harvard professors. Having established ramifications of significance belied by the un-planned appearance of this athletic-looking foreign holiday-maker who turned out to be a high-level expert, with a smart Chinese woman in tow, the Department Head (called Cao) obliged. She jotted down notes and quizzed further, this time about the foreigner's connections with Professor Hsu Chien Lung.

Wally said merely that he wished to pass on the warm regards of a common American friend.

Scribbling, the Department Head nodded. Her face grew a little tighter.

"His condition is not good. What a pity!" She sniffed.

"You mean we can't see him?"

"Of course you can see him, but I'm afraid he will not appreciate your message. Let's go," she said, coming out from behind the desk.

As they walked the sunlit dismal corridors, Wally's skin tingled. To have tracked Professor Hsu through many obstacles brought a sense of adventure and imminent achievement. The path that had taken Hsu to Harvard in the first place, where he left an impression on young Harvey Heilmann, and the path that had taken Wally to Cambridge, England and Cambridge, Massachusetts, and now to China, were about to intersect. He was an agent of the larger meeting. The somewhat arbitrary determination to rediscover Hsu had brought about the kind of connection that might happen or might not, and that makes the world take one shape and not another, and Wally was aware of a single man's direct participation in the unboundedly complex fate of the planet, as he followed Department Head Cao through the curiously inactive institution.

During his time in China he had encountered time and again the disorganization of the place. So much seemed to be a formless, fluid mess; a sluggish, surging river of mud and sand and fertile slime and debris pouring itself into the sea of a present that was endlessly disappearing into the past, always threatening to burst its banks, sometimes doing so, recording its progress by the silt deposited. In response the people were salty, sarcastic, quick-humored, laughing at disaster rather than preventing it, in supreme anti-perfectionism. Yet that was not all. Somewhere in this stir-fry was genius, Wally was convinced. Somewhere was a spirit of knowledge and understanding, hidden certainly, dormant or suffocated perhaps, un-self-advertizing, imperceptible to the foreigner's gaze; yet it existed, and for Wally, with his particular expertise, the genius had come to reside in Professor Hsu Chien Lung.

They passed through locked double doors into a corridor of doors also locked. Through one, left ajar, was a glimpse of a ward of four beds, clothes, ornaments, furniture, luggage, that suggested long-stay patients. In the window was a big red paper cut-out of the character for long life. They came to a little sitting-room with the usual armchairs, the usual loose brown covers, the usual mugs for tea. Wally, Jin Juan and Department Head Cao sat while an orderly went to fetch the Professor. After a time, the frail old figure appeared in the doorway. He was short, quite fat, with sloping shoulders, rounded stomach and splayed feet as he shuffled forward. His head was near bald save for silver spikes above the ears and on the left was a big pink birthmark. His very pink lips hung loosely. Striped pajamas showed beneath his loose gray serge trousers. On his feet, scraping across the terrazzo floor, were black corduroy slippers and sheer nylon socks worked with butterflies. What Wally noticed especially was his wristwatch that hung loose on a band of metal links and told the wrong time.

In a loud voice Department Head Cao made formal introductions, and the old man grinned enthusiastically. Jin Juan came forward and placed her slender hand in the Professor's pudgy hand. Her cool, bitter expression ignited into shock at the squeeze he gave her. After giggles all round they sat, and Wally began to speak in slow clear English.

"I'm very happy to meet you . . ." His speech had advanced three sentences and the jolly, vacant grin on the old man's face was unchanged. "You remember Harvey Heilmann? At Harvard?" Wally repeated, with exaggerated inflection. The old man appeared not to register. "Perhaps his English is rusty," Wally said to Jin Juan.

Department Head Cao spoke up. "He can't speak English. He can't speak Chinese either. He can't speak anything now."

"He's lost his marbles," said Jin Juan. Once remarked on, the fact was obvious.

The old man had started to dribble. As the spittle fell in a long thread from his lip to his jacket, the Department Head watched unperturbed. "He does not know who we are or where he is or who he is himself. But he's quiet. Our *qigong* therapy has helped but he has not been able to regain the power of comprehension or speech. We continue the treatment."

"What results have you had?"

"He has a good appetite, and regular bowel movement,"

she said with satisfaction. "He is strong and should live for a long time."

The man's fleshy features and bulging pink eyes struck Wally as the very expression of absence; there was scarcely a human individual there, not a spark of intelligence, but a dough dumpling in official drag. He pitied the poor old man, and lamented the absence of what he had hoped to encounter.

The Department Head nodded. "Okay." The visit was over. Once again there were grins, nods, handshakings, goodbyes. From the international world of medical research Wally brought greetings and honor to the slobbering, jolly dumpling.

"What a sad end," said Wally as they retraced their steps through corridors and locked doors.

Jin Juan still walked behind, her hands clasped in front as if she were spectator at a pageant. Was that a sardonic smile on her pressed lips?

"It hurts to see a man who could once produce such fine work reduced to that state," continued Wally. "Do you know his papers on traditional treatments for cancer in the Zhejiang region? I believe Hangzhou is his home town. He has collected remarkable data from the villages in that region. That's what he worked on at Harvard back in the 1930s. I guess I was half hoping to collaborate with him even now at the College. So it's all very distressing." Wally chattered garrulously.

Department Head Cao absorbed his words and waited for Jin Juan's clarification. To the woman she said that perhaps Wally had misremembered. She said that Professor Hsu Chien Lung was not from the South, from Hangzhou: he was from the extreme North-East, from Harbin. He had studied in the Soviet Union in the 1950s, he had never studied in the United States. She thought perhaps he had made the acquaintance of some American professors at conferences. He was not a cancer specialist, he was a brain surgeon—or had been.

"Really? Really? Oh I see!" Jin Juan responded matter-of-

factly, and passed the information on to Wally, who was flab-
bergasted and furious.

"You mean that old guy's not Hsu Chien Lung."

"He is called Hsu Chien Lung," the Department Head said
categorically. "How do you write it?"

"The same."

"He is Hsu Chien Lung originally from Peking Union Medical College."

"There must be some mistake."

"Maybe there are two professors with that name."

Again the Department Head suggested to Jin Juan that the
foreigner had misremembered.

Wally swore. "Mrs. Gu—I'll kill her."

Jin Juan was quite calm. "It's a mistake. The wrong Hsu. If
the Hsu fits, wear it. It doesn't, so don't get upset. We've been
taken for a ride. But if he was the right Hsu, it would not have
helped you much. Hey? It's better we beat a retreat."

"You're right." Wally turned to the Department Head and
bowed. "Forgive me. My mistake. I'm a stupid foreigner."

Department Head Cao was dignified as they took farewells.
She evidently agreed with the distinguished foreign guest's
self-assessment.

Wally and Jin Juan walked down the hill from the *Qigong*
Rest and Recreation Institute and cut through to the waterfront.
Everywhere trees were in bud, acacias, plane trees and poplars,
everywhere new residences were under construction, as if the
retired hacks herded to holiday in the place would never cease
coming. On street corners cherry-cheeked women sold ice
blocks and drowsy youths sold porcupines made of cockle
shells. Occasionally a Cantonese construction worker would
fly past on a Suzuki motorbike. And everywhere the elderly
officials waddled with their unique blend of smugness, vacancy, busybodyness and undeviating rectitude, sea lions
washed up on the beach.

A road ran along between wind-bent tamarisks festooned

with blazing convolvulus and crossed at intervals the rank marshy streams or sewer drains that flowed into the foam where people frolicked. Wally and Jin Juan came out onto the sand and took their shoes off, enjoying the sun on wintry skin.

"What can it mean?" He pondered. "What are they up to? Can that man be Hsu Chien Lung?"

"You think they don't want you to meet the real McCoy?"

"Or don't they know what I'm after? Is it a question of crossed wires?"

"Not likely," said the woman with hot confidence that verged on anger. "Better wait and see. I guess that Hsu is a decoy."

"I just want to talk to the old guy. I don't bite!"

"You're a foreigner. You're all spies. You want the truth, but maybe your truth goes against the glory of China."

"Come off it."

"You want this thing badly. There must be a reason. They cannot see your reason. The safest response is to stop you. Don't lose your temper with them. Wait."

"Maybe I'm the crazy one with this fantasy that I must meet up with old Hsu."

"Perhaps you should wait for Hsu to find you. I guess he knows you're coming."

"How can you be so sure he's alive?" He looked at her inquisitively. "The guy's probably kicked the bucket, or an old fraud like all the others. But it's my way through this country."

"The old man is fond of dragons," she said. "It's one of our sayings. This old guy was a dragon fanatic. He studied them, painted them, filled his house with toy dragons. One day a real dragon popped its head in the window. The old guy died of fright. It means you like the idea of a thing, but you can't cope with the reality."

"I'm like that?"

"Many foreigners are like that about China. We Chinese

are like that about foreign things too. We want them—want you—on our terms. We're timid."

"Your English is really incredible. It must be wasted in the middle school."

"I was assigned there."

The angle of her pointed chin had the capacity to suggest negative emotions without any ostensible change. A few faint lines round her eyes tautened, her eyes perhaps narrowed a fraction, her lips, sitting together, clenched, as if she had sucked on vinegar. Resistance, bitterness, anger were communicated in a mute form that had been internalized and almost, but not quite, dispensed with. Useless ineffectual negative emotion passed through her in a shudder and was gone again to leave her serene and ironically sparkling.

"How old are you?" He took a Chinese liberty.

"Twenty-nine."

"Married? Not married?"

"Not married yet." The shudder once again.

"Strange, someone like you." It didn't fit. A job with low status, and no career prospects to speak of. A dazzling sophistication and command of the foreign language, such as only the best Chinese background and education can achieve in the most gifted and diligent students. Style, attractions—sharp-temperedness. No husband, no kid. Most Chinese women by Jin Juan's age had taken care of those things or were panicking. Something was wrong. He hesitated to pry, but pursued the line of his questions.

"Have you got a boyfriend?"

"I have," she said, holding up a finger with a ring. She lowered her eyelids and looked at him humorously. "Can't get married till we find an apartment. That's no simple matter in Peking."

He had judged her wrongly then.

"What about your parents?"

83

"My parents died some years ago."

"Oh. So there's only you."

"My grandfather is still alive. He's in the South. You know?" At that her face became fully expressionless and she turned to look at the waves. Some girls in what looked like cocktail dresses, in stockings and high-heeled leather shoes, with chains round their waists and shells round their necks, were prancing in the sea up to their thighs, shrieking from cold, clutching each other and laughing as spume broke over their bodies and their drenched clothes, trying to steady themselves and pose for the photograph that a chap on the beach was lining up. The romantic bedraggled look, a mermaid flung ashore in a party hostess's rags: that was the image they were after.

"Shall we swim?" cried Jin Juan.

"Too cold!"

"You can keep your clothes on." She bubbled with laughter.

"You people are bananas."

3

At dusk Wally sat on the balcony of the Diplomatic Guesthouse watching tea-colored waves break. At the tip of the western promontory of the bay was famous Tiger Rock, an object of holidaymakers' pilgrimage which, for those with active imaginations, had the shape of a tiger. As the crowd swarmed over it in monochrome clothes and the tide rose, Wally was reminded of those nuns who sang "O God Our Help In Ages Past" while the ship sank.

For the first time since he had been in China his loneliness took a new form. It was no longer the steady, standard condition which he was confident of enduring, but the more puzzling and sweeter absence of a companion who had made him happily forgetful of himself and his situation.

Jin Juan had asked about his wife and in straightforward terms he had told her the truth about Bets. His present feelings of tender emptiness came from having unburdened himself. But it was impossible to render the images that were growing stronger and stronger in his memory.

Bets had bowled up to him in the dark cramped stairwell of a Cambridge party nearly twenty years ago, a big-boned young woman in a peasant jumper, with a clippety-clopping New Zealand accent.

"A little Antipodean girlie just lobbed in at the station," said the waspish, equally Antipodean culture critic who had her suitcase to stow.

She greeted Wally with the enthusiasm of an old friend, automatically, though they'd never met, and at once lapsed into embarrassed silence.

"What brings you to Cambridge on such a night?"

"I had his address"—gesturing at the culture critic, Charles—"and wanted to hear the choir. You're living here?" She had a chipped front tooth and a wild mass of wavy blonde hair.

"Nice!" she exclaimed when he laid out his situation. "So you can hear the choir whenever you want."

"Actually, to be honest, I've never got round to it. It's more a thing for tourists."

He had not meant to sound condescending, to imply that the girl was as shallow as sparkling seawater; but his own Cambridge had so narrowed down that the famous choir was scarcely part of the place.

He had narrowed himself, crawled into the inner recesses of his work. His PhD routine permitted mild inebriation once a week, no more; and usually in the form of these Cambridge parties, where in cold dim rooms in workingmen's cottages furiously intelligent students pursued pungent arguments about revolution, antimatter, sexual distress, while Chairman Mao's picture was pinned to a wall of the crumbling loo down the back.

It was a change from black things to hear the girl's confident account of her English pleasures: towpaths, Devonshire teas, domestic interiors, voices, curtain calls, old stones. She had been in the country for two months.

Late into the night they danced to *Jumping Jack Flash*, worked up a sweat then collapsed. Next afternoon they went together to King's to hear the choir. She would be called nothing but Bets, and gave a low wheezy laugh.

They sat on hard seats in white light from high windows. Wally could not get inside the music no matter how hard he concentrated. He shuffled and frowned; his thoughts roamed; images and dreams came to him seemingly unconnected with the music; yet afterwards, clapping and beaming, he knew he had experienced something. Bets sat expressionlessly throughout, as if it meant nothing to her, and as soon as it was over said she was starving. They walked, found a tearoom, walked again, found a pub, and talked easily, humorously, till closing time. Wally forgot about work that seemed, all of a sudden, shamefully self-absorbing, or found a new enthusiasm in explaining it simply. Towards the end Bets made some matter-of-fact comments about the concert, which showed specialized and discerning judgment.

She confessed, "I studied for a year at the Con. Didn't have the voice—and now I'm traveling."

Wally felt tricked by her uncomplicated directness; he had earlier made some pompous remarks about the music. Seeing how she undersold herself, he would not be such a fool as to take her at face value again.

Nor had he enjoyed a day so much in ages, and when they were back at his college rooms he hugged her, in sheer delight at her solid enlivening presence rather than intending seduction; though seduction followed, as if it were the simplest thing in the world. Neither for young Wally nor Bets was it casual or common. But Bets showed not a trace of embarrassment, even when Charles popped his head round the door next morning to escort her back to London.

The next weekend Wally traveled down to see her and she took him to a Lieder recital. Some of it—the Schumann—she had once studied, but she refused to sing for him. He loved being with her, especially in the mornings, lazing through passages of time filled with one another. She was bouncy, exuberant, wonderfully crude at times, and she had fallen in love with him. At the end of the year he moved into the top story of a subdivided Victorian family mansion, and Bets came too: provisionally, on her own terms, keeping her own plans.

When the summer arrived, Wally agreed to wind up his experiment and they went wandering, from Cambridge to Land's End in a borrowed car, staying in bed-and-breakfasts when it rained, or camping by embowered streams when the weather was fine, sitting shirtless till late. They never needed to apologize for what they were, a shy serious socialist boy from Australia whose clothes hung on his man's frame and whose conceptions were at the forefront of science; a pilgrim girl from New Zealand whose lack of awe was salt in the stew. When they visited William Morris's house, approving his union of artisanship, organicism and creativity—which tied in with Wally's theory of the body's organicist intervention in its own processes—seeing the charcoal of Beatrice on the wall, Wally knew he had his own, a muscular candid woman with the gold of the sun in her eyes.

On the night of the summer solstice they camped at Tintagel and saw a student performance of *The Tempest* in the ruins of what might have been Camelot. Radiant moonlight attended on the players, scrawny or puppy-fat in tights, and their fuzzy voices echoing among the gaping, moon-shadowed battlements turned to powerful legend the Bard's conviction that all strife, even in love, can be reconciled. *Thought is free! Thought is free!* They chanted in hippie dance.

Afterwards Bets and Wally climbed down the cliff to the beach with a great group of actors and spectators and stage hands, and a mighty bonfire was built. Callow Ferdinand, Caliban, Miranda, stripped off their clothes and pranced into the frothing, icy western sea, and others followed—Wally—Bets—trilling, shrieking, their bodies coated in silver scales of moonshine.

They sang then while they warmed themselves round the fire. A lone voice started: *And did those feet, In ancient time* . . . and others joined. The night never grew dark; by four a.m. auroral lights were poking through the gap-toothed castle walls from the east. It was midsummer 1968, and as dawn rose the young people, gypsy-like, with long tendrils of hair tangling in the breeze off the sea, in frayed jeans with embroidered red stars and flowers, in t-shirts and denim jackets, arm in arm took the rocky path up the cliff, while a single voice still tried to sing, *bandiera rossa trionfera* . . .

It was late the next day when Wally at last stirred, to find the space beside him in the tent empty. Bets was drying her hair in the afternoon sun. He heard her singing alone for the first time then. Her voice sounded different: low-throated, distant, darker, bluer, singing that old song, *You-izz, You-izz* . . . He loved her.

"Hi sport!" she said screwing up her eyes.

In the autumn they were married, in a friend's back garden. Why marriage? Because in those days there was no need to worry, nothing to fear. They wanted to entwine like the honeysuckle and the vine.

4

Bets did have a voice but no discipline, which was lucky because Wally had discipline enough for three. Always his work
came first. He was the hard-working genius, the scholarship
boy, and a child when it came to looking after himself. He
would sew on a button with the wrong color thread, crack the
egg he was trying to boil. But he needed Bets less for material
provision than to keep alive in him the sympathy and respon-
siveness that would otherwise have dried out in his research
work. She was the only human being he was close to. Because
she loved him, she fell in with that role. Her attendance at
musicology lectures diminished and she couldn't be bothered
with the prissy competitive workshops. Sometimes she ren-
dered a piece so perfectly that the top of her head blew off,
and she would collapse afterwards in shocked, blushing,
breathy chuckles. Other times she sounded as asthmatic as a
whistling kettle, as musical as a mosquito. She had no control—
and because she knew what perfection was, she felt weak
before the amount of self-inflicted suffering needed to achieve
it—when life was too much fun. She took a job as a barmaid,
and was happiest singing blues in the pub on occasional evenings. The blues voice stayed with her, and blues was the cradle
song when Jerome was born.

That year Wally got his doctorate and they crossed the
Atlantic to the other Cambridge. The Vietnam War was in full
cry and Bets came to believe that the war was invented especially to indulge operatic American agonizing. She despised
the war, and the United States for it, and wretched Australia,
and her own gutless homeland too; she hated anything that
bullied in the name of ideology. The Pope, Stalin, Uncle Sam,
the wire photos of the tear-stained faces of Chinese Red Guards

adoring their leader: all alike made her shudder. She was a political agnostic; she believed only in the anarchy of growth, which was how she reared her son. She stood for an eccentric, resistant individualism far removed from Wally's kindly, lofty ameliorism. They ranted a lot about the issues in those days and Bets often gave offence at faculty dinners by snorting at some pompous professorial remark. They survived Harvard only by joining their own personal discussions with the general fight by which values were thrashed out for the Republic and the world. There was simply no escape in the place. Despite the liberal reverence for all forms of personal choice, all antiquarian highways and byways, all useless and irrelevant pursuits, in spite of venerable, salvation-seeking, perpetually pilgrim New England on all sides, there was no private nook to which to retreat.

But in the end they were outsiders. An attractive offer came from Prince Henry's Hospital in Sydney. For Wally it was not an easy choice to forsake center stage. How many Nobel prize-winners came from the North Shore, while in Cambridge, Massachusetts, every block had its own? But he acknowledged the facts of geography, the nearness of Bets's family across the Tasman. And they wanted their child to be Antipodean.

Aged five, Jerome was brought home to Australia speaking of cookies and cook-outs, of "small is beautiful" and "do your own thing" in a Hahvahd drawl. Now, more than fifteen years later, he spoke Strine. He'd hung on to his United States passport. He had a London haircut and Japanese clothes and a global knowledge of fast food and cocktails, a mingy computer hacker's physique and an expression when he looked at his father that was—Aztec. *Aiya!* He was a citizen of the world.

The gaps had widened after the nuclear family returned to Australia. Why? Who or what was to blame? He and Bets had shared a little fancy that their roots were common, though, unlike him, she came from a well-heeled family that frittered its capital away on self-fulfilment. Wally used to joke that when

90

they were kids he and Bets must have been lovesick for each other across the Tasman Sea. As a youth he had been drawn to the peak of beloved Pigeonhouse Mountain to dream eastwards, and Bets as a teenager on family holidays at the beach had loved to stray to the western tip of the headland, to dive fearlessly off the rocks into the ocean, already knowing their direction, already seeking their center.

But Wally's time in Sydney became allotted to committees for good works, always on the side of the angels, while Bets preferred the Angel, a pub where her motley friends hung out. She had few responsibilities. Teaching had been tried; no one faulted her performance, but the labored nurturing ran against the grain for her—especially when she ended up teaching music, which she hated. They had money anyway, since Wally got the Chair of Oncology over the heads of his elders. He was a haggard social reformer now in his own sphere, in strife with numerous administrative bodies, sticky with the politics of New South Wales and always feeling he had no time over for his Real Work. Bets laughed at him with her wide mouth. What passed for social reform in Australia was a kind of white sugar on which a new mendacious class would have grown obese had they ever stopped jogging. Bets did not believe in solutions, and Wally waged his battles alone. Carried along by the undying love of a baggy gang of happy social misfits, Bets would sometimes, at the Angel, sing the blues. They told her she should go professional; she threw back her shoulders and laughed till she coughed.

Her other pregnancies miscarried till she gave up trying. Jerome was always there when she needed him. Otherwise he was down on the beach or up to something.

Bets was bony, golden. Always she was restive, sometimes brittle and destructive and hilariously angry. She got drunk and shocked friends with her reckless, often reactionary opinions. When the black mood was on her she jeered at the Royal Commission into Human Relationships and scoffed at the Whit-

91

lamites, and got an earful of gutter language in return. "Just get nucked," she would counter in flattest Kiwi. She blamed people—society—herself, for handing over the individual quest to a government—an official—a husband—who would take the matter out of your hands with the ringing conviction of progress ever onwards. In these moods she turned to her special friend Aldo, a joiner turned harpsichord maker, who was plump, jesting, kind to a fault. She rang him every day and he wouldn't let her hang up till the hard edges softened.

Wally never stopped needing her, yet their separate and irreconcilable lives divided them by a space wider than the Tasman. If he lifted his head even a minute from his commitments, which went on twenty-four hours a day across the nation and round the globe, Wally froze. He had failed to come up with the goods. The papers he still managed to churn out added not a hair to the mountain of human knowledge. All the challenges were still in place, budged not an inch, as pressing as ever. He got in the habit of ringing Cindy, a nurse. They would go to her flat at Coogee where she would roll a joint; she patted him—"Relax, relax"—as she chased cockroaches off her mattress.

Once he came home at three o'clock in the morning. He never told Bets when he would be home. His was the only car on the northbound highway. The lights were on in their bedroom and bathroom, and—it was a cool night—Bets was outside on the terrace that opened off their bedroom. Below on Whale Beach the white surf and black sea pounded steadily under the stars. She was in her nightie. He couldn't guess what reverie and rancor was upon her, or deeper passion that would not let her sleep.

From the roar of ocean he distinguished her singing in full low voice the old song, fragment without words. She had not heard the car, and only stopped when he came into the bedroom—and she came towards him, to meet him, her gold hair brushed down, her figure straight and strong, her eyes

92

almost smiling, her mouth half open, not quite daring to break into speech. What could she utter? Not a word of complaint, of recrimination, not even the dead calm of resignation. She was entirely beautiful, in her thirty-seventh year. She loved him. And he had not been there.

Now she was not here.

5

The day Wally and his friends returned to Peking was the Festival of Pure Brightness, a Chinese All Souls Day when, as Jin Juan explained cheerfully, you should sweep the graves of your ancestors and step on green. But the original pilgrimage to dilapidated country graves had given way nowadays to a park visit or even a token stroll on roadside grass. Around the Medical College the old white tufts of grass at the corners of the buildings had green tips. He placed his big feet on the young grass, and asked Jin Juan if that would do. The magnolia tree, however, that stood outside his window, was unchanged.

He wanted to invite his friends in for tea, but Song and David's child was playing up so they agreed to separate. He shook hands with each of them in turn, thanking them, with awkward sincerity.

Then waiting for him in his room he found a thick letter from Uncle Lionel that began,

"My dear boy—"

CHAPTER SIX

Extraterritorial

1

Western feet tread a beat in Peking between the Friendship Store that supplies needs and the Hong Kong-run hotel that offers comforts at a price. The beat is featureless save for the determined dragging of feet and the hiss of the scruffy Central Asian money-changers: "Change your money, change your money." Frozen in winter, windswept in spring, dustblown in summer, Mongolian boy soldiers guard the fenced compounds of uninspired tower blocks along the way. Inside live the eyes and ears of Outside, the diplomats and journalists who are paid to know China's image. At night from high in the darkness the boom of rock and roll or of orchestras descends, for they are partying people.

Word comes as an encoded address that leads to an entrance, a lift attendant (desultory informant), a doorbell behind which a "personalized" space is made as un-Chinese as a stage set, Africa or Manhattan, a plastic magic carpet on which extraterritorials float over the dark street.

Wally needed an evening out. He arrived early, and the

familiars were already there: the Bostonian economist whose hair rose above her head like the top of a Corinthian column, the tired, gracious Australian Cultural Attaché in his yellow suit, the sharp-witted Canadian Trade Commissioner with her punk son. Already vigorous on the dance floor were Dulcia and Jumbo, together. They had become a couple. The man from ABC was there; the teachers of English; the ex-Maoist who advised the Pentagon; and others Wally could classify among the Five Foreigns.

Included in Type One were the diplomats and embassy types who had opted for China and were neither illusioned nor disillusioned as they battled on beneath a required gloss of optimism and discretion; or those who came to China as to any post, hoping to bank all their pay and live on allowances while enjoying an exalted station, miserable, sarcastic, half-mad as they shopped in vain for the washing powder, the breakfast cereal, the beer to which they were accustomed.

Category Two covered the journalists who hated no-news no-information China, but loved her because by sheer dint of hanging on they became lone authorities to a gullible world. Clubbable, joking creatures with a magnanimous streak, they became weirder as the restrictions and surveillance pressed in on them, driving them eventually to drink, sex, paranoia, outrage and outrageousness.

Sleekest and most disgruntled were Type Three, the business operatives, victims of the notorious joint ventures and other forms of economic cooperation, with a fund of stories as to how the Chinese screw without being screwed. They were young men and women mostly, who, seeking gainful employment in the People's Republic, found themselves as go-betweens in multinational arms deals or struggling with projects of gargantuan fantasy designed to save the company's bacon back home. How their scorn brimmed!

Number Four were the teachers, on their wanderers' passports, expert in anything from artificial intelligence to light opera that was deemed relevant to China's Four Modernizations. They were specimens to be studied, balls in the global game of educational pingpong that China wished to join. Confucius stressed education. In New Age China there were more institutes, research centers, universities, colleges, think tanks, scholarly societies, more underpaid and idly employed "intellectuals" than there were green vegetables. The intellectuals would not make the mistake again of suffering as they had done during the Cultural Revolution. To enlist the help of foreign teachers was one way of feathering the nest.

Fifth came students and scholars of all kinds, the lubricating oil. Because they spoke Chinese and lived on a pittance, the city turned to them a different face. They served no one but themselves; had nothing to lose; dared anything. They boasted of explorations, fights, schemes, lovers. A girl student from West Germany might stride into a noodle shop at midnight and sit down to get drunk with the truck drivers, just for the language experience. For those like her, the wall dividing the two worlds in Peking was at its most porous.

There was also a sixth category, absent from the party, of tourists and transit passengers, short-term visitors who would hear no word against China, who marveled at having seen a peasant, who prided themselves on having traveled for three weeks without paying a cent to the hospitable locals, who loved the simplicity and sincerity of the Chinese people, who neither knew nor cared about Deng Xiaoping, for whom the politics meant nothing more than a chipped coffee cup at breakfast, who on return to their country of origin wrote letters to the highest authorities urging the dear, dear people of China to never, never change. Long-stayers would snuggle up to such visitors in the hope that the jaundice of years would fade and first love be rekindled. But Category Sixers avoided the expatriate residents like the plague. Why bother, when they could go out to enjoy a real Chinese experience?

All categories were insulated, all were exposed.

It was Clarence's party. One of his photographs had been used by the agency around the world and he had been paid his highest ever fee. It was a personal satisfaction that could not be shared, so he threw a party instead and invited everyone he knew. He came up to the Doctor with welcoming light in his eyes, purring all over.

"You got the word, I see. Glad you could make it. Got a drink? Help yourself anyway. I'm just popping down to let the Chinese in. Back in a mo."

Wally poured himself a Stolichnaya, sparing the ice. When foreign friends came up to him beaming, he was faintly suspicious. Since he was known as the Doctor, parties were apt to turn into consultations on anything from bloodshot eyes to Japanese encephalitis or worse. He wasn't in the mood. Creeping round, he plomped down on the sofa beside Sabina, the zany Jewish correspondent for *Der Spiegel* who, as always, wore black.

"You know," she said, "I have cut all my ties with Chinese. Every time I go to visit a Chinese friend I am followed by a limo and a motorcycle. For three weeks now. I tell my friends not to call me, not to visit. The Public Security Bureau is on to me."

"Do you know why?"

"There's no point wasting brain power to guess how their crazy minds work. You know I was expelled from Taiwan for writing nasty things about the military dictatorship."

"They should love you here."

"No-oo," she made a long German no-oo. "It's one country, don't you know? We foreign devils are not supposed to meddle with internal affairs."

"Have you written anything nasty lately?"

"I wrote a review ridiculing a film that the propaganda people want to win the Golden Cock. I said there were technical problems. The film was not in focus, the soundtrack was out of sync. That wasn't nasty, was it? I didn't say the film was utterly banal and xenophobic. Shit! I know too many people here anyway. They hate that." Sabina knew everyone from Party leaders to prostitutes. "At least their techniques are obvious. I know that motorcycle *shifu* who trails me. And the big black limo is incredibly obvious. I love to go into the narrow lanes where the limo can't follow. Make them miss out on the fun. Last week I visited some friends in the evening, in a tiny little *hutong* near the Drum Tower. We were talking and laughing together when the knock came. Some busybody from the Neighborhood Committee and the *shifu* with the motorcycle. My friend went out to speak with them. The security guy said, 'Where's that German in black you got in there?' " Sabina was in fits. "Where's that Jew in black you got in there? Too much!"

"So what can you do about it?"

"Nothing—I stay at home like a bad girl."

The Chinese contingent had arrived. If there were the Five Foreigns, there were also the Three Chineses at such parties. They were mostly Category One, the self-styled artists: people protected through family or profession from the dangers of contact with foreigners. Some were at the cutting edge of thought and style, as Westernized in the head as it was possible to be; others were parasites with something to gain, if only in esteem, from mimicking the imported lifestyle, people who maybe hoped to go abroad to study, who could avail themselves of foreign patronage. Neo-expressionist painters just behind the beat, poets more published abroad than at home, pianists of exemplary technique, a drummer with a James Dean hairdo, members of a Mongolian dance troupe and their hangers-on, boys, girls, sisters, cousins, some of whom had

studied at Peking's prime institutions and could act as inter-
preters, Chinese men outnumbering the Chinese women three
to one, the women holding hands in protective pairs.

The naifs were Category Two, those brought on the arm
of a new-found foreign friend, drawn like fish to a bait. Since
Peking was a honeycomb of secret worlds within worlds, courtyards behind locked doors, the unperturbed naifs accepted
the affluence and decadence of the foreigners' compound as
one more privilege beyond their reach. The naifs were rejected
as pariahs by the artists of Category One. They spoke no English. They roamed the room like ghosts or stood alone or
clung tight to their foreign friend. They did not know what
spies or informants or foreign nutters might lurk.

Clarence returned with a couple of naifs under his wing.
As they headed towards the sound system, Clarence gave a
stoned giggle. He was the perfect host, as he had been brought
up to be, indulging his guests absolutely. He only longed for
the stage in the evening when he could let himself go too,
and express through tipsy tenderness the affection he felt towards his Chinese friends. His photography had absorbed
something of the Chinese aesthetic, moods rather than analysis;
he was catching moments in a performance rather than making
a factual record, and that contributed to his success, to the
point where the social reality was melting, and he saw the
Chinese as a billion aesthetic permutations of pathos or
absurdity.

Category Three (Chinese) were the New Age barracudas,
the moneyed and lawless taxi-drivers, bellboys, waitresses and
import-export people who could cruise anywhere at no risk
to themselves. The foreigners' parties simply provided a medium where they could crack on to each other.

Wally felt himself to be among a crowd of energetic, frantic
kids. Some Chinese boys were drunk already and jumping
about. He was pouring another drink himself when Dulcia

accosted him with a clink of her glass and asked how he'd been doing.

He started to tell the story of Beidaihe but she interrupted, having a more urgent story of her own. Jumbo, she related, her abstract artist, had turned out to be a fast learner and more than a match for her competitiveness. Underneath he had the energy of a combustion engine. If he didn't get out of China, his drive would destroy him. But with Dulcia Jumbo had to subjugate himself. Much as he hated it, his head was still Confucian. Although he had read Freud and physiological tomes and the Chinese classics of pornography and even stumbled through the copy of *The Joy of Sex* she gave him, his language remained puritanical. What two bodies might do, drifting into his imagination in distressing dreams, came under the sinister shadow of terminology as cold and disapproving as any Victorian circumlocution.

The first night her patience had been exhausted rapidly. She yawned and lay down on his bed and as he covered her with the quilt they came neck to neck; he switched off the light and they were in bed. But he lay stiff as a board, not understanding her body rhetoric, and gradually the power was consigned to her. He shriveled into himself and she used him as a massage mannikin. Afterwards he sat up in the dark for a smoke, sighing deeply in self-criticism.

From then on he became her student. In her apartment at the Friendship Hotel she showed him, when the Do Not Disturb sign was out and Tina Turner on the machine, how *The Golden Lotus* could be made their own and the "mouth evil," the "hand evil" and the "back entrance evil" became delicious liberating impulses. He learned to take and give any amount, and stayed after hours in her quarters, and she in his, until their relationship was seen to transgress the bounds of what a decent Chinese citizen might do with a Red-Bristled Devil (Dulcia's bristles were very red). The spies were put to work.

One was stationed by Dulcia's stairwell and the half-witted porter at Central TV—a poor kid who ate white rice for lunch because he couldn't afford vegetables or meat—was instructed to report. The staff at Central TV were forbidden to speak freely to the probable foreign-agent woman.

She told Wally she could look after herself but feared for Jumbo. Should she stop seeing him? Perhaps Jumbo's aim was only to get a visa for the States, but she didn't care. She wanted to have his baby and write a novel in which the American heroine and Chinese hero communicate purely through body language. If her divorce had come through, she would have married him, only he refused to marry her because he was determined to reach America without taking that step, to arrive free in the Land of the Free.

"Should I give'm up? Should I stop seein'm?" Dulcia appealed to Wally, sweat beading her brow.

"Can you do that?" he asked.

She stamped her foot. "No, I can't. It would kill me."

He held up the palm of his hand, smiling wryly. "There's your answer then."

"But Jumbo could be in big trouble."

"You'll have to make sure you stand by him. If he wants out, you'll have to work harder for it. He'll get no support from his unit if he's under suspicion. It's one fish against the ocean. Not easy."

"I'll stand by him, Doc, but he won't take my help. I respect that. Only since I'm the one got him into this mess, so I'm the one's gonna have to get him out."

"You're a good woman. You probably understand more about this game than he does."

"I doubt it. China's China." Dulcia would take on anything as long as she knew the strength of the opposition. Here the enemy was impossible to estimate.

"Hi," said Jumbo, rolling his eyes as he came up. He looked like Al Jolson. "I never understand the foreigner party. Every person puts on the best clothes and stand around looking so serious and don't want to have fun."

"I'm warming up," Wally excused himself.

"Hey, what's your idea of fun?" Dulcia accused Jumbo. "Shakin' up the fizzy drink cans and throwin' creamcakes at your friends? We call that a kids' party."

Jumbo raised his eyebrows. A glacial young woman in red velvet opera cap skewered with silver prongs glided by, her mouth downcast—as if to prove his point.

"The foreigner takes a lot of warming up," said Wally. "Three vodkas to be precise. Cheers all." He drained his glass.

"Okay, let's dance," cried Dulcia—and they did so, until they were hot and breathless, and Wally's shirt was unbuttoned to the waist and the dancing space became so packed with bumpers and grinders that someone compared it to the Peking bus at rush hour.

"I say, Professor!" cried a mock-toffy Australian voice when Wally staggered against the drinks table. Wally dropped his arms with a sigh of pleasure to see the leering presence of Ralph the Rhino with his protruding eyes and horn-like nose.

"Howsa doing, old cock!" With exaggeration Ralph shook Wally's hand.

"I'm surprised they let you in."

"Had a bit of fun with the lift sheila—a real goer." Ralph's face dropped into a caricature of the sullen lift attendant and made Wally laugh again.

"Have you got a drink?"

They scrounged for a glass, then the two men wandered out to the cooler, quieter balcony to talk. Below, the Embassy grid of grandiose 1950s piles and stately trees lay lightless and the city stretched.

"Fuckin' beautiful," said Ralph. "Makes Sydney Harbor look like a sewer, eh?"

Wally laughed again. "Beautiful and mysterious. But seriously, Ralph, I want your opinion." And he launched into the story of his visit to Beidaihe.

(There was no one more knowledgeable about China than Ralph the Rhino. He had got himself tangled up with the country in the early days and had blazed his trail through many a drab revolutionary meet. His style was *sui generis*. In the 1970s when the ideological clamps were on, his larrikinism gave him sufficient anti-bourgeois, anti-imperialist credentials for him to be welcomed as a Friend of China. With the recent changes his frankness and ingenuity and sheer sticking power endeared him to his contacts. A compulsively inquisitive intellectual anarchist, Ralph wasn't trying to get anything out of China, nor concerned with making a "success" of it. His first and last love was herbal medicine. Originally, back in Sydney, he had trained as a doctor, but he never did things properly. A side track took him to Chinese medicine, the Chinese pharmacopoeia, the ancient script, and ever more esoteric explorations of ancient science and philosophy, all pursued with an amateur's passion. At one stage he detoured into Australian Aboriginal culture, testing the theory that Peking Man was kin to the gracile-skulled skeletons of 40,000 years ago unearthed near Lake Mungo in western New South Wales. He financed these explorations and travels by any means to hand, living like a nomad on the smell of an oil rag. In Australia he beat around in an old van with few possessions, and always retreated to the avocado plantation he had established. He lived in a big army disposal tent there that kept things simple. A chest suspended on ropes from a pole stored his dictionaries and encyclopedias. He feared mildew. When the rains came, he sat under the tent flaps hacking a path through Chinese *materia medica*, until a return to the Middle Kingdom became essential, for six months or a year, in order to follow up inquiries. A citified bush Australian with the shyness of a snake, skeptical to his big toenail, an oblique bullshit artist to the last drop in the bottle, and open-heartedly surging with a benign and munificent life-current, crazy Ralph was respected.

From the barrage of recommendations and counter-recommendations that Wally gathered before leaving for China, Ralph's was the voice that loomed loudest and wisest. They had clicked on first meeting over a cappucino in Sydney's Chinatown. In high summer Ralph wore a flame-colored Hawaiian shirt over his khaki shorts and Wally was in a safari suit, coming from a university committee. Their talk turned on the power of certain organically derived substances to change the red-white blood cell ratio for purposes of sickness or slow death, and was so mutually illuminating that it generated a second meeting in a pub, then a third and a fourth. Wally was knocked out by Ralph's acuity, and Ralph was impressed by Wally's clinical experience and access to official medical knowledge. Towards the establishment Ralph was perpetually irreverent, but he valued what its funding could underwrite. Wally, disillusioned by the medical powers-that-be, loved his guerrilla raids on Real Truth.

"In China anything is possible," was Ralph's motto. Tonight for the journalists he had the story about Radio Peking broadcasting the archaeological discovery of a stone disc with inscribed grooves that when hooked up with an iron needle and a hollowed-out buffalo's horn and spun at high speed produced the voice of Confucius dictating the *Analects*. Forget Thomas Edison. The Chinese had invented the gramophone three thousand years ago. When a foreigner declared the story to be a hoax, the patriotic broadcaster shrugged, "In China anything is possible."

Ralph's greatest feat had been his lone motorcycle ride from Peking to an unvisited Tibetan lamasery two thousand kilometers west. He had dyed his hair black and cropped it like a Chinese, and became dirty and determined enough to convince the locals he was one of them. At any point he could have been arrested, attacked or stranded, but the people on the way were delightful and the trip was serendipitous. When he climbed the last stretch of winding road, through stunted conifers and scattered boulders and drowsy Tibetan shepherds tending hairy po-faced flocks, to temple structures that were weirdly amphibian, scarcely distinct from the rocky peak yet afloat in the sky, the solitary monk on the hillside took out a horn as long as himself to blare a timeless, toneless welcome to the growling Yamaha. Ralph got off his machine and was received through painted carved gates and offered a bed for the evening, as an honored pilgrim from the fabled oppressive capital. Later over cigars and tea savoring the perfection of the place's geomantic setting, its *fengshui*, and the completion of his goal, Ralph felt just like a man who has taken one step, and the right one, off a plank into depths from which there is no return.

Word of his exploit spread like wildfire through the foreign community, and journalists and photographers vowed to repeat it. But no one except Ralph would ever do it again. So discreet had he been that when the story reached the Public Security Bureau and he was called in, he managed to convince his questioner that he had never left Peking. All he brought back from the lamasery was an ordinary piece of quartz. But no one doubted the story because Ralph was Ralph.)

"Good one," he said, when Wally had told his story. "So you were sent on a wild goose chase to Beidaihe? And the old prof turned out to be a veggie? Good one."

"Does it make sense to you?"

Ralph scratched his chin. "Have you confronted your minder with the fact that it's the wrong Hsu?"

"Oh, a waste of time absolutely with Mrs. Gu."

"Wonder what they're up to? They're up to something, that's for sure. Let's think. They're trying to throw you off the trail of the real Prof. Hsu, right?"

"Right."

"Which means they've got something to hide. Either something shameful to cover up or something valuable they don't want to share."

"Right."

"I'd opt for the latter. The Chinese are great ones at hoarding their goodies. You say the original Hsu had important things to say in his youth. Who knows what brilliance he may have produced later. They'd be frightened you'd steal it."

Ralph put the matter clearly. Wally's problem lay in bamboozling himself with the most complex of explanations. Too often he did not see the wood for the spreading trees of his own verbiage.

"What could be so important that I would steal it?"

"You don't know Chinese pride, mate. Chinese tenacity. The other day I read a survey done in the streets of Moscow. The main gripe of the man in the street over there against China is that the Chinese have a secret cure for cancer which they are gradually leaking to the United States but withholding from the Soviet Union. That's true. That's what the Soviets believe. There could be something in it. The ultimate arms race."

"Fantastic!"

"The point is that Chinese medicine is a great source of national pride, as much a unifier of the culture as the written script. It has survived into the twentieth century because it works, first of all, but also because the Chinese are great mystifiers and because when it comes to sickness human beings will accept any amount of mystification and mumbo-jumbo in their desperation to get better. Medicine is the great secret weapon of China. Once again the great men of the West are coming to pay homage to the Mighty Empire in hope of learning her secrets. Where you are, since it's a Western medicine center, you probably don't see this. But where I am, at the Academy, the religious certitude and secrecy with which they enshrine their knowledge has to be seen to be believed."

107

Ralph concluded, "They might just have something important at your place. Ninety-nine per cent unlikely, but you never know. They're making fools of themselves to protect it, that's obvious. You better find out what they have, lad."

Ralph made it sound easy.

"How?"

"Avoid confrontation. Ingratiate yourself with the boss. Ingratiate yourself with the disaffected."

"Grease up to Director Kang."

"That's the spirit."

"Can the Chinese really be so peculiar?" asked Wally. "Why do we always end up talking of them as 'the Chinese,' 'they,' 'them,' as if they're a different species? As individuals they're as different from each other as chalk and cheese. But it's the larger organism that fascinates us, the group thing, the nation, the race. What laws does it operate by with its revolutions and counter-revolutions, the fanaticism and the inertia that drives you up the wall? How do you know what they want? They don't seem to want anything for its own sake, but only as a way to somewhere else, as a way of keeping in the swim. They slide past us, round us, through us, but afterwards you feel there's been no contact at all."

Wally was thinking of Jin Juan.

"Hey man," said Ralph. "You gotta stop thinking about China. Them, us. Forget it. Restore peace to your mind. Settle your heart. Day by day. Step by step. Specifics only. Come and visit me some time at the Trad. Med. Academy. We gotta go in now." He led the way in from the balcony.

But the party was fading. The Canadian Trade Commissioner was dancing with a Chinese poet whose creased face gave him the name of Monkey. The Australian Cultural Attaché was singing Peking opera in falsetto. Dulcia and Jumbo were necking on the couch. Clarence and the two Caravaggesque naifs were twirling each other in a high jive to cheers and whistles from the room. The time had come when Clarence was wild, his hair awry and sweat running down his bared chest, and he could horse around with his Chinese friends as if they had all been boys in the same public school.

Sabina's face was white as flour against her black hair and clothes.

"Shit, I gotta go home and write a story," she said to Wally. "This time not the Chinese but the Germans. All governments are shit! One of the Baader-Meinhof group has been working here as a foreign expert for seven years with no passport. The Germans offered him a pardon to go back home, then sprung him at Frankfurt Airport," she gabbled to Wally. "We must hold our mistrust. Mistrust always!" She looked at her watch. "At least the German prisons have hot water. My apartment has no hot water after midnight. I go. You come?"

"Out of the frying pan into the hot water. No, no." As a middle-aged man he was flattered by Sabina's interest, and regretted for a moment. But he too would turn into a pumpkin if he stayed and drank more.

2

As he cycled home, he enjoyed his release. He passed a man keeping guard over a pile of cabbages. China this, China that. Ralph the Rhino was right. Settle his heart. Put his mind at rest. He could no more understand China than he could understand himself. Journalists, diplomats, photographers, China was too big for their lenses. The Five Foreigns met the Three Chineses and had the Four Conversations. Was the political line really Right but pretending Left, or really Left and pretending Right? Was China booming like the new Japan or struggling to hang on? What was the latest absurdity of the currency apartheid that obliged foreigners to use expensive funny money? And there was always so-and-so's claim to have discovered the Real China, where "they had never seen a foreigner before," as if to see a foreigner rocketed people into a new kind of space-time. All under the same moon, he thought, noticing the sky.

The night porter stirred as he came through the College gate and the boy sleeping on duty on his stairwell grunted. Entering his empty flat, Wally fell into the armchair and stared upwards with a feeling of tension and strangeness. He felt detached and free-floating, cut loose. He stared for a while at the air, then snapped himself into a different posture, adjusted the lamp, and took out the thick envelope from Uncle Lionel.

"My dear boy—"

3

From his treetop in tropical North Queensland Uncle Lionel sent an apology. He was too busy in his hedonistic dotage to concern himself with stray family doings. Like Wally's father, Lionel had gone early into the world, after Retta's death and Waldemar's second marriage. By the time the family papers came down to him, there was little family relationship left, and Lionel's own silver-whiskered gallivanting was in full career as he found second, third and fourth winds. Posterity could decide whether the records should be maintained or returned to earth—altogether too dry a matter for Lionel. He packaged up the relics and dumped them on the post office counter.

As Wally flicked through the badly typed pages of his grandfather's memoir, "Postscript to Turn-of-the-Century China," his eye caught a sentence he remembered having liked. "Not for the last time was I accused of being a heathen."

In a village in the South near where Waldemar, at twenty-five, was a lay medic-missionary, a traveling Baptist woman from Georgia had "gone mental." She smashed up the plaster guardians of the local Daoist temple and, muttering prayers and obscenities, had decapitated the gargoyles along the eaves, put a match to the paper lanterns and fanned the flames with revered embroidered banners. The monks had lifted their robes in the easiest way to extinguish the fire while old mongoloid women restrained the American, and the abbot of dubious virtue hurried to the *yamen*. Subsequently, in a charade of a trial prolonged by nasal high-toned officialese, and despite a plea of insanity, the visitor was sentenced to death. She had no consciousness of her crime. Her traveling companion, a foreign devil from Alabama in a pin-striped suit, was at a loss. Executions could be summarily carried out— not to mention the rumors of exquisite tortures when death was not summary. The gent begged for the nearest Sinophone foreigner to be summoned, and next day young Waldemar was borne in by litter. The circumstances were recited several times over while he spied out an avenue for compromise. At last it was agreed that the Baptists should pay for a new and better temple to be built, assisting personally in the painting of the spirit heads; and a banquet would be given where the abbot and his monks, the Magistrate and his family, would be invited to dine like gods, and in the glow of repletion enmity would lose its edge. Waldemar hoped that fermented grain liquor, like the waters of Jordan, would wash away sin. He was learning, however, that there were no final solutions. What passed for forgiveness was often stored away to be remembered another time.

Imprinted in Wally's memory was also the reference to his grandmother's diary. "Once Retta wrote in her diary that she had counted over a hundred corpses in the river. Possibly exaggerated, but suggestively true." The image of his grandmother counting corpses had caught Wally's imagination as a young boy. Retta must have been twenty-three or -four at the time. Her diary had not been preserved, so it was thought, until reckless Uncle Lionel committed to the mail a swatch of

111

lined yellow pages torn from a notebook and covered in a Victorian handwriting that crept over the paper like a tiny translucent crab.

W. says I must turn the other cheek. I suppose I must. I have seen a trader in the marketplace maintain his dignity while in the presence of angry creditors and afterwards slap his own face very hard, once on each cheek. Is it worse to inflict punishment on oneself or to offer oneself to another's malice? I do not know. The Chinaman's way is an advance payment against whatever suffering must come. No satisfaction is afforded the enemy, although a Christian knows anyway that an enemy's satisfaction must be hollow. My thoughts are rebellious, but I write them. W. left this morning in the chair with Lionel all excited. They are to visit the site for a new hospital on the plateau. If rains come, they will be gone for many days. So far sunshine. May is at her lessons and wee Jeremiah playing in his basket in the sunny corner of the courtyard. I raised my voice when Wang refused to go shopping. He asked me to pray for the pains in his legs. I shall pray for his idleness. They make such a fuss of the children in the marketplace, yet I dare not leave them behind. May takes the basket, she can carry our purchases, Jeremiah must be carried in my arms. The ruts are too rough for his cart. I hope the oranges are in. We need strength. I should not sit here writing. Yet I feel safe at my table by the upper window. Over the wall today the mountains are sharp, like a broken frilly cockleshell. The rice terraces are aglow, the water asparkle. My eyes dazzle if I try to pick out the black things afloat in that shining mirror.

CHAPTER SEVEN

Greasing Up

1

Eagle knew his faults. When he was unsure of himself he exuded too much optimism. He already regretted his swaggering entrance to the office of the Party Secretary of the Sports Institute. But the coach had encouraged him. The same man who had sacked him from the team greeted him like a prodigal son and praised his physical condition, repeating over and over how he hoped Eagle would return to fill a vacancy in the squad. No problem, no problem, insisted the coach, rubbing Eagle's bad ankle. The carton of duty-free cigarettes that Eagle had got from the foreigner was zipped inside the coach's carry-bag. But it was not the coach's decision. Eagle would need to speak to the Party Secretary. She was a slim middle-aged woman who wore red chiffon scarves with her Japanese running shoes. Eagle adopted a clownish certainty of success and made the fatal mistake of trying to charm her. He had no cigarettes left.

The Party Secretary gave a cold and precise recitation of Eagle's relations with the Sports Institute. He had asked for holidays at inconvenient times. He played the fool with his teammates, putting fun above disciplined team spirit. He blamed luck when the team was defeated, rather than criticizing his own performance, and he lost heart when the opposition was impossibly superior. His injury had been caused by his own carelessness, at great cost to the Institute. He was not a Party member.

"Your attitude has not been good," said the Party Secretary.

"I'm sorry."

"Is there any change?"

"My attitude has changed. I have learned from my mistakes."

"Fine," said the woman. "Okay. You can rejoin the team." It was her tactic to leaven kindness with a bitter moral. "As long as you have your unit's approval, you can start training tomorrow."

"Oh," said Eagle as his rising heart sank again, "don't you look after that?"

"The responsibility for releasing you lies with your work unit. We have nothing to do with that. Haven't you spoken with them?"

Feeling the hopelessness of his situation, Eagle smiled his broadest fake smile like a goody-goody child.

"Thank you, Party Secretary."

As if from the Emperor's throne, he backed from the room. The coach was scurrying out of sight, but Eagle chased him. If the unit would not release him, maybe the coach could help.

The coach knew a friend who knew a friend; it was not impossible. His words trailed off as Eagle sloped down the corridor in the strange good mood that came over him when his heart hit bottom. As his mother said, he was too happy. He couldn't take life seriously.

In the street, despite himself, his step quickened—quite in contrast to the compliant position he had been forced to adopt in the Party Secretary's office. The question of whether he could rejoin the team was out of his mind, proof itself of bad attitude. He slithered aboard a bus and sprang off at one of the most crowded places of the city, where he could rub shoulders, move like a fish, look and be seen. He streamed into a department store, peered at ugly shoes, streamed out again into the sunshine. He bumped into a girl on a bicycle who abused him. "You stupid idiot, strolling along in a dream . . ." He abused her back, both of them laughing. "You can't even ride straight!" The old-fashioned gray brick shopfronts had bright vertical panels of characters announcing that they sold medicine or hardware or fish. Some old shops had tacked aluminium frames, sheet glass and neon to the front, and sold computers and photocopiers. Eagle deviated from the main street, passed a theater and racks of potted daffodils and hyacinths outside a florist, and followed deeper into sun-slashed alleys. Everywhere people were basking, busying and budding like flowers at the onset of spring. The emerald sprouts on the pruned trees along the way were turning to catkins and the sky was joyfully blue. He knew as he knew himself the gray uneasy heart of the city that contracted to frozen wounding rock, then thawed in uncomfortable negotiations, sluggish, adaptive, and at last awakened with an irrepressible smile. He pranced into the little dumpling shop as he turned a last corner. The queue of empty stomachs growled and wisecracked and behind the counter his classmate Lotus sat taking the money. She saw him and looked down, showing no expression. He stood in the queue, impatiently shifting his weight in a kind of jig, as if he were one of those kids listening to foreign music on a Walkman. Lotus waited till he reached the head of the queue before she looked up and rolled her Rs at him as only a Peking girl can.

"Eat half a jin of dumplings," was his taciturn reply.

His ticket passed through the window to the back of the shop where they kneaded and rolled the dough, stirred the filling, stuffed the dumplings and placed them in huge steamers over boiling water: hot, hard, never-ending work. There were no empty stools round the tables in the little shop. No matter how quickly one ate and left, another was always waiting for the place. The city was insatiable. Eagle poured some vinegar into his bowl and leaned against the wall: they made good dumplings here.

He liked Lotus too, who gave a slight smile from under her white hygiene cap as juice dribbled down his chin. They came from the same neighborhood. Although not directly affected by the Cultural Revolution, most ordinary kids had grown up in an atmosphere of violent mistrustfulness, ignorant and unskilled. Eagle and Lotus had played kids' games through it all. He would sneak out to meet her on the ruined bit of city wall behind the station where they could scramble and hide as long as daylight lasted. By the time they were teenagers, in the terrible months before Premier Chou En-lai died, they could no longer be innocent of the world around them. The streets were full of vagrants, delinquents and untended children. Eagle and Lotus stuck together. Their relationship, though uncondoned, was protective and loving at the base of that crumbling bit of wall. They saved themselves from the destructive despair that overwhelmed many others, and had a great time.

But Mother Lin thought the girl was scarcely better than a peasant. She could not know the moments of beauty that Eagle and Lotus discovered amidst social chaos in the stormy years of their adolescence. Then as things settled, they drifted apart. Lotus was married to a factory worker and moved to the western suburbs. Her husband worked hard and made little. She produced a son and went to work in the dumpling shop. Some days she chopped, some days she rolled, some days she served, some days she took the money. Though she got fat and lost her prettiness, she had no complaints.

The door of the shop was wide open to the air, and across the way carnations and geraniums bloomed. After hibernation

116

the beginning of spring brought restlessness and the desire to test new powers of body and spirit. No more than two or three times a year Eagle came to see Lotus, when he needed comfort or pleasure. When the feeling came, his feet, like a homing device, took him to her. At first it brought shame to both, but eventually it became an understanding. For her he was an opening of the window, a night out, a treat. She came from behind the counter to walk him to the corner. In that snatched private moment he said, "Tonight at the canal."

No more words, no contact. The dough-rollers in the shop were all eyes and ears, and the old lady selling ice-blocks from her trolley was an informant. Eagle vanished, and Lotus returned to her workaday self.

He figured that at night it was warm enough if they wore their coats, and there were enough leaves on the trees for them not to be seen if they leant against a tree in the scrubby area at the far end of the wasteland beside the canal. After going to his unit, he would call at his friend's to pick up some rubbers. Lotus would leave a message at her husband's factory to say that she was staying at her mother's overnight. To go home and change would take too long, but she could go to the bathhouse and perhaps buy a scarf on the way. Anyhow she must ask Eagle to get a pair of shoes for her husband through his friend at the leather factory.

As he walked away, Eagle's thoughts switched to the basketball team. As a child he had studied martial arts. He enjoyed rolling on the old mattresses in the yard, shaping and toning his young body with the other boys, until martial arts were discouraged as a stinking vestige of feudal superstition and he switched to other sports. After his ankle injury, he had taken it up again, determined the office job would not make him soft. The friend with whom he trained was a martial arts champion, and by the time he came to reapply for the basketball team, Eagle was in good shape. But could he get a release from his job? If he didn't, it was goodbye to his chances of winning the ex-model Pearl and a new flat. His step leadened as he reached his work unit.

It was Chief Hou who had got Eagle the job in the state office as a favor to Old Lin that turned out to be an exercise in not showing undue favoritism. Knowing that the young man had come into the office through the back door, everyone was satisfied to see him bored, humiliated and wasted. And once inside, the door shut behind you.

Chief Hou explained that a government office could not be seen to release an employee on the employee's own request, especially on a youthful whim to play sport. That was a bad precedent that might lead to chaos. Eagle protested that basketball was part of the Four Modernizations, raising China's sport to a high level of international prestige.

Chief Hou prickled at the boy's rationalizations. A great rationalizer himself, he was not swayed. It was a question of "work need." Eagle was essential to the office, said Hou, preparing to embroider the palpable lie. In China, service personnel, especially the military and their dependents, relied on the promise of early retirement and a cushy unthinking afterlife, which it was the duty of Chief Hou's office to take care of. From the age of twenty-five the needs of service personnel, retired out due to injury, were catered for from the Ministry's "iron rice bowl." Eagle's task, once a week, was to take the senior citizens to the park where they could quaver pieces of Peking opera to each other. Someone young and fit was needed to herd the elderly to and from the park. Eagle was indispensable.

There was no arguing. The only recourse to a leader's God-like decision was prostration, a series of return visits until God's mood changed or His price was found. Eagle bowed his head, not angrily, and left.

On the way to the bus stop he executed a whirling martial arts movement, a foolproof device for bringing your opponent to the ground in agonizing submission. Then he shrugged and

118

shook his shoulders like a bird ruffling its feathers, and scrambled aboard the bus. Lotus was waiting by the canal.

2

It was not clear who was treating whom. Mother Lin wanted to introduce the Doctor to Peking opera, the Doctor wanted to give Mother Lin a night out. Eagle scoffed, but came along for the ride. There was much fretting about tickets. Wally insisted that he could get them. Mother Lin put on her best jacket and slacks, and mother and son caught the bus to the theater where the Doctor was waiting as planned. Eagle considered it a major sacrifice to sit through an evening of Peking opera. It was an unpopular art. He was glad when interval came and he could join the scrum for icecream. Mother Lin was content with faint praise for the performance, not as good as it used to be. Wally's head was ringing. He had understood nothing but cacophonous, kinaesthetic sensation. Eagle had mistranslated the opera's title as "The King of Bah Says Goodbye to His Cucumber," and Wally improvised accordingly. At interval he was still trying to sort out the pieces.

Then suddenly Jin Juan came bumping through the crowded foyer, exclaiming with surprise to see him there. The man at her side, standing confidently in a smart beige trenchcoat, gave Wally's hand a firm Western shake.

"What's your opinion?" asked Jin Juan.

Wally said he was there with his friends and looked round for Eagle and Mother Lin, who had vanished. He was on a mission to achieve a little understanding of even the most impossible things Chinese, such as shrieking Peking opera. Jin Juan relished its stylized energy. Her cousin was one of the performers, so she often came. Tonight, she explained, after interval, her cousin would perform an extract from the ancient

119

tragedy *Snow in Summer* in which a young woman is falsely accused of trying to murder her mother-in-law. As Jin Juan talked with animation, her companion, Zhang, took no part, grinning at the woman's foreign-language fluency with incomprehension and a degree of hostility.

As they were drifting back to their seats, Eagle returned. He didn't notice Zhang at first, and was delighted to see the Doctor escorting the elegant woman down the aisle. But Zhang came from behind and placed his hand possessively in the small of Jin Juan's back, provoking her, it seemed, to suggest that they should all sit together so she could explain the plot to Wally. Zhang acquiesced, self-importantly proper, and further disconcerted to find an old woman, Mother Lin, included in the party. He scarcely humored Jin Juan's taste for Peking opera. He had been happier as a firebrand adolescent chanting "Down with the Stinking Olds," of which opera was one of the rankest. Now he was into Democracy with Chinese Characterics at the prestigious Center for Research into Economic Structures.

How could she have any feeling for him left, thought Jin Juan. He had been late, as usual. They had planned to eat together, but he had changed the arrangement, as usual. She had waited outside the theater in Goldfish Lane, and Zhang had been sublimely unflustered when eventually he arrived. She had stiffened to his touch before releasing inevitably into its warmth. He could be romantic, turning his serious eyes to her. He was self-preoccupied, but zealous and bright; not indolent like some of his ilk, nor knotted and strained with political resentment and ill-will. He existed happily on the egotistical enthusiasm of an unsoured princeling.

On stage a prison scene takes place, the deep-voiced gaol matron as impervious to the bride's pleas for help as a tree-stump in winter; the tyrannous mother-in-law demanding judgment, not for herself but in recognition of the law; the innocent bride, removing her jewels and brocade, sorrowing

120

as she flutters nearer to her death, like a moth to the flame.

As Jin Juan explained the characters, the story of *Snow in Summer* emerged in archetypal outline for Wally, the distortions of voice and rising anxiety of percussive sound became expressive and the nuances of the three performances shaped a bride's tragedy as moving as it was tautly artificial. His eyes were on the girl, the cousin, who had Jin Juan's long Sui-dynasty face and swanlike neck. She wore a sky-blue dress and silver lollipops quivered in her hair. She was a puce and white mask of purity and her voice shrilled like a reed. Her body seemed to shudder with outraged virtue as if it were a set of vibrating fibers, and with self-sacrifice that grew more erotic as more defiant. When she was led off to wrongful execution at the last, it was as if stretched elastic had snapped—and the opera was over.

The clapping was perfunctory. The performers stood in full light on the bare stage before rows of rapidly emptying chairs. Jin Juan tugged Wally up on stage to meet the three principals. Their eyes were like glimmering pools of oil in hard masks and they stayed in character as they greeted and nodded. Jin Juan's cousin whispered only a few words in her ear as they left the stage. Wally was intrigued by the power of their characters, offstage in their bulky costumes as well as onstage, and especially he was taken by the slim sorrowing bride into whose eyes he was permitted to stare deeply as she made her exit.

Zhang smoothed down his trenchcoat as Wally and Juan said their goodbyes on the street corner. They were speaking in English, but Wally dropped his voice nevertheless when he asked her how they could make contact in future.

"I have no way of reaching you," he said, "so I'm relying on you to get in touch with me. You know you can find me through your friends at the Medical College."

"That's right," responded Jin Juan with a discreet little nod.

Whether or not Zhang understood the communication,

Eagle noticed and took his farewell in high spirits. Zhang wore his rank imposingly, and Jin Juan was a dish, and Wally laughed when Eagle told him frankly, as they walked with Mother Lin to the bus stop, that he approved of the woman.

3

Ralph the Rhino was waiting for Wally in the New Age Bar. Sitting alone, he'd been pestered. Foreign Trader had joined him for a drink and offered Han bronzes, Sung porcelain, girls, boys, dope, heroin and excellent exchange rates. But Ralph kept his hands clean—unlike Party Greenhorn, who was developing a paunch and sat in the dark with a white hand appearing from behind to rub his trouser front. He must have been sitting on the girl.

"Extracting the honey," snickered Bi the bartender as he fixed Ralph's favorite drink. "Is it all right?" asked Young Bi respectfully.

"Better and better, mate."

Wally rescued Ralph not a moment too soon. The Doctor was tingling with electric sensations from the evening at the opera and Ralph greeted his enthusiasm like a satisfied parent. Then, laughing all the way, Ralph quickly got down to business. "You got the stuff?" His big balding pate shone.

Wally pulled from inside his jacket a swatch of blurred gray photocopies.

"The usual high-quality reproduction," commented Ralph, bringing the sheets closer to his eyes. "You don't want an instant translation, I hope. This is technical stuff. I'll need reference books for medical terms—musk, mug-wort, toad's venom—you know the sort of thing. Can you give me some time? This one looks good. *Cervical Cancer Removed by Witch-doctor: a Scientific Investigation.*"

Wally pricked up his ears. "What are the other titles?"

"Let's see. *Remission of Tumors through Herbal Medicine and Acupuncture.* Interesting. *Malignancy-bearing Genomes and the Impact of Certain Tree Fungi of Southern China. Radiation, the New Moxybustion?* A whole host of goodies. All the work of your Director Kang? Impressive. And you say Kang's the bogus Yankee? This looks like traditional Chinese medicine to me. I'm surprised to see it emanating from the Peking Union Medical College. It's usually a case of never the twain shall meet. What's the rest of Kang's stuff like, the stuff in English?"

"Impressive in places. The data is exceptional. Sometimes there's an inspired hypothesis, other times he makes ludicrous, totally implausible links between the Chinese data and modern Western practice. It's full of contradictions. At places he doesn't have a clue what he's dealing with."

"The stuff's published abroad?"

"A fraction, and that's the more modest part, though plausible for that reason. The pieces published in the English-language journals in China do a lot of trumpet-blowing, with great insistence on the need for the latest Western technology, scanners, chemotherapy, radiology, all that."

"A bid for funding?"

"Presumably."

Ralph shuffled the pages together and slipped them inside his coat. The translations would be hard work, but he had no greater love than to ferret his way through the esoterica of Chinese wisdom or fantasy.

"By the way," he said, "Hsu Chien Lung was the name of your old boy, right? I asked one of my trusty colleagues at the Trad. Med. Academy, dear sweet Emeritus Professor Wu, a real honey of an eighty-year-old. She wouldn't come up to the height of the bar here, bent double by the weight of her knowledge, looks like a Maori tiki, a totem face cut with a chisel. Anyway, she's a love, even if she does go in for ellipsis.

She said of your Hsu Chien Lung, and I quote, 'He could not be surpassed.' High praise. She said they had carbon copies of his original papers in the archives. Never-published things. If I'm very nice to her, she might just arrange for me to see them."

"Does she know what happened to him?"

"I asked. She just shook her head with that special Chinese mixture of horror, wonder and resolute fatalism."

"Hm. Well, drink up. Another Black Chinaman?"

4

Wally was drinking too much in China. Tea and booze. Booze and tea. Booze brought him closer to the people, as if his wild drunken fire of impulses, wishes, hallucinations and flights reflected the rainbow-colored dream-world flaring in everyone's head; as if, despite drab exteriors, everyone were secretly the Monkey King in a drama that could be entered upon through drink. His work failed to exhaust his energies, and his determination to research China had expanded in an unruly fashion to include what Ralph called The Deep Structure. His behavior was becoming more and more peculiar. What was the committee man, the concerned doctor, the administrator of yore doing ambling along an empty midnight street waving at any car that passed? He had no objections, suddenly, to wasting his life. But he had misjudged Director Kang, letting surface impressions get the better of reasoned assessment, and he must make the appropriate amends. He thought of the tiki totem's comment on Professor Hsu Chien Lung. "He could not be surpassed." Playing with words produced another reading. "He was in the way." He had surprised Jin Juan tonight with her callow chap. As he thought of Jin Juan, her face metamorphosed into the exquisite sorrowing mask of the opera princess, Emperor's Cucumber in a salad of snow.

5

"Who's he?" snapped Zhang as he and Jin Juan walked away from the lighted foodstall where a long-whiskered man in a night cap was turning kebabs over a brazier. "How did you meet him?"

"Song introduced us."

"What's her aim?"

"He's helping with her work."

"You should keep away from foreigners."

"You're a typical suspicious Chinese. Aren't we supposed to be learning from them?"

Once in the darkness he put his arm tightly around her waist. The shadowy east gate of the Imperial Palace loomed, where they turned to follow the moat. In the air was the sharp fragrance of mimosa beginning to bud.

"Have you thought about us?" she asked.

"I always think about you. I love you." Perhaps five hundred times before in the ten years of their never-ending courtship he had said those words to her. When was it he had promised to marry her?

Zhang's father was in a high cadre in the Ministry of Aeronautics and Astronautics, one of the ultra-leftists of fifteen years ago who had turned himself inside out and kept on top. His mother was a Vice-Mayor of Tianjin. The family went back to the Manchu rulers, which accounted for Zhang's cruel cheekbones. He had been protected from everything, Jin Juan judged, and was a glossy, moody, self-concerned young ram. She had not forgiven him for being late and unapologetic, and contrasted his behavior with the foreigner's straightforward friendliness.

They turned the corner of the moat and climbed the crumbling steps by the boathouse to reach an alcove that was exposed only to tranquil water, their trysting place. He pushed her against the wall.

"Easy!" she protested.

"I love you. Really. Truly. I love you. Say you love me. Say it."

She could never resist their passion, although she hated it now. Ten years ago when she came back young and confused from the countryside, she had admired his brash undentable student's optimism. At the time she was starving for some friendship, some opening out, after the cut-off years in the work camp. They had joked together on those days when they met by the lake and ice glittered. She had pretended to be a student at the Foreign Languages Institute and he was amazed by her English, which he wanted to study. They became committed intellectual partners and prudent, demanding lovers. With Zhang's help she got into the Foreign Languages Institute after all; he was the more impressed by her lie.

Her fingers behind his back counted ten years of sweet, necessary, efficient lovemaking as he held her against the boathouse wall. Afterwards, walking back along the moat, she raised once more the question of the flat, which was the question of their marriage.

"It's fallen through," he said. "Mum doesn't agree."

"I'll talk to her then."

"She's in Tianjin."

"I'll go to Tianjin."

"No."

It was the custom that Jin Juan did not contact Zhang's family, whose high position made them strictly out of bounds.

"You mean you haven't spoken to her."

126

"They oppose." Zhang had staved her off for years, by sharing the hope that in time all obstacles to their marriage would be overcome. He used her as his mistress, sympathizing with her problems, sharing with her the difficulties he faced with his family. But Zhang was growing older. He wanted to marry and have a son. The relationship had grown stagnant despite the sexual satisfaction. He could find another, a younger girl who suited his prospects; he could start again. He knew that he had no will to fight his parents, and each year Jin Juan sensed the hardening impasse.

On this ordinary evening, as they walked back along the moat as on a hundred other evenings, for no apparent reason, except that there had been nothing else between them but sex, and Zhang had been bored by the opera, and irked by the foreigner and Jin Juan's animated English, and that she had been a little more removed, for whatever reason, Zhang said words that could not be retracted.

"We'll never be able to get married. Let's forget it."

She did not reply at once. The reply was not worth the effort. At last she said feebly, "I'll talk to your mother."

"Forget it. No use. Let's call it quits."

"No!" Stopping, she addressed to his face loud savage words. "No, that's not possible. You promised. You'll carry it through."

As she threatened him, he felt piteous and hostile. "I won't be ruled by you or anyone."

"Does your mother rule you?" she spat.

"It's the end."

"It's certainly not the end. You're a seducer."

"Don't say that."

"I say it. It's the truth, that's why!"

She stamped the ground with her sharp heels as she walked quickly away from him. He did not follow. It was as easy as that. He stopped again, lingering at the kebab stall. Jin Juan sat head erect and dry-eyed all the way home on the bus. In Chinese law to sleep with a woman on the promise of marriage and to break the promise was rape. The thought that for ten years she had been raped by young Zhang gave her a certain despicable satisfaction. Her fingers felt around her eyes for wrinkles. She was no longer young. Because of the years in the countryside she had aged fast. There would be no other man for her if Zhang got away. Whether he liked it or not she was his for life. On her beautiful face the strain showed not a flicker. Her tumultuous emotions were calmed by some lines from the earliest Chinese book of songs. Three thousand years ago, women had lamented.

> *I had hoped to grow old with you,*
> *Now the thought of old age grieves my heart.*
> *The Qi has its shores,*
> *The Shi its banks;*
> *How happy we were, our hair in tufts,*
> *How fondly we talked and laughed,*
> *How solemnly swore to be true!*
> *I must think no more of the past;*
> *The past is done with—*
> *Better let it end like this!*

6

Flattery did not come easily to Wally. He considered that to remark on another's virtue implied astonishment that such virtue could exist. Director Kang had no such scruples, however, and launched into fulsome praise of Wally's work in the College. Wally countered that he had not been giving his full attention to supervision in the lab because he had been work-

ing through the pile of the Director's papers given him by
Mrs. Gu.

"Fascinating, remarkable stuff," Wally declared. "You've
been hiding your light under a bushel, Director."

"Oh no, that is not my recent work. Those were my salad
days. A few speculations on the conjunction of Chinese and
Western medicine. You see, Professor Doctor, I do not believe
we can command Chinese medicine unless it is thoroughly
integrated into the discipline of Western critical science. Our
aim here—I speak broadly—is to root out superstition, to
destroy false science, and to establish watertight findings com-
patible with the latest Western technology."

"All very laudable," smiled Wally with a sense of the ground
sinking under him.

Kang spoke in high-falutin' terms, with an eccentric version
of a laid-back East-coast scholarly manner, all the time beaming, twinkling and flopping open his fleshy mouth. He was
perhaps sixty and the Italian shoes he had newly procured in
Chicago sparkled.

"When you have time, perhaps," broached Wally, "there
are a couple of steps in the clinical data itself—a couple of
stages in the application process of Chinese drugs where I
don't follow the leaps—no doubt dependent on knowing the
traditional method of treatment, which I don't. I am concerned
with how precisely the hormone or embryo treatment works
that you indicate in your papers— If you could spare the
time—"

This was the closest Wally came to a technical question.
Kang rubbed his hands gleefully. "Nothing I like better than
an exchange of ideas— Oh, if only there were sufficient time!
I am honored, Professor Doctor, most honored. The details
of course are a little fuzzy—it was all some time ago now."

Wally stared into Kang's jolly eyes that gave nothing away.

"I'm interested in learning something of your testing
procedures."

"Of course, of course. Time is so precious, you know, Professor Doctor. I can gladly invite one of my assistants to work with you on the matter."

Wally paused. It was a snow job. He rose to his feet and shook Kang's hand with an excess of joviality.

CHAPTER EIGHT

In Harness

1

China was in a hurry. Every month a hundred new concrete shells sprang from the earth of Peking, cylinders, wedges, cubes, like children's building blocks. Around the clock by every available means materials were carted across a city that had become one big construction site. Teams of Mongolian ponies hauled trayloads of bricks, donkeys brayed against barrowloads of gravel. Glass window fittings, stacked like last week's newspapers on the back of green army trucks, slid and shuddered. Old codgers on pedicabs lugged girders three times their length and twenty times their weight. Burping hand-tooled contraptions carried mounds of cement that blew away in the wind. Sooty-faced boys pushed coal. So the haulage went on. At dawn as the police vans turned in, food suppliers set off for the market. Trucks of freshly pulled spinach and horses carting the first peaches of the season queued at intersections with the buses and bicycles of commuters. A big black pig trussed in a wicker canoe was ferried from suburb to suburb. Fish dangled from handlebars. Poultry rode squawking in panniers. Newlyweds hauled plush two-seaters and washing machines smelling freshly of Japan, the proud groom clenching his teeth as he pedaled forward. Child coffins attached to bicycles bore haughty Young Master or Miss of the one-child family to school, while at work their parents transferred to unit car or minibus to be conveyed again to meeting or shop; their conveyances became softer as they rose higher in the system until they approached the condition of their leaders who glided past, visible through the black windows of Benzes at an angle of semi-recline, hauling the country into the future. What if the ropes broke? What if the horse threw the rider? Gazing straight ahead of themselves after lunch the leaders in their back seats dared not think beyond the pure pronouncement of their decrees. The old lady heaves her trolley to the corner where she sells dirty iceblocks for five cents each. The ancient ragpicker creeps along like a tortoise to find a couple of dry dumplings, a plastic bag, a crumpled culture magazine, a piss-sodden greatcoat, a discarded electric hair-drier. And so movement continues till morning, when young Eagle jogs by on his regular run.

Gently does it, says Eagle, convinced that training, rest, diet and Chinese medicine will strengthen his weak ankle. Each afternoon he works out at martial arts to achieve not only a peak of physical fitness but also a depth of spiritual determination. Given the chance to try, he would now perform so well that he could never be excluded from the team again.

2

To test the water, Eagle visited Pearl's house and presented her mother with the bags of bananas and dried bamboo shoots that his brother Sunshine had brought up from the South. He chatted and smoked with Pearl's young uncle while her mother poured hot water and Pearl sat button-lipped. She wore the mauve mohair cardigan from Paris and a slinky foreign frock that had been washed too many times. Her hair was in a chignon too complicated for someone staying at home and her face was professionally made up. She was displayed as one of the assets of a prosperous family. There were few occasions on which Pearl could dress up, now that modeling jobs came less frequently. If she displayed her foreign beauty techniques in public around Peking, people would get the wrong idea. Nor, being unmarried, would she go to the city's nightspots. Practical not ethical considerations forced her to sit home by the television. The maintenance of virtue was an investment in her future.

When Eagle arrived, rather than showing her pleasure, she looked pinched. Her mother's welcome was enough for two. Pearl merely sat by, wondering if she had cast him aside too lightly. It had been many months. During his brief stint in the model troupe, Eagle and Pearl had been leading boy and girl. She was hard and cold and needed a good-looking man. But modeling accorded ill with "socialist spiritual civilization," and when the troupe was disbanded, only Pearl got to stay on as a professional, apparently because Pierre Cardin personally had insisted on using her. She was placed in the Department of Product Popularization at the Ministry and went to Paris several times. She detested foreign men. She always returned to Peking and once upon a time it had been to Eagle, who as a prospective basketball hero suited her. When she found out about his ankle injury and his sacking from the Sports Institute, she joined the others in blaming his bad attitude. She said that only if he worked to join the Party would the team take him back, and only if the team took him back would she do likewise. It was her ultimatum. She didn't want her man out of a job. She didn't want a man with an injury that would cripple his chances for life. After all, there were other fish in the sea. The marriage their talk had been tending towards faded, and with it the large new flat with water and gas and heating and a lift that came as Pearl's dowry. Diplomatically they stopped seeing each other. But Pearl had not found a replacement. Her modeling work was thinning out, and she was wearing the same clothes she had been given in Paris two years before.

Yarning, laughing, feeding one piece of information after another to Pearl's uncle, Eagle made the deal clear. He was in top physical condition. The team was sure to take him back. What about it?

This was business. There was no immediate answer, but the provisos were in place.

Draping the mauve cardigan over her shoulders, Pearl stood in the doorway to see him off.

"Come back when you've got time," she said.

"The man came again today from the neighborhood committee," said Mother Lin, knitting when Eagle got home. Sweet summer air filled the room through the open door. "About the demolition of our street."

3

The Doctor and Song turned to small talk as they completed the experiment. He was fishing for news. Song said that Jin

Juan was unwell and had gone out of town. As they changed out of their lab coats, Wally told Song about his initiation into Peking opera. "Jin Juan and her cousin seem very similar," he observed.

"Two brothers married two sisters," explained Song. "They are double cousins."

"Jin Juan should have been a singer too," he joked, sensing that Song was in the mood for gossip.

"Jin Juan could do many things."

"She seems wasted in the middle school, with such marvelous English."

"She is too unlucky—" Once they were through the door to outside, where there was no chance of being overheard, talk loosened. "At graduation from the Foreign Languages Institute Jin Juan was the top student. She should have become a research student and gone abroad. But there was no chance."

"Why ever not?"

"She was asked to work here at the hospital translating medical journals and training doctors in English. But the decision was reversed."

"Why?"

Song shrugged. "On high."

"Was someone out to get her? Someone from the College? What was her crime?"

"You don't need a crime."

"You've known Jin Juan a long time, haven't you? How can her situation be so different from yours?"

"Her background is different."

And a different personality, Wally noted, imagining in Jin Juan a stubborn, principled streak, whereas Song was a flexible practitioner and probably the cleverer of the two. Something about Jin Juan invited trouble . . . He remembered her at the theater, sharp towards the arrogant fellow on her arm.

"She's not married?" asked Wally, adding quickly, "She had a chap at the opera—I wasn't sure who he was."

"Her fiancé," said Song, "of long standing."

Wally took the inference. "Long engagements are the custom in China."

"Not so long as this one," Song commented sourly. She despised Zhang. Her own parents were peasants. The turbulence of the Cultural Revolution had opened up opportunities which she had utilized with hard work and brains. Now she saw her country being destroyed by smooth privileged parasites like Zhang. She put it bluntly: "They should have married years ago. He's taken advantage of her. Now she's too old and too inconvenient and because his family's gone up in the world he can do better. His family has made difficulties. I blame Zhang." The story made sense, though Song would not be more specific. Instead she invited him home, for "a very simple dinner."

Once again her husband David did the cooking while the colleagues talked, Wally's offers of help being thoroughly overpowered. The daughter bounced on the sofa chanting, "Mogadishu, Moscow, Monte Carlo."

"The creche does a fine job," said Song, raising her eyebrows.

Also present was David's younger brother, a law student at Peking University. As the mood progressed, and food and beer were consumed, Wally asked whether the boy studied Chinese law or Western law.

"There is no Chinese law," he answered smartly.

"What do you study then? Are we not developing the legal system?" David laughed.

This light-hearted approach was as a red flag to the bull. "We are developing rules," said the boy. "We are strangling ourselves with rules, but there is no law to protect the people, to safeguard justice and confer rights. Power is the only law."

"That is so in the West too," offered Wally.

"I don't know about the West. I'm not allowed to go there. I know there is no law in China."

David, shiny-faced from the cooking, began to admonish his brother in heated Chinese for spouting heretical opinions in front of the guest. The boy called David a coward. An argument developed in crossfire over Wally's head as the brothers grew passionate. From the key words, Party, economics, modernization, democracy, freedom, Wally could guess at its general drift.

The boy argued that China's failure to develop an effective legal system arose from a deep antagonism to the divesting of authoritarian power that law implied. Similar failures in scientific and technological development, in the economy and in culture, stemmed from the same refusal of the political system to budge. The Reforms were welcome, of course, but were too slow, too cautious, often sabotaged, and fundamentally half-hearted. In the West, in Hong Kong, in Taiwan, development had occurred rapidly because people were free from the repressions of socialist central planning. If freedom of speech could be protected in law, then a true new people's China could be created. What the Party most feared, however, was the release of the potential for continuing change on which it had ridden to power itself.

David did not particularly dispute his brother's opinions. Yet he urged him not to voice them. Caution and gradualism were to be recommended. Intellectuals could see a long way into the future, David said, too far sometimes, to a future that would never exist. They should also make the effort to look back. He understood that for his brother there was no past. What beckoned was a fresh start for a generation that had been spared disillusionment and which, encountering obstacles for the first time, swore to abolish them. David had spent the years from fifteen to twenty-five in the countryside, never quite achieving the desired state of perfect re-education. On his return to the capital he had wept tears of hope at a Democracy Wall that was rapidly cemented over. Now he recognized the dream of reform as a calenture. He contented himself with the rhetoric of democracy as an infinitely-to-be-postponed goal. The greater danger lay in too much complaining, too much demanding, too much belittling the past of the martyrs. If the old men on high were piqued by the ingratitude of their offspring and underlings, then the thunderbolts would fly. History could only be reversed in a patient manner that would save the face of the people. Within the shell of his idealism, David had found a place for what experience had taught him, that the world cannot be improved and that life must be endured. Or perhaps that was the contempt of middle age.

The kid took David's views as a provocation, appalled to see his brother only ten years older already maneuvering himself into the robes of a Confucian elder. Why did all Chinese feel the need to preach rectitude to those "under" them? How could his brother bear to promote the older generation's world-weary apathy in the name of order and acquiescence and don't-rock-the-lousy-leaking-boat? The kid scowled.

"The truth is we would be better off today if the Kuomintang had beaten the Communists shitless. We could have used our energy to go forward instead of constructing this palace of terrors!"

"Now don't get too crazy." David wagged a finger. "Don't forget that before Liberation our country was also backward and feeble. Anyway, I'm fed up with politics. Put more money in my pocket and I'll be content. Just like the masses—and a bit of cash would shut you students up too," he said sulkily.

"That's where your thinking is deficient. There ain't no more money, and there ain't going to be no more until we change the system. It's politics first." The boy was flushed. Changing tactics, he appealed to the visitor.

Wally wished he had not been asked. But it would be pusillanimous not to make a stab.

"Well, I'm a doctor first of all. I believe in health, which is really another name for the opportunity to continue growing.

We'll never know what the perfect conditions for growth are, and that's lucky because we could never achieve them anyway, but we do know what's harmful in an environment and we can recognize which conditions are good enough. I guess I believe a good society ensures those opportunities for healthy growth—food, shelter, security, education enough, equality enough, love enough—but what it really boils down to is room to move. Freedom to think about things and act on your thoughts. Space to create, to continue. I believe in space. I'm an Australian. We have lots of space and we haven't had to think very hard about what happens when space is constantly encroached on, about the kind of organization and adjudication necessary. The harness of community is not a big thing with us."

Was it gibberish? He scratched his head. The kid seemed to warm into a fuzzy drunken happiness, thick hair flopping round his eyes and ears. He wore faded jeans and a bulky black sweater. From his wrist hung a silver bracelet, and a paisley rayon scarf was stuffed around his neck. He looked for all the world like types Wally had hung out with in Cambridge; rosy red cheeks after a couple of pints, wispy sideburns and moustache, a sullen underlip and the same tense body language. In the Cambridge of 1968 Wally had been unswervingly convinced of what he believed. Had he uttered such woolly benign thoughts back then he would have been hooted from the pub. The trouble was, his present formulations lacked all ardor, because he knew no way to guarantee the growth and continuance of creativity that he valued. The fact of life was sickness, not health. Unable to get round that fact, doctors became in the end the most indifferent or the most despairing of people—which was why he had reverted to research. Was he giving up the fight? He had always resisted the tribal assumption that firebrand youth led on inevitably to crusty conservative old age, had always kept in mind those elders who defied the rule by luxuriating in their old age like tropical blooms. But was he now, like David, preparing to change his clothes and his colors—shuffling off?

The kid stood up and bowed to Wally. He had to catch the last bus back to the students' dormitory. He said that on May Day he and his friends were having a picnic at the Old Summer Palace. His brother and sister-in-law were invited, and he hoped the Doctor would come too, with other foreign friends. Wally was courteous in reply, shook the kid's hand heartily, and asked him to repeat his name. He was called Build-the-Country.

David apologized afterwards for the loose talk that had flown. "It's all fun," he said. "The kids like to shoot off, but in reality there's no commitment to their ideas. Life has been too easy for them. They're innocent of society."

"That's what us oldies always say."

Song, playing with her daughter, had been happy to keep out of the argument. After ten hours in the lab, she longed to close her ears and eyes completely. "Lab again tomorrow," she said coming from the bedroom. "At least our pigs can't give us their opinions. I prefer pigs to humans sometimes. Tomorrow Director Kang reports too. I wonder what news."

Wally stretched himself from the cramped corner where he had been sitting all evening. He had not raised the question of Kang's work with Song yet.

"Vila, Vienna, Vientiane," came a sing-song voice.

"Oh that naughty child!" sighed Song.

"Look, I'll be going. Thanks, David," he called to the kitchen, and to Song on the landing he gabbled, "I hope to catch up with Jin Juan. Will you tell her? Do you think I could contact her through the cousin? Do you know where the cousin lives?" But Song was not much help.

When the foreigner was gone Song warned her husband that he would have to do something about his kid brother before they all got into trouble.

4

The concourse outside Peking Station was quilted with bodies
of peasants, long-exiled residents and those waiting for trains,
forgotten kids drifting back from the countryside, criminals,
innocents and wearybones bedding down together on the
pavement. The boy was bleary-eyed after his cramped night
in the smoky train. His hair was like a dried pat of buffalo
dung, his eyes rubbed red. He ran his tongue over his furry
upper lip and spat. He had traveled by horse-cart to the next
village and by broken-down bus to the market town, through
mountains of flinty stone and spurs of caked yellow dust where
no trees grew, to the plain where water ran in channels, producing emerald rice crops and fat white ducks. He had a mute
sensation of regret at leaving home. At New Year he had written
to his sister in the city telling her that one day he would come.
She didn't reply. She had married out of the village many years
ago. Then he had gone to the father of the other boy from the
village who had gone to Peking. He had the address in his
head, money in his pocket, and news to pass on.

He was eighteen, youngest of six brothers, a sturdy round-
faced boy of medium height who had brown farmer's hands
with stained yellow fingers and limbs that swung so freely that
he seemed loose in the joints. He wore his best cotton jacket
with a tear at the pocket and a cigarette burn on the sleeve.
He carried only a bag of flat pancakes. His schooling had
stopped when he was twelve. Their land was poor and the
work unremitting. But as the youngest of the boys he was the
least indispensable, and the expectation had grown up that he
might perhaps take another road. He was often sent down to
the market town to sell produce or buy fertilizers and salt. He
liked to stay and watch television in the street there, even if

it meant he had to walk all night up the mountain track to get home. On television he saw one colorful event after another jump into a mysterious narrative chain, and weird-looking heroes and villains, green, orange and crystalline blue who waged glorious battle and danced some cosmic dance that re-created for the boy in magical form the legends that had surrounded his village and his people, in sky and earth and water, for generations. None of these visions had been uppermost, however, when he lay down to sleep the previous evening, uncertain whether he would go or not. But when the rooster crowed and he opened his eyes, the dawn air laden with the damp smell of mud walls nipped him into action. He clambered quickly from his place between his sleeping brothers. He sat on the great clay urn out the back beside the pigs. He splashed his face with icy water from the bucket. Through razor mountain peaks a tender light was pushing towards the little human settlement, offering a protective bond between his home and the faraway world so pink and promising. His belly stirred hungrily, but there was no time to eat. He laced up his canvas shoes, buttoned his jacket to the neck, called into the dark that he was going. His father echoed the words gruffly. Only the dog, whining and leaping in the street, shared the adventure.

Arriving in Peking, he stared at the many cars and people; he had never seen traffic lights or tall buildings or cranes, and he felt tall himself as he walked. He kept expecting to turn a corner and have the city end. But the streets went on, until he stopped noticing single things. He was going to the No. 3 Vehicle Plant on the West Third Ring Road and assumed that he would arrive at his destination automatically. In the countryside he never had to ask or be told where things were. He walked for several hours before it dawned on him that he had not got anywhere. A bristling peasant instinct made him steer away from asking directions, and when he did speak, his heavily accented language was more demand than question. At last, disconsolate, he found a dumpling shop and spent the remains of his money filling up on dumplings that were of thinner dough and more expensive than at home. The girl who took the money had a patient attitude. The West Third Ring Road she knew: go west, turn north. She came to the shop door to point him on the way, explaining about buses. But when he reached the bus stop, he just kept on walking, and when the bus route finished, he sat down on a step feeling that the city was stuck to his body like tar and feathers. He had one coin left. He crossed to the old woman on the corner who pulled an iceblock from her canvas box and said as always, "Go straight ahead." Where it was she had no notion, and as the country bumpkin headed west, she toddled back inside the limits of her world.

Night fell, and the wind picked up, rasping the city with sand off the Gobi desert. At evening rush hour the streets milled with people whose heads were bagged and masked against the wind. Then the streets emptied again. His stomach growling, his head aching, he screwed up his gritty eyes and placed one foot before the other with no thought of where. Faces were closed as firmly as shopfronts and courtyard walls to shut out the sandpaper wind. He had no knack of eliciting sympathy and walked doggedly forward, slower and more aimless, with an empty grin on his mouth, until he found a bare patch of trees and earth with an edifice in the corner, an open door to a large unlit bog. He squatted inside out of the wind, ignoring the stench, and wondered if there was a clean dry spot where he could curl up to sleep.

His eyelids were drooping when a man came in. The man humped his shoulders away from the draft to light up his smoke, coughed painfully, a tall figure in greatcoat and cap astride one of the trenches. The smell of smoke suggested pleasure. From his squatting position the boy asked whether the man knew the West Third Ring Road.

The man peered down into the dark. "What?"

"The West Third Ring Road."

"I know it. Go west."

He swept the coat around him and was already striding towards the door when the boy came up behind him and asked for a cigarette. Without a word one was offered. The boy grabbed it in the darkness. The match flared up and he concentrated on lighting the cigarette. Only when he leaned back with a grateful smile as the match burned out did he meet the foreigner's face.

In other circumstances there might have been panic. But here a relationship had been initiated and they were brothers before they were Chinaman and Devil. The boy followed the man outside in order to see clearly the pale funny-shaped face, like a kind of horse. Clarence was equally struck by the face of the boy. He had expected another scrounging late-night Peking prowler. The ruddy face in the match flame was a dirty cherub's. But he had learned to be suspicious. He repeated the directions and turned to go. The boy came after him.

"No, no," said Clarence. "That way is west."

But the boy continued to walk beside him. Clarence coughed convulsively. The wind burned his throat. He could tell from the accent that the boy was from out of town, but there was something else. He did not bombard Clarence with the usual questions he encountered on his camera-less nocturnal rambles, and saved Clarence telling lies.

"Are you cold?"

"No, no!" The boy was shuddering. Clarence suddenly pulled off his greatcoat and draped it over the boy's shoulders, and a spirited tussle broke out, the boy refusing, flailing about, pushing Clarence away, throwing off the unwanted garment, and Clarence insisting, smiling, wrapping the coat round the boy's body and holding him squirming—until polite refusal was enough and the boy slipped his arms into the engulfing coat. Clarence was cold, but didn't care.

The boy's story emerged through the Shandong burr. He

144

had no possessions and no money and had spent his first day in Peking looking for the place where his friend lived. The only information he had to save himself was the name of the No. 3 Vehicle Plant on the West Third Ring Road. Clarence took the boy inside a late-night noodle shop where he emptied two bowls of noodles in ravenous slurps. The old proprietor was bemused at the partnership and reduced the size of the portion. The only other customers, two slick youths, made exaggerated compliments on Clarence's Chinese, to which he replied: "Don't pull my leg." And the boy jumped up, angrily, offering his fists.

There was a cheap inn behind the noodle shop, where the night porter made difficulties.

"The rules, the rules," he muttered as he shut the smooth-talking foreigner and the moron yokel out into the night. He had lost the place in his *kungfu* novel.

The wind sliced into Clarence's chest. The boy squeezed his hand, kissing it sometimes like a puppy. When a lone taxi appeared, Clarence ran into the middle of the road and waved his arms. Seeing the pale face, the taxi stopped, and for a price agreed to take them to where the No. 3 Vehicle Plant was supposed to be.

They were dumped in an area like a ghostly airfield with the odd red flower of a light drooping above; low brick hovels, stretches of rubble, ditches, abandoned construction projects, iron fences, concrete walls, high iron gates labeled with names—and not a soul. A soft bundle turned out to be a sleeping guard who curtly said go west—a hundred meters.

The boy padded off.

"Hey," said Clarence, "that's east."

"West," said the boy.

"East!" said Clarence.

They stopped in the dead center of the broad road, and the wind drove through their bodies as if they were shreds of rag caught on a wire.

Clarence spoke firmly. "That is north."
The boy echoed agreement.
"That is south."
Nods.
"Then that is east, and this is west."
The boy granted north and south. He would not grant east and west.

Clarence imposed his will and they marched west by the compass to an obscure opening in the barrier behind which was a yard of puddles, mounds, shards surrounded on three sides by barracks. The boy shouted the name of his friend from the village. A bony figure in long johns came to the door and pissed voluminously on the step. The boy called and called. They tried another door. In a room of a few square meters a dim bulb revealed perhaps twenty-five tousle-haired gray-faced snoring snuffling bodies side by side, head to toe, toe to head, pressed against each other in their greatcoats on a wide platform where there was no room to lie flat. On shelves round the walls, on every hook, in every cranny, were their meager towels and bags. The boy peered at each sleeping face in search of his friend. An eye opened to meet their investigations. They were all Shandong peasants come to work at the plant—but the friend was not there.

Clarence and the boy conferred outside. The boy was confident he would find his friend in the morning, and that his friend would get him a job shoveling coal at the plant for one yuan a day, which was why he had come to the city.

"I don't know your name," said Clarence. "What's your name?"

"Autumn," said the boy. "I was born in the autumn."

Then Clarence broke with his usual practice and wrote down a telephone number. He told the boy to hang up if anyone else answered, but to keep trying, if he needed help. Clarence left the boy with his greatcoat and some money in the pocket, and started his own long coughing journey home.

146

The boy yawned. He lay down on a ledge of the platform of bodies, squeezing against the outside man. Gradually the pressure of one more body was taken up by the others. Each adjusted his position a fraction, and by morning the boy was sleeping just like the others, a sardine, but one whose heart glowed with his adventure, and the telephone number on a scrap of paper in his innermost pocket.

5

It started when the winder in Wally's camera jammed; in trying to fix it he wiped out thirty-six memorable moments. He couldn't remember them anyway. A few days later he lost his address book. Deliberately? Ties were severed. Letters remained unwritten. He stopped bothering to listen to the World Service or read *Newsweek*. The world was slipping away. Whose fault? Was all-mothering China drawing him into its soma? Gray on gray. Or was withdrawal his own expression of the state his existence had reached? His work ceased to be in earnest. The days went by and nothing was asked of him. Whether he exercised among the blooming magnolias in the park or stayed sedentary, whether he drank Scotch or sipped tea, made no difference. He slept for eight or ten hours at a stretch, his sleep weighted with accidie. His bones ached from too much sleep. Friends, acquaintances, the mystery of China— what nonsense!—all were forgotten in his submersion in the strangling web of sleep. And his dreams were drab, as if the power had been cut.

Until there came a singular, baffling dream.

He was a horse galloping swift as mind down a long drive that wound through snug hills and golding vistas, a landscape of promise delivered, spring and autumn. His own motion, and a larger motion beyond his power, carried him eagerly through pine-covered cleft and wooded park, rain forest and open country where cattle lay beneath mighty spreading trees, through awesome wilderness and great good places to warm Arcadian Eden. As the horse galloped the scenes revolved, down a turning drive, back, to a place (he could not place it), a mansion of many rooms, one added to another over the years, in a declivity of scarlet earth, in a sea of ripe wheat, with the sound of ocean beyond.

It was a museum with polished floors and watery light cast through long windows onto worn country timber in well-proportioned rooms. On tables, melons and peaches nested in porcelain, and stars floated in crystal glasses of half-drunk wine. On a dining board by each place-setting sat a small bronze fox, blackened, after Donatello.

The horse's hooves struck the floor with a din. Through windows a sloping greensward and terraced Italian garden were visible where men in white togas were dotted about. Despite their theatrical whiskers, worn to make them look old and stately—graybeards of powder and greasepaint they were, with penciled wrinkles and receding latex hairlines—he recognized among them his best friend from high school who was a trade union leader; he saw those of his contemporaries who had become doctors, and those thinkers who had become tax lawyers and media managers. He saw those bright sparks from the lab in Cambridge who were professors and professionals. And there was Harvey Heilmann bent like a tree for all his swimming. The men on the lawn conferred with solemn animation, colleagues, but boys all, in their silly robes. Arranged in Socratic dialogue on the grass, the figures were attending a symposium. They represented Western Mind—high-toned blokes with painted faces. Was it in Athens? The westering sun soaked garden and hills in apricot nectar. Had they gone outside Florence to escape the plague? Somewhere on holiday? Beyond the shrubbery was a stand of soughing white gums, and a kookaburra cackling.

The horse stood by the window and from the half-filled glasses on the table came an ethereal kind of music that should have been inaudible. A cavity of his horse-brain noted the music as Mozart's for glass harmonica. Then suddenly, quite oblivious of the docile stallion, girls and women swept through the room as if summoned by the current of sound.

The women wore light, gathered robes that revealed their bodies through gauze, as in frescoes by Ghirlandaio. They laughed and whispered, reaching for each other as they hurried, mothers and grown daughters in a wise, passionate sisterhood. And the men on the lawn one by one cast their gaze towards the house, rubbing their hands, and one by one broke from their debate. *Ewig' Weiblich zieht uns hinan . . .*

And the horse nosed forward after the rustle of women, through long dream corridors as the crystal music died away and another music was heard—earthly fleshy sound. He came to the last crowded room, with men craning at the back, women at the front, and at the very front not visions but the women he knew—Bets's friends, the dancer, the abortionist, his mother-in-law, Cindy from Coogee, all in a solid phalanx— and leaning against the grand piano, her silver-blonde hair streaming, tanned shoulders bare, head high, mouth delivering that song was Bets—his wife.

A hand seemed to grab and wring his guts. The room was empty. The toga'd men and gowned women had vanished. He was a man again, and across the empty polished boards of the long sunroom he stared at her, in jeans and singlet, singing from the piano the old song.

Where was she? They? As day closed the hills burned with warmth and light, yet were cooled by zephyrs laced with sea tang. The nip of eucalyptus, the sweetness of hawthorn, the perfume of magnolia reached the mind from some displaced garden. Where was this dream that combined in one present too many enchanted stages of the past?—the house at Whale Beach, the upstairs in Cambridge, Massachusetts, the rented

Tuscan villa, the flat in the other Cambridge, Tintagel, the holiday shack near Pigeonhouse Mountain, the city pub where he found her that night at the piano, with her friends around, singing her lungs out. Then it became that other night on the terrace above the growling sea, and she was there not in jeans and singlet or quattrocento gown; just in her flimsy nightie.

6

"I didn't want you to know before I did," she said. "I've been seeing Geoffrey Mithers."

Wally blinked.

"Darling—" she said, reaching both her hands.

His own felt grubby after his night out, but she was sweeping aside such trivialities. She had floated free of accusation. At least that was her tone, a wafting lightness reserved for matters of utmost gravity. Mithers? He had never imagined, allowed for, a serious adultery. For all their separateness, he and she were too mature for that. One of his own colleagues?

"Geoffrey wants me to go into the hospital," she continued, "for tests. A biopsy."

The facts so briefly recounted were commonplace in Wally's line of work. It was as if she had told him of a minor domestic problem she had trouble with and he as a man could fix in a jiff; the kind of thing that need never become calamitous for sensible informed people like themselves. He refused to follow the implications, refused at first to respond.

"Well?"

He was squeezing her hands with all his pressure and her hands were cold, his hands moved up her arms, he hugged her, as if to hoard the precious warmth of their two bodies, two drumming heartbeats. Over her shoulder the white fringe of the black sea was like a line of fatty tissue attached to the monstrous heaving organ.

She'd had pains, chronic indigestion, she'd been passing blood. Knowing something was up, she'd gone to see Geoffrey—poor man!—asking him to say nothing to her husband. She hadn't wanted to burden Wally. Anyway an intuition or fear, a possibility like the present, had to be faced alone. She wanted to know first. Geoffrey's preliminary tests had determined the need for acting straight away. And Wally wasn't there.

"Bloody hell. Mithers is a goon!"

From the tone of her singing that he heard as he came into the house, and the heavy serenity of her body, he guessed that she already renounced all alternatives but the worst; the patient's clinical reaction, that usually intensified into guilt or anger, the power of her spirit was even now turning to a kind of gildedness, in the early hours of this cool, clear morning. Dawn would come . . .

By first light Wally was talking professionally. They should not jump to conclusions; if the diagnosis was made early enough . . . ; there was no one path for disease but an infinite number of permutations in which medical science could intervene at many stages. Nothing was irreversible. He was the committee man selectively dealing out the Janus-faced news. Bets nodded at the plausibility of his trade. At last she yawned and said she needed a shower. They made love instead and as the new day stirred they ignored the first of the telephone calls and sprinted down to the beach with long skidding steps.

There was never a point at which the truth was spoken. Perhaps there was no truth: as Wally kept insisting, the situation must be considered multivalent. His optimism was resolute, Bets's light-hearted hopefulness the attitude required. Only once, without Wally's knowledge, did she talk candidly with Jerome. The kid shunned her at first, involuntarily resisting the wound; then came very close.

151

For month-long stretches of almost normality, the cancer did not change, as all held their breath before the next lurch downwards. And there was always the possibility of a remission, in no one's power to effect, though Wally believed it should be in his if anyone's (even as Mithers continued to handle the case). Wally committed more and more medical improprieties. He got at Mithers. He called for second and third opinions, and scoured the latest publications in the journals. On flying trips to the States, Britain and Germany, he consulted with the best and worst of his colleagues and old mates, some of whom were moved by his uxorious devotion while others regarded his behavior as a frantic quest to salvage *amour-propre*: a campaign to vindicate his life's work in medical science and his faith in humanity's capacity to side with growth.

Bets submitted with good grace to a punishing regime of treatments, from diet to radiation to the latest complicated hormone manipulation. Most she resented being discussed as a case. Among her friends she confided only in Aldo, who knew a miracle worker who used strenuous meditation to achieve remissions in forty per cent. In the end Wally looked to quackery too. Only partly submerged in the relentless pursuit of a cure, his anger was directed chiefly against himself— the mockery of his idealism—and himself as a representative of the fat vanity of the medical fraternity whose knowledge had scarcely advanced a step since Hippocrates—and himself as a member of a species that was nature's whipping-boy. There was no case here for dignified philosophical acceptance of the inevitable. A fine healthy woman in her thirty-seventh year struck down by a stray biological bullet that did not kill cleanly but inflicted the most humiliating wastage.

Half her insides were cut out and reorganized with clamps. Then followed another plateau of laughing lunches on the terrace above Whale Beach in a capricious winter of sunshine and squalls. Then another lurch, a metastasis. A stepped-up course of chemotherapy was set up using technology of greatly improved accuracy, the famous silver bullets that the hospital had specially flown in. Wally was to meet Bets in the clinic for the first session; only she didn't turn up.

He had not even known where the place was, and when none of the numbers on her telephone pad answered he had to look up the Angel in the yellow pages. On the corner where he parked streetwalkers stood wearing raincoats over their mini-skirts. The voice came to him as soon as he was inside the door, in the rowdy, muggy downstairs bar that opened to the street. The voice came from over his head, and he stomped towards it up the wooden stairs.

She leant against the upright piano, her thinning gray-gold hair brushed out and frizzy from rain earlier in the day, her shoulders and fleshless arms tanned like polished wood. She wore a scrap of a singlet that hardly covered her scars, and tight jeans, and her brilliantly made-up face was red from drink and gray from chemicals. She gave the impression of hot bronze. Slipping a bit, she reached for her glass and propped herself against the piano's vertical, while around, basking in the radiance they conferred on her, were the original communist, the ex-nun, the abortionist, the Liberal politician, the drag queen, the richest woman in Edgecliff. An intrigued young audience hung about, kept in line by the woman who ran the pub. Aldo was at the keys.

Bets was singing that old love song. She sang both the man's part and the woman's, and her voice achieved extraordinary depths and colors. She sang as she had never sung before, in ultimate self-delivery; bound and yet released, so beautiful and sad. Her mouth was taut, her eyes a caked mess of tears. Her smile lines stretched as she saw Wally standing impotently behind the crowd. And for him, who would remember all the other times, she sang *Bess, you-izz my woman*

*now, you-izz, you-izz! And you must learn to sing and dance
for* TWO IN-STEAD OF ONNNNE! Rejecting further treatment, she
was on her own.

7

The new leaves on the little magnolia they planted in the drive
were burned by salt. After the trip from the crematorium father
and son looked morosely across the food they were obliged
to eat, searching each other's eyes for rescue, hating the sunshine. A year passed before Wally could decently extricate
himself. His grief took the form of scathing disgruntlement
with the vanity of medicine. The certain way to convey that
sentiment, needling his colleagues to his immense satisfaction,
was to suggest that Western medicine had exhausted itself.
Though his colleagues lost patience, he half came to believe
in his new attitude. From deep in his memory, from a pregnant
time in his career, he fastened on a Chinese name and, bur-
rowing through his files, came to those old papers as signposts
to the road not taken. He proposed, as Chairman of the Department, to invite this Professor Hsu Chien Lung to be a
Faculty Visitor. Letters were written, the quest began. But to
the Faculty's relief the fellow never materialized. Wally's colleagues wanted no venerable Chinaman, and facetiously advised Wally to go to China himself. He surprised them by
agreeing. He believed the Chinese could offer some useful
pointers. He needed a change of scene. In his heart of hearts
he also knew that the stake was greater. If he didn't get away
from that terrace overlooking the ocean, he would go crazy.
He must escape the depths of his emptiness, and the knives
of his guilt.

154

8

The dream singer became mute, as if the dream's sound was turned off, and Wally heard his own guttural moan as he rolled over and grasped at the empty space beside him in the bed. Dreams come from nowhere to taunt with intimations beyond our powers, creativities we cannot possess. From the gray vacancy of his existence Wally had summoned up such colors and presences as made him sweat. Better if they left him alone? That would mean he was dead. He caught as he could at the crumpled rope of bedclothes, the dream that had been his torture his only comforter.

With the lights on, he fell asleep again. There was a knock at the door. He answered in his dragon-embroidered robe, and frowned when he saw the woman who had slipped in past the attendant and up the stairs. Before he could express his surprise she had taken up a position in the center of his room where her head drooped modestly. By way of introduction she spoke one or two phrases of compressed Chinese that Wally missed. Apart from Mrs. Gu, he had never had a female caller at the College before. This one, in a black slacks-suit and hair up inside a cap, could have passed for a boy except for the mask-like made-up face. Pink and puce shadings over the cheeks; green, black and white in a zebra pattern around the eyes.

The visitor did not respond when Wally addressed her in English as Jin Juan. Quickly he grasped that she was Jin Juan's cousin, who must have come straight from a performance at the opera theater: the imperial cucumber. To appear at his door so late in the evening was an act of temerity and high courage. Perhaps Jin Juan had encouraged her. She was a striking creature, maintaining her stage stylization as she moved about his rooms and responded to his remarks in a high-pitched voice, sparing with the information she revealed. Her long-term motives would emerge with time; now, she said, it was just a visit between friends. Wally re-tied the cord of his satin dressing-gown low around his hips. Over tea they chatted in the same stilted, uncommunicative manner. Azalea she was called. Her long neck drooped, and lights seemed to be struck from her paint-framed eyes. He could smell her as she sat side-saddle on the couch beside him. His bare hairy legs were staked apart on the floor, and a knee contrived to touch hers. Azalea was as graceful, as refined, as could be, and her purpose was apparent. Had she by some mistake made her entrance into the wrong scene of the wrong opera? Certainly, he began convincing himself, he had been bewitched by her from the start. Nature abhors a vacuum, so Wally's emptiness had called and Azalea answered. What price would she exact? He wondered who might be watching. When he put his arm on her, she kept him at bay with the most extravagant gestures and wicked, delightful flashes of her eyes. Why not, thought Wally frankly, it's been a long time? And he hugged her to him, held her slender body against his in the empty space of the bed, grew rapturous at the feel of her skin, kissed the paint from her eyes. So much he had forgotten.

She went as secretively as she had come. In the morning the other side of the bed was empty.

CHAPTER NINE

Things Fall Apart

1

"When life has no interest, dreams matter," shouted the young man who was ten meters above the ground. He had shinned his way to the top of one of the ruined stone columns in the Old Summer Palace. His friends were picnicking below. Looking down, he feigned dizziness and swayed a little, as if he really might fall.

"He's okay," laughed Build-the-Country, tilting his chin towards the column.

"How did he do it? One minute he was sitting here brooding over his beer, next minute he's up on that thing."

Against the blazing blue sky, the young man's figure was distorted like a modernistic statue. His skinny arms flailed at peculiar angles in homage to the sun. Baggy cotton trousers rolled to the knee billowed in the breeze, and only his feet seemed firmly planted.

"Put on your own heart!" he declaimed, and the groundlings cheered, recognizing the line. The monkey-faced poet who had penned it threw a bread roll, and a volley of cans, apple cores and orange peel followed.

But climbing to heaven was one thing, getting back to stable earth quite another. There were no footholds on the worn fluted column. His friends were calling from below. He was drunk, they yelled, he should be careful.

A couple of the guys dragged out the large quilt on which they were sitting and held it up as a safety net. On top of the column the young man pushed back his glasses and scratched his head. Others joined in holding the edges of the colored square taut.

"I'm coming," he shouted, took a breath—and jumped.

"Ouch!" He bumped his arse and sprawled like a baby on the quilt, and laughed and laughed.

How easy it was!

What was his name?

The Philosopher Horse.

Huh? "Ma Zhe," it was explained to Wally. "Meaning Horse Philosophical. He's an unemployed kid from the South. A thinker, a writer. Not bad, eh? He's got guts."

Watching the animated rosy face of Philosopher Horse, with the bumfluff on his upper lip as he sipped another beer and straightened his wild black hair and frayed yellow t-shirt, Wally thought: a holy child.

The party grew more disorderly. The weather was warm, as evening came on. The grounds of the Old Summer Palace, chiefly given over to farming, were rich green, with figures in bright blue coats bobbing in the green as they pulled weeds or cut vetch. On paths crisscrossing the hillocks and mounds loitered lovers and solitaries. The willows' jade nipples were bursting and crepe myrtle was headily in flower. You could see clear across to the western hills, as lucent as candy sculpture.

The friends poked fun at one another as they lay about on the ground, picking over the last of the fruit and meat.

158

"The Doctor likes Peking opera!" they pronounced in disbelief when attention turned to Wally.

They were students, unemployed, writers and artists. He was Build-the-Country's guest. Song and David had stayed home with their child, perhaps fearing the unruly company. Wally had heard that Jin Juan might be there, but she was not, and without her he lost his zest for the party. She had not been in touch with him, nor had her cousin since the curious visit. He had been to the opera on several occasions, and had even gone snooping around backstage during the daylight. But the company was not resident at the theater in Goldfish Lane, and by the time he tracked them down to other theaters they had each time moved on. He was embarrassed to keep asking Song to deliver messages, but since it was on his mind, he had asked Build-the-Country how he might locate a Peking opera singer. He was behaving, perhaps, like a naughty old man. But that was not his real purpose. Somehow, for reasons he could not define, he was beginning to be aware of, to be compelled by, a set of parallels, or even connections, between his—desire, was that the word?—for the beautiful singer, for Jin Juan, and his quest for Hsu.

The curling baroque stones looked like the playthings of a giant child abandoned in the grass. On Jesuit advice, the pleasure palace of the Chien Lung Emperor had been filled with scaled-down replicas of the European architecture of the day. Removed from native soil, the eloquence of Rome was translated into swirling plastic pomposities of fantastic silliness. Yet, despoiled and desecrated, becoming ruins proper, the remaining fragments regained their dignity as the sorry traces of Europe's dream of the City of God on Earth, and China's dream of Europe as her illustrious vassal. The place had become the locus of a cult, where young Pekingers held meetings, or basked like lizards on the stones.

And Philosopher Horse guided them, scruffy southern kid that he was.

Jumbo was there with the artists, and Dulcia, who had brought Clarence along. Jumbo was in a sulk and went off with his friends to row boats on the lake.

"The shit's hit the fan," Dulcia confessed to the Doctor. She was red around the eyes.

"He's in a huff?"

"Well, his passport still hasn't come through and they won't tell him anything. The Public Security Bureau is investigating him and the spies at the Friendship Hotel have been reporting. Every time he visits me they take down his details and ask what our relations are. I tell 'em I'm his English teacher. But they're playing it by the book and we're waiting for the knock on the door. It's really having a negative effect on my functions. They've been to Central TV. You know, Central TV was going to pay for him to study art design in the States. Now they turn around and say he can pay it himself. They don't trust him any more. Where's he gonna get that kind of money? He'll have to sell a lot of pictures."

Wally commiserated. He knew the obstacles she was up against.

"What pisses me is that I'm sure somewhere in his head he blames me for all this trouble, when I'm only trying to help. He's pretty arrogant. He believes he could do all this by himself—contacting schools in the States, getting references, preparing résumés; he believes he is doing it himself. Or he resents me if I take short cuts through the Embassy, as if I'm trying to trap'm. He thinks I'm a spy too. I've said to'm really honestly that I'm helping'm because we're friends and I don't *expect* anything in return. I'm not working the Chinese way. He says that he wants to go to America as a free man. He doesn't want to marry me for the sake of the passport. He says we can decide what we do when we get there, when we're equals. But they won't ever give him the passport unless we do get married. And there's the problem. I can't marry'm anyway till my divorce comes through. Jeezus! But the basic problem is that he doesn't trust me."

"Maybe you're expecting too much of him," said Wally.

"I'll be frank with you. The first few times Jumbo and I made out it wasn't a good experience. He really had no idea what was happening. He would just lie there being very gentle, but no good for a woman like me. I know Chinese men. You gotta get tough with 'em, tell 'em, show 'em, and they learn real quick. I gave Jumbo a copy of *The Joy of Sex* that I brought from the States. Things got really interesting after that. There are things the human body can do that don't exist in the Chinese language.

"That was our honeymoon period. Then one day at my apartment at the Friendship he found the box under the bed. You see, I imported a whole shipment of *The Joy of Sex* and I give one to every Chinese guy who needs it. Jumbo counted how many were left from the original five dozen. And he turned on me! It's crazy. Well, we made up. Wow! But he doesn't trust me."

"Do you trust him?"

"How can you? I like him. I don't ask about trust, whether he likes me for myself or for what I can get'm, you mean? If you want Chinese friends, you gotta understand that helping people is like the very heart of friendship. And that kind of friendship gives me power, which I kinda like."

Wally smiled. Dulcia was a tribute to Sino-American relations. As she rolled on to her front, she concluded, "Right now I hope we both get out of this country before something ugly happens."

The others returned through the trees, exhilarated from their larrikin rowing. They were lugging fresh supplies of beer to drink in the summer dusk. Jumbo's moodiness was gone. He pranced ahead of the troupe, his hair flying about like ruffled feathers, and flopped down in the woman's lap. A girl pulled out her guitar and sang a Chinese version of Simon and Garfunkel, and when it came to the chorus they sang and shouted and clapped and stamped under the trees. *"Lai-lai lai! COME, COME, COME!"*

It was a rare opportunity for unabashed enjoyment, out of reach of surveillance. There was no need to talk politics. Their longings were shared with unspoken intensity and they drew strength from suffering together as far-seeing exiles in their own land.

When the singing and dancing died down, one of the poets, the youngest of them all, a boy with thick curled locks like a Persian lamb, with a black silk jacket over his black trousers, a Beardsley bohemian reincarnate in Peking who drank like his hero Dylan Thomas, sprang up on a pediment and shouted out the language of his heart to a crescent moon that seemed to hang over his shoulder:

> *I am he who from this darling earth*
> *chokes out poems*
> *as if retching on bitter flowers,*
> *the drunkard of springtime!*

His admirers hooted and roared.

Towards midnight a girl said she felt like swimming. They found a deserted edge of the lake, pulled off their clothes and ran scrabbling and shoving into the chilly water, swimming towards the center of the lake like so many glossy water rats. They cheered Wally for his hundred meters' Australian crawl. Then they scrambled back on shore and covered wet bodies with clothes that were still warm. It was Philosopher Horse who said that the time had come to scatter like clouds blown by the wind—but they must remember! They must remember the spirit of their gathering. They must remember their common cause, help and protect each other. He gazed around at his friends imploringly. He stared at the American, the Englishman and the Australian, who looked solemn and embarrassed. He pulled each of them by the hand into a firm huddle of fellowship. "Freedom!" he roared.

On bicycles, on foot, they fanned out from their picnic place. Jumbo and Dulcia picked a path through the fields to Jumbo's house. Build-the-Country and Philosopher Horse stumbled in their wake. Clarence was on his motorbike. He coughed, and winced from a pain in his gut. As he revved, he discreetly asked the Doctor if he could arrange to see him professionally.

"Not now," grinned Wally, who had miles to pedal before he slept.

2

Eagle had reached an agreement with Pearl. With the help of two more cartons of cigarettes, he had also reached an agreement with the coach. He started training with the squad and easily proved himself good enough to be in line for the national team. The coach then cleared the matter with the Party Secretary of the Sports Institute, and with Eagle's work unit, and only Eagle's ability stood between himself and his goal. Marriage was talked of again, and the furnished flat that Eagle and Pearl would move into, and with the flat squarely in view, Mother Lin could set her heart at ease—fortunately, since her heart gave trouble.

Eagle trained energetically. He erred on the side of incaution and caused errors by taking too many risks, by not allowing his teammates time to prepare. Blunted by overfamiliarity, the other players welcomed the extra competitiveness Eagle brought, but were quick to criticize. When Pearl came to watch their practice matches, Eagle couldn't resist showing off and his teammates passed white-eyed glances. Eagle was one of the stars.

The formalities for his transfer from the state office to the Sports Institute had not been finalized, however, before he put in his most extraordinary performance in a match between two city districts. He seemed to harness all his power, working with his teammates, passing, connecting, in perfect synchronization. By the start of the second half, the game looked sewn up, when the balance changed. The opposition turned bullish at the prospect of defeat and their play became angry. And in a subtle, unconscious maneuver Eagle's own teammates bonded together to block their own best player. Eagle was too busy, too tired and too high to notice. As things started going wrong, he tried hard to counter the adverse pressure. The opposition lured him into an outlandish sideways lunge. He leapt into the air after the ball. When he landed on one foot his balance was not quite right. It was his weak ankle. The weight of several of his teammates crashed down on him. Under the impact of his own motion and the momentum of his fellow-players, his knee gave way. He tumbled in ungainly motions of pain across the ground. When they tried to straighten him out, he screamed. The kneecap was smashed and the leg fractured below the knee.

Eagle was suspended from the squad with no compensation; and according to their agreement, Pearl had no choice but to call off the engagement. The new flat was lost.

Mother Lin was silent as she nursed her beloved son. The doctors applied their routine treatment to reunite the bone and patch up the knee. But she feared her son would pine away with shame. He would be laid up for many months. The sky had fallen and crushed him.

3

An overgrown Boy Scout was waiting for Wally when he arrived outside the Peking Observatory at the appointed time. With his crewcut, his flat cotton shoes, his loose nylon shirt and baggy Baden Powell trunks, Ralph stood in a sliver of shadow against the high gray wall. Black glasses concealed his expression, and a black plastic document holder was slipped under his arm.

"G'day cobber. Fighting fit, eh? You're looking great, sport. Don't tell me this place agrees with you!"

The Observatory was flanked by a shaded courtyard garden where peonies bloomed. Ralph told how the Empress Wu, one of China's terrible ladies, had ordered all the flowers to bloom in winter as a tribute to her power. The helpless plum blossom, the fawning rose, the shameless dahlia, the resilient chrysanthemum complied. Only the peony refused, having a majesty above the Empress's, and was exiled to the Western city of Luoyang. Admiring the large layered blooms, vermilion with gold coronets, Wally could see why the peony was made sovereign of Chinese flowers.

They sat on a stone bench in a drooping arbor and Ralph began his report.

On perusing Director Kang's writings in English and Chinese, and reading through Professor Hsu's early papers from the *New England Journal of Medicine* and the manuscript pages from the archives of the Traditional Medicine Academy, he had been struck by similarities. A more systematic study, with attention paid to the probable dates of composition and publication, led to the inescapable conclusion that the larger part of Director Kang's work was lifted from Professor Hsu's.

"All the good bits in Kang come straight from Hsu. It's a blatant act of plagiarism committed not just once but carried on methodically over many years. In those cases where Hsu's original also exists it's crystal clear that what is not Hsu is rubbish, either Kang's own padding or lifted from another ill-chosen source. Where there's no Hsu original one can only guess that the good stuff comes from papers of Hsu's which are missing. To my mind, there's not a shred of doubt that Kang is a fraud and a crook. The only thing that can be said in his favor is that he recognized the value of what he was lifting. Even that may not be to his credit, since he might merely have been reacting to other people's acclaim of Hsu's work—probably other professors from abroad many many years ago."

The surmises Ralph presented made sense of the cool reception that Wally's quest for Professor Hsu had received from Director Kang and Mrs. Gu. But Wally displayed a scholarly reluctance to jump to conclusions. He said that acts of plagiarism were often hard to distinguish from similarities in work emerging from different people within the same lab or institution. And he understood that originality and plagiarism had not the same meaning in China as outside.

Ralph countered that the lifting in some cases was total—character by character—and carried out too pervasively over too many documents to be a case of influence, reciprocal or otherwise. It was possible, however, that Hsu, by reason of some political taint, might not have been allowed to publish his research findings and that Kang in a nice piece of side-stepping was putting out the work under his own name for the greater glory of the Medical College and the motherland. But this in itself made something of a mockery of the College's pretences to be engaging in experimental science and seeking verifiable or falsifiable conclusions according to international procedures and standards. Worse, the fact remained that Kang was swanning round the world receiving accolades under false pretences, when the political problem, if there had been one, had surely ceased to apply—and meanwhile Professor Hsu had disappeared without trace. The more likely explanation was that Director Kang had engineered Professor Hsu's removal once he had his hands on enough material to ensure his own rise.

"The bastard." Wally was profoundly shocked.

Then Ralph presented another bit of news. Dear old Emeritus Professor Wu at the Traditional Medicine Academy had let slip that, as far as she had been able to find out, Professor Hsu was alive and well and living in retirement in the South. He had gone back to his old home.

The two men strolled together through the courtyard of peonies and up the stairs to the roof of the cube-shaped building where astronomical instruments were on display. The instruments provided an elegant frame for photographs of the new Academy of Social Sciences across the way, on the site where once the imperial examinations had been held. The beautiful, enigmatic objects had been presented to the Ching Emperor by scientifically minded Jesuits who hoped to exchange their knowledge for religious conversion. In the end the Chinese had taken neither form of enslavement, but later devised their own, also in the name of deliverance, and now were once again seeking knowledge as the way out of economic disablement. The instruments had been looted and sent back to Europe during the Boxer Rebellion, then returned to China under the Treaty of Versailles. Under a brilliant blue sky they stood as a rusted cat's cradle of irony.

"We've stumbled on to something big," said Wally. "It's a major academic crime."

"It's news to us, but not in the inner circles of the Chinese medical world, I bet."

"You mean they condone it?"

"I mean they conveniently don't know about it and wouldn't thank you if you rubbed their noses in it. They'd have difficulty feigning surprise for a start."

"Kang should be hounded for this. Hsu deserves justice." For Wally, as a medical scientist, the very possibility of knowledge rested on the most scrupulous adherence to the principles of intellectual honesty.

"Whoa boy, before you start breathing fire you need to think carefully. First put all ideas of sweet revenge right out of your mind. Revenge is pretty well impossible for us in China, because the Chinese simply don't allow us to feel the emotional satisfactions we need to make revenge work. That's why in the past a lot of Westerners have just gone crazy and beaten the shit out of them. Kang is morally untouchable. You can't shame him. If he can be brought to feel shame, which is unlikely, it will only be by that inner grouping of his own people to which he feels accountable. You're nothing to him. Your only satisfaction can be in discovering what this information, assuming it's true, is worth to you—how you can play it to maximum advantage. Its value can massively increase if it's held back for the right opportunity, like a card placed nicely in a game. That's China I'm afraid. The joy of revenge has to give way to the cooler pleasure of a deal well made. Are you with me?"

"You're saying we should sit on this information?"

"Only till we know where we are."

"I'd still like to get Professor Hsu back from the beyond. More than ever now."

4

Jin Juan was still in Peking, finishing up her teaching for the summer. She stayed in her dormitory. It was prudent, for the sake of her grandfather, to continue to give the honorably inquisitive foreigner a wide berth. She could observe him satisfactorily from a distance through her friend Song's reports.

168

She had, in any case, a more immediate matter to deal with.

She wrote to Zhang that there was something she needed to discuss, concerning him, and stipulated a time and a meeting place. He didn't show up. A few days later his letter came explaining that he had been called away on business but that he would be available if she so desired. She wrote again making the place the edge of the lake north of the Forbidden City where they had met as young lovers, the time a summer afternoon when the pleasure boats jostled. She saw no reason to spare him.

Zhang looked officious. "How have you been?"

"Not very well," she said. "Busy with examinations."

He was contemptuous, not of her diligence but of her arrogant expectation of something better.

"What's up?"

"I've been unwell, for a woman's reason that perhaps you understand."

"Hmh." It took him a moment to realize she was talking matter-of-factly, not sentimentally.

"Do you understand? It's already two months."

He sat rigidly.

She continued with sudden self-pity, "We've been separated two months and now this."

"It's very convenient," he commented sarcastically. "It never happened before."

Not that she would have told him about, she thought savagely to herself, then said, "I must have had foresight. It's a coincidence."

"I suppose you want my help," he replied, staring away. Half the boats seemed to hold fathers with their babies. "I can arrange for it to be taken care of for you. No problem."

He turned to face her, using the act of taking her hand as a pretext to press her belly. He felt full himself, a sensation of distinct pride. "After all these years," he said, grinning at her.

169

Her narrow eyes bore an expression of dependence stiffened by dignity. He could not fault her. She would not ask directly for the thing she wanted, and now he could not break away from her into indifference.

He laughed bitterly, out loud. "We'll need to consider the situation," he announced, as at a committee meeting. "Examine." He squeezed her hand desirously. "First you must have an ultrasound test. If it's a boy—"

The shouts and laughter of kids in the pleasure boats joined the slapping wavelets, the cicadas and the whispering leaves.

"Sooner rather than later," she said at parting. "I can't wait too long."

5

Along the canal fishing rods stuck up from the bank. The road ran due north through a sun-slashed avenue of trees. On the back of the bike Autumn hugged Clarence's waist as they flashed between farmland and factories. On small peaks were lookout towers and tiled pavilions that shone like honey. At a certain point Clarence ducked his head and they passed the sign that said in Chinese, Russian and English *Foreigners Forbidden to Enter*.

The road led through orchards towards the hills, and the plain, as they left it behind, became a checkerboard of water mirrors and green rectangles, with an earth station protruding like a mushroom. Clarence turned his imagination to the romance of foothills and mountains. For centuries temples had been built, one rivaling another, to oblige wanderers on those magical, not-so-rugged slopes. Most were dilapidated, ambiguously protected by their irrelevance to the present; the Forestry Institute's negligence had allowed one wing of the most ancient Buddhist temple to burn down.

"Shoo! Shoo!" said the guard. A person-in-charge waddled over. "Go back!" He did not say where.

A track wound down from the monastery across a rivulet to a set of lower courtyards where a mighty eunuch had once presided. It was now part of a rivet factory. The entrance to the main hall was colorfully decorated with characters, urns, tiles and little ceramic gargoyles. Bells on the topknot of a stupa tinkled in the wind, weeds sprouted through the damp flagstones, and to recline there in the shade was delicious. Behind an embankment ran the railway line to Peking. Where the geomantic setting was most auspicious, along the hills' line of jewels, progress had dictated the fire chariot.

Halfway up a hill of dwarfed, pruned trees, across the railway track, beside a revolutionary coalyard manned by two indifferent guards, they found the flight of stone steps that led steeply up to the Tomb of Prince Chun. They climbed until they reached a landing with a small temple, crossed a stone bridge and climbed again to the terrace where stood a mortar and brick plinth that looked like a filled-in water tank. When he was regent uncle to the last boy emperor, Prince Chun had lavishly ordained his own funerary mound—but not a century had passed and the tomb was derelict and disregarded even by scholars. Only the conifers and gingkos tattled over the pile of rubble.

A woman in a blue cotton smock herded white goats through the golden grass. Into a niche of the terrace wall leaned a courting couple. Graffiti were scratched in the clear spaces, and a pink Maoist slogan had not yet faded from the tomb itself. Bits of green-glazed dragon tiles were scattered on the ground where Clarence and Autumn spread their great-coats. Clarence uncorked the wine and Autumn spread out food from the panniers. They lay beside each other in a sunny patch. Over their heads birds circled like gliders in the mountain breezes. A little drunk, a little sleepy, Autumn smoked a cigarette. He had come to enjoy his Saturday outings with his

English friend. His drooping eyelids showed the line of soot he had not quite cleaned off. Most of the day he shoveled coal into the boiler at the No. 3 Vehicle Plant. No matter how thoroughly he washed in the bathhouse, the ingrained coal-dust never came away. He rolled his jeans up to the knee, his t-shirt to his nipples. Black curls spread out from his head, like snakes running into the grass, as he sprawled on his back. One of his first city novelties had been to get his hair waved.

Clarence never slept after lunch. He sipped his wine, coughing occasionally the cough he could never get rid of, and took out the pre-Liberation tome that was his chosen guidebook. Alone with the remains of Prince Chun, his sleeping friend and the susurrating pines, he read aloud the mannered periods:

> It is pleasant to look at the brocade of autumn tints from the pretty pavilions on the hillside, to linger near the pond where tame goldfish rise to the surface to be fed at the sound of a wooden rattle, to gossip with lonely old men who have cut themselves off from family life by the nature of their calling, but who served Empresses and princesses and remember many things . . . The old regime may have had its sins both of omission and commission, but it certainly cultivated refined tastes. Alas, these Manchu grandees—so typical of the faults and virtues of the past—have nothing to offer the new world except a wonderful but unwanted elegance of living which still permits them to accept with calm dignity the fate of failures.

As the afternoon wore on, the sun exposed golds and greens on the slope above the tomb. On a rocky hill face a spring issued from a clump of boulders, and around its waters were gathered stone tablets invoking the virtues of dastardly

Prince Chun. On one stone Clarence picked out the Buddhist injunction to cleanse one's heart.

They clambered higher, among thorny flowering gorse, stunted pines that clawed for position in the soil, and slender oaks with great clappers of leaves. Birds and insects, a rare sight, leapt among the branches, not just sparrows but tuxe-doed Chinese magpies and butterflies and hornets. There was no one about, which was even rarer. They climbed above the tree line to a burrow in the earth where a fort was overgrown. Power and communications lines sagged and spun overhead. The different layers of agriculture were evident up the slope, from cabbages at the foot through fruit trees to hardy pines for timber, before the mountain became a forbidding rocky challenge that the peasants shunned. Clarence and Autumn continued to climb, on animal tracks, up the windswept spur.

The peak was elusive. Higher and higher they climbed, until the wood around the tomb of Prince Chun looked like a tame courtyard garden. They met no other person. The path gave out and they were forced to crawl up rock ladders on hand and foot. At last they reached the highest point. Beyond was a slight dip, then another rise, and beyond that the same again. In corners of rock, snow sat white and hard. They found remnants of what looked like hide-outs or guard posts, where sensitive souls had escaped the grind of reform-through-labor during the Cultural Revolution, or landlords fled the Com-munists, or republicans the Manchu Emperor. Or earlier, much earlier, had boy soldiers been sent to keep perpetual vigilance against the hordes from the North, Manchus, Mongols, or any-thing from outside? Men who spent a lifetime watching, or turned their backs on duty to light a cigarette and huddle to the warmth of fire and companionship inside a rude hut, un-prepared when the wolf at last came down?

Gradually the mountain slope was cast into glitterless shadow, gloomy and cold, and Clarence and Autumn retreated. It was dark when they reached the grove above Prince Chun's tomb where they rested, and Clarence lit a match to peer at his guidebook:

> When the heavy shadows close in on this deep walled valley, where the sun rises hours later and sets hours earlier than it does below on the open plains, and dim the burning blue of the wild larkspurs, ghostly shrieks are heard—so the peasants say; war cries of the wild Khitans who knew no law but the sword, no home but the saddle, no faith but the "Black Magic" of their "Shaman" priests.

They squatted in their greatcoats in the grassed-over bunker of the ruined fort. They dared not light a fire. There were some fruit and biscuits left, some cigarettes, and a pocket flask of whiskey. Listening for the howling of wolves, they heard no noise but the wind that wailed from on high or rustled with the spirit of Prince Chun. The clear sky lit by moon and stars was the property of a ruler from whom no secrets were hid, and seemed to promise a universe that would run with the unmysterious precision of a jeweled timepiece, if the mortal would only give up trying to understand and simply salute its power; a fascist brightness, to which ordinary people were of no greater significance than rabbits or sheep.

Clarence and Autumn felt ordinary and animal—tired, sun-exhausted, not quite satisfied by their food, light-headed and drowsy from the whiskey; and cold. They squeezed closer to each other and were nodding asleep like Tweedledum and Tweedledee when Clarence suggested they should improvise a bed and stretch out.

He pulled off his greatcoat and laid it on the ground, stuffed the panniers with dry grass as pillows, and got Autumn's greatcoat to provide a cover. They lay down side by side on one greatcoat, Clarence cupping Autumn to his shape, and settled the other greatcoat round their shoulders. Their lower legs stuck out. Heat, the heat of the day, flowed from one body to the other. Smelling of sweat, with heavy breath and heartbeat, they nestled close, like two puppies. Clarence's hand found the burning hot skin under Autumn's t-shirt, and followed the smooth hard stomach to the tight knot of his navel. Autumn poked his bum into Clarence's groin. Clarence grunted in surprised, excited assent. The full moon was like bath water glistening on the bare patches of their skin as the greatcoat covering slipped off. Distant, totalitarian, arctic was the sky. They turned their backs to it. Autumn's nose pressed the ground. Clarence's mouth rooted in Autumn's hair. Face downwards, they were hot and animal in their hidden burrow of earth. They stirred again only when the new sun melted into existence across the plain.

6

Wally returned from another fruitless search for the opera company. He had suggested to Song that he would like to organize a dinner and include Jin Juan and Zhang, but Song said that it would not be appropriate, and added hastily that Jin Juan had gone to visit her family in the South. Summer was all in the air and Wally needed a companion. He needed Jin Juan who spoke the language with such sophistication that she could satisfy his questions with answers, he needed her to create a sense of contact, he needed her to give him China. As he went round Peking he couldn't stop believing he might accidentally come across her. In the evenings he went to the opera. But once again tonight there had been no sign of Jin Juan in the audience, nor of Azalea among the screeching beauties on stage. Disgruntled in his armchair, he placed Retta's diary on his lap as the only thing guaranteed to seduce him. The magnolia was in blowsy bloom; its scent seeped into his stale quarters.

Today great excitement. Patriarch Lu has purchased a cannon. Whisperings have been abroad for months. His son has been writing letters to men in the South—scholars they call them. And then his nephew was sent out to complete the transaction. One knows not whether the nephew is sly or gullible. Certainly he is not to be trusted, but charity attributes his untrustworthiness to weak judgment rather than intentional malice. His face is long, unhappy. From his eyes one might suspect him of weeping in private. Why? The son is a far more wholesome creature. But nephew was entrusted with the arrangements and working through middlemen of doubtful reputation purchased the beauty from a yet more dishonest Yankee. The cannon is a Krupp. Perhaps it came direct from Hong Kong on that rotten little low-bottomed boat that stuck in the mud today as she sidled towards the shore. Much hilarity as coolies drowned like ducks shouldered the inestimable Prussian treasure onto a flat barge to bring her on land. Patriarch Lu had sent out the klaxons, drums and gongs, and bangers were set off incessantly to welcome the brute. There is no secret about his new toy, less (W. surmises) because of his boastfulness than to warn the Magistrate. He struts around in a tight silk sheath like a pig who has managed to stand on hind legs. On whose side is the Patriarch? Peg calls him Uncle.

A minor catastrophe. Every day they play with the cannon yet not so much as a pop comes out. Lionel is full of excitement. I climb the wall with him and Baby to look down on the parade ground. Patriarch Lu has a band of youths drilling each morning. They do a special kind of exercise, waving their arms and silver swords through the air in slow motion, that is believed to make them invincible to bullets. Foreign bullets? Just to be on the safe side they also have the cannon. For the first few days the mere presence of the beast was imposing enough. No one knew how it worked, so a great range of capacities could be attributed. Then loss of face set in. A demonstration was required. They must have lost patience too, because this morning when we were at lessons there was a high-pitched crack then a thud. By the time I got to my look-out window all I could see was a crowd around Lu's blackened, cursing Jack-of-all-Trades. Wang reports that a cannon ball was indeed emitted and flew a neat fifty-yard arc before making a crater in the middle of the parade ground. All were greatly impressed. Since one is still uncertain of the Patriarch's allegiances, one knows not whether to commiserate or rejoice in his military feebleness. Wang relates with glee that the Jack-of-all-Trades had his pigtail blown off.

Waldemar hears that in consequence of the singeing of Jack's hair, which was ignited along with the fuse, all the Patriarch's men have been ordered to snip off their pigtails. This is interpreted favorably as a gesture against the Manchus.

How far we are from any center of news. Our town is hemmed between mountains with roads that are dusty and stony in summer or miry and snow-covered in winter, and bandit-ridden all year round. The variably navigable river issues into the sea at a place with no proper port. As the crow flies—surely no Chinese bird—we are close to Ningpo which boasts splendid modern institutions and even Shanghai to which all the world pays tribute. In reality we are as far from anywhere as if we were in the deepest hinterland. Dr. Morrison's dispatches from the *Times* reach us by a roundabout route, weeks or months late; a matter of little moment, since we are in blissful ignorance of the dramatic events of which he writes. For this thanks be. Had I known when nursing my first-born, and I a girl bride fresh from Home, full of faith and confidence in our work, had I known in those days of the slaughter of the innocents in the North, the savagery of the Boxers, the siege of our Legation heroically withstood—the thrilling narrative has at last reached us—I should . . . but really one knows not at such extremity what one should have done. Is it not wiser to spare one's imagination remote horrors and instead place one's trust in the Lord? At the height of the xenophobic crises my Wee One was absorbing all my attention. We were as dazed and confused as the Chinese, as one calamity after another rains down on their heads.

I remember how the Boy from the Roman mission came, and later one of the local nuns, and out of much jabbering the message was clear that we should flee. This occasioned much anxiety, since, being our first settled home in China, the place had received our loving attention. W. built the walls with his own hands, and the house was the one example in the district of an edifice built according to modern science. Such was the haste urged on us in our flight that I happily assumed the matter to be temporary. One is willingly deceived. There was our little family of three, and Peg and her mother, and a few of W.'s students whose eyes were rolling with terror. Wang insisted on staying. The rest of us were simply bundled over the back wall and bumped on to the muddy ground in the darkness. I remember passing Wee One to Waldemar while I held out my arms to catch Peg. The Roman Boy then led us through a maze of "safe" houses until we arrived at the inner sanctum, which was crowded with Chinese who for reasons un-known had been lumped together with us, the only for-eigners except for the porcupine-faced Sardinian priest who kept bustling to the main door to receive word. We waited and waited. I assumed that a fire had broken out in our corner of the town. That was the most rational and most innocuous explanation. But from W.'s agitation as he learned more, and concealed his knowledge, my own fears unwillingly took to smoldering. Then sud-denly, before noon on the second day, a piratical-looking soldier was admitted who told us to go back to our homes in peace.

The morning was as pretty and sunny a summer morning as Taichow had ever offered, which fostered trust in our safety. I rocked Wee One and made goo-goo, and so completely my motherly love allowed me to forget the danger that it has never been relived since. How bounteous is His Mercy. We learned that the over-lord of the province had thrown his support behind the Boxers as an act of fealty to the Emperor (the Dowager in fact). To carry out his vow of exterminating all foreign influence, he sent one of his captains over the moun-tains to Taichow. The Magistrate, anxious to preserve both his position, which the overlord allowed him, and his power in the locality, which was unchallengeable, embroiled the captain in negotiation; his aim being to obstruct the warlord's intent. Whether he was persuaded to this aim by Patriarch Lu, we never could discover. Post-haste the captain reported Taichow's defiance, and from over the mountains the warlord breathed fire and thunder. That was when the Magistrate had the offend-ing elements rounded up for safekeeping. Special intelli-gence, argued the magistrate, suggested that the Empress Dowager's support for the Boxers was itself an uncertain quality, and if the Old Buddha was playing a double game it was surely wiser for lesser Buddhas to emulate her. The Magistrate agreed with the overlord beyond the mountains that depending which way the wind blew he would either dutifully massacre all of us gathered in the Catholic sanctuary or allow us a lease of safety. When the Empress herself succumbed to the Great Powers' wrath, following the Siege at Peking, the overlord of Chekiang was beholden to the Magistrate's caution. And the Magistrate became more than ever suspicious of Patriarch Lu, who had, we guess, been wise all along.

Our execution was stayed. Yet not knowing, I could not enjoy the sensation of relief. For which may greater thanks be given. I write for the benefit of my posterity, should they wonder how their mother (or their grandmother!) survived. Yet have I survived entirely? The heathen Dr. Morrison writes (old news now) that the throne has been shaken again by a mighty general. The rebels want a constitution. Or that is their pretext. How far away we are. Today a farmer was brought in with thigh gashed by a hoe. I showed Peg how to disinfect and stitch the wound. Twenty-five stitches.

Today I taught Peg to churn butter. Servant's work, but she wanted to learn. Milk still a difficulty. W. is away at the new hospital. I made him leave Lionel this time. He promised to investigate at Heaven's Terrace. Surely the cows there have first-class milk, so lush are the paddies.

He called my name. Retta! I heard his voice but it seemed as if we did not inhabit the same place. I could neither rise from my chair nor turn to greet him. Shame! May I be forgiven! Some power had my mind, my body, or both, in its wilful possession. He said I ignored him.

180

That is not the truth. Every day I watch the river. I sit. Baby Jerry sleeps in his cot without a peep. Lionel plays with amah or Peg. My love for the boys is boundless. I tell myself that I live for my husband and my boys. I pray for strength to do my duty. Pray? That, I tremble to confess, is the problem. I pray to nothing. Emptiness. Then the spirits tease me. They pluck the hair and stick pins into the person that is mine. In broad daylight they present the faces of bad dreams—the men in the marketplace, the ailing children in the hospital and their grief-stricken, accusatory parents, the agony of young women passing in the alley with expressionless masks and bound feet. Their faces become distorted like the demons in their temples. Then they begin to torment my Wee One. I am sure her grave is unhallowed in this soil. Her spirit has been taken by theirs. When I sit in my corner by the window these imaginings and feelings occupy me. While I am about my tasks they remain sealed up. Only when I settle to rest in the afternoon, gazing at the river while Baby Jerry sleeps, do I join that world behind the brightness of day, where dwell beings who belong to the rotting faces of the corpses floating by in the river. I was unaware until this occasion when W., having returned early home, called to me in vain, that each afternoon as I sit on my chair, I must enter some kind of trance. Has God left me? Waldemar spoke harsh, uncomprehending words. He says I should busy myself. We busy ourselves in vain here. Yet Peg is my comfort.

It is Peg's birthday. W. says I care for her more than for my own children. I love my boys. Amah made noodles for her and I a birthday cake. Before retiring I found her in the courtyard, against a post, staring at her feet. Must they be bound soon? When she is lonely she shows no expression. She was remembering her mother. Does she love me? Or does she detach herself?

I continue to be in awe of my husband's idealism. Let us consider our eight years here. We have built our residence and a small place of worship. We have established a rudimentary school and a clinic. At Heaven's Terrace we have also built a hospital. We have treated hundreds, perhaps thousands, of bodies and souls; taught English, hygiene, religion, to many. We have helped to settle disputes. We have been honored guests and despised curs, founts of wisdom and spectacles of folly, as circumstances arose. What remains? All this we have done ourselves. Our teaching has been no more than commerce on the river. The people return to their own ways as naturally as their curiosity drew them in the first place. They remain what they are. And our architecture remains, that is all, as long as we do. I do not say the eight years have been wasted. But I must keep my eyes open, which empties my spirit. W. is filled by the spirit. He says it is our duty to be here, that we ought not question His ways, His mysterious ways, and tells the parable of the mustard seed. One knows not what fruit our labors may bear. W.'s faith is unswerving. Yet such a very little knowledge . . . We are unaware even of the lessons they draw from our teaching . . . is not this a dangerous thing? W. says that at the very least we are agents of science, and asks if I would deny our people the knowledge of antiseptic medicine. My husband can be remarkably insistent.

I consider I have taught Peg something deeper. She with her endless questions has awakened my interest in the wonders of nature. The other day she took me to a latticed shop at the crossroads where there were drawers and drawers of herbs, stones and other scrapings. A dreadful place. Peg convinced me that the vendor had the remedy for Baby Jerry's spots.

In the afternoon to the river again, a flock of a hundred brown ducks skittering across the mud. I parked the pram on the path, trusting no one would snatch poor Baby Jerry, and went with Lionel in my high boots across the mud. He threw crumbs and they came voraciously.

W. casts his bread upon the waters. My idealism is lost. I were better not to write.

Raining cats and dogs. I vow to write no more, but I am boarded up inside. Peg is poring over the books that have arrived from Shanghai: Dickens, Gray's *Anatomy*, Mr. Darwin. I count that after eight years we have only three reliable disciples here. And Peg, to whom I refrain from preaching the Gospel. I justify this action by telling myself that she is ours only by accident. Ours was not the environment her mother chose for her. Every day I see how gifted she is, how intelligent, how completely Chinese. She is demure, polite, shrewd, skeptical, at twelve years old, like the best Chinese women. I see now that Patriarch Lu only sent her mother to us because she was a superfluous widow woman in his clan. The woman was wholly bound by the Patriarch's command and probably regarded it as the grossest humiliation to be bundled with her young daughter into the foreign devils' service. Waldemar was grateful for a most civilized and fitting act of good will, I being expectant. I suspect that Patriarch Lu merely wanted a spy in our midst. The woman helped me no end with Wee One. The birth, W. noted, lasted 36 hours. Our little girl, our first-born, May, who tolerated the evacuation in 1900 without a bleat. Ah, we are tossed on a river. The violent surges carry us through safely, the calms prove fatal. I did not feel May's death in my heart. Why? I shall never understand. Waldemar refused to relinquish the post. We could have carried Wee One over the mountains to escape the cholera, but he refused, solacing me with the hope of finding peace in His Will. Did he assume we must all perish? His Will made me numb. I consigned Wee One to God as if setting her body into the murky river. I see her black body in the little open box revolving in the whirlpools, with the face-down dead baby girls flung by wretched Chinese mothers into the same river. With sobs and lamentations, in black crepe, I committed my child to the grave. No Pharoah's daughter for my baby girl Moses. Yet it was an act I did not understand, a shadow play, therefore the grief went around my heart like a knot. I walked numb, airy, ethereal, along the top of the wall beside the river, and on the embankments between the rice paddies, through the groves of purple bamboo flowering with large white dishes of flowers with black centers, like staring black eyes, and believed, how foolishly, that a life was no more than a flower to fade and die. Piety and acceptance numbed my natural mother's feelings. From there my defiance has slowly, imperceptibly grown.

The woman also was carried off by the disease, another plucked bloom, and her six-year-old daughter Pei was left us. Beside the clothes line I made as if to snip off her nose and showed her the dread instrument. She said my nose was big, hers small. Mine should be snipped. She picked up one and laughed. Hence I named her—Peg.

She has been my joy, my daughter. When we retire after lunch to my bed beneath the mosquito net, and wiggle our stockinged feet together, I talk and tell her everything. She listens, sometimes speaks her opinions, always questions. Something of the soul is shared. Yet

184

what a traditional little Chinese woman she is! Her lot is a yoke. I will take her with me when I leave.

A break in the diary followed, and Wally did not read on. He speculated instead about the living, with whom the ghosts on the page seemed to whisper their connections.

7

Zhang sat on the narrow bed in Jin Juan's dormitory. He had brought gifts of Chinese medicine, like a suitor once more, and commented vainly that the woman had put on weight. He talked animatedly about his travels, in a sharp northern style. In the coastal cities the economy was booming, he said. Foreign exchange was flooding in and flashy international hotels were going up.

"The peasants are profiting already. They love the Reforms. But the change won't mean much unless the urban masses can accept it with their hearts and minds as well as turn an advantage in their pockets. Many are growing rich," he said.

"Many are growing poor," said Jin Juan.

She offered him tea, but refused his invitation to dinner. She did not wish to appear wholly accepting of his turnaround. He found it irksome that she was not more grateful. After all, it was he who had shown magnanimity by returning to her in her condition. He did not consider further because if a woman was able to fulfill her primary function of mothering a son, then the rest could be overlooked. What he owed his parents was not the correct choice of a wife, but posterity. And he would not find another beauty like Jin Juan among the silly grasping girls he met in trade offices and foreign hotels. She was superior among Chinese, he admitted; she was a true Chinese.

"I think you understand me," he bowed his head as he took her hand, pinching her skin a little, "I believe that we understand each other."

She told him that she was going away for a while, making a trip to her home town in the South. It was her duty, and natural enough. Yet he distrusted her family connections.

"Is it safe for you to travel?"

"I need to see my grandfather. I'll be gone only two or three weeks."

Zhang nodded. "There's not much time." He wanted to trap her now, to make certain. "Well, hurry back."

Her long neck curved in ironic deference to his will.

8

Clarence and Autumn always met secretly, in public places—bars, eating-houses, parks and the half-rural reaches of Peking's suburbs, and at each meeting made sotto voce arrangements for the next meeting, so as to avoid surveillance—so Clarence was alarmed to get a note demanding that they meet at once.

He waited on the assigned street corner while the traffic rushed past. The boy was late. Then Clarence saw him—and, shocked, noted a yellow plastic windjacket, synthetic pillar-box red running tights with a GT stripe down the leg, white "Italian" running shoes made in Taiwan, hair freshly permed, and a turquoise neckerchief ruffled at his throat. Autumn came grinning like an idiot, a bird of paradise among the drab workers. He always bubbled happily at seeing his friend, and today he had spent all of Clarence's money on new clothes.

Clarence shrank inside. Himself he wore Chinese cotton shoes, jeans and a gray jacket, to be as inconspicuous as possible—though nothing was as obtrusive as his long nose. He always urged discretion on Autumn. Yet he knew he shrank less from Autumn's imprudence than his sheer bad taste. The peasant lad was yellow-stockinged and cross-gartered!

"New clothes," commented Clarence bluntly, planning a safe place for them to go. "Nice color." He tweaked the jacket.

"Yes, very fashionable," Autumn purred.

In a corner of the zoo, near the browbeaten hyenas that no one wanted to see, Autumn revealed his discovery. He was too excited to keep it to himself. At last he had found a way of doing a favor for his beloved Big Brother.

Excavations were being carried out at the No. 3 Vehicle Plant. While he was digging a trench, Autumn's spade had scraped against a pot buried deep in the clay. He quickly covered it up and later, after dark, returned to dig it out. It was a large unbroken earthenware pot that his instincts told him was ancient and valuable. He unbuckled his khaki satchel and let Clarence peek.

Autumn giggled, pushing the satchel into Clarence's lap as a gift. The satchel nearly tumbled to the ground. Autumn kept giggling, while Clarence's face became strange with thoughtfulness. Probably he could not carry it out of the country himself. Perhaps, however, he could arrange for it to be sold. He would make inquiries. Valuable it certainly was. Han dynasty, perhaps. And the money must go to Autumn.

"No, no, no," protested the boy.

Clarence thought of leather-jacketed Foreign Trader at the New Age Bar.

Autumn looked so healthy, happy and trusting. When Clarence looked at his rough, boyish face, and the smile, and the ridiculous new clothes, he felt like a defiler.

9

A gaudy profusion of scarlet and yellow flowers marked summer along Changan Avenue, and perpetual crowds streamed
into the Forbidden City where the tiles seemed to crackle and
the blood-colored walls to smoulder in the heat. In a secluded
courtyard at the side Clarence and Wally began with gossip
and generalizations, the warp and weft of Peking talk. The
personal existed uncomfortably at the intersection. Clarence
was chain-smoking and coughing. His slight build and London
face, alert with intelligence, his hair like a chewed toothbrush,
and the shirt of Nile green silk, made him seem like an eccentric court attendant of yore as they sauntered among dry
pines to the Flowing Music Belvedere.

"That's nasty," remarked the Doctor of Clarence's cough.

"I can't seem to shake it off."

"Smoking doesn't help."

Clarence nervously chucked the cigarette to the ground.

"My health's bad in China. A constant succession of colds
and flu, headaches, bone aches, and nonstop Delhi belly.
Mouth ulcers, weight loss, bleeding from the bowel. I seem
to get everything that's going."

Wally adopted his avuncular consulting manner. "China's
a pretty stressful place. The stress strikes at the points of vulnerability in your system. Reactivates things that would otherwise lie dormant. Maybe you need a break."

"I think I should have a good check-up. Who knows what
could be lurking?"

"You may have picked up a tropical disease. It could be
attributable to any one of a number of causes. Are you sexually
active here?" continued the Doctor.

Clarence grinned stiffly.

"I see," said Wally, not probing further. "We're not in a position to do all the tests here, but I can put you on to a doctor in Hong Kong next time you're down. That can be arranged." He turned to the sky. Those who had dwelt in the Forbidden City had seen only the sky. They had no proof that the outside world existed. Nor could the millions of subjects of the empire, for thousands of miles, ever guess what lay within those walls. Yet both had gazed at the same sky.

"I want to make sure I haven't got anything I could pass on." Like a corporal facing his CO after he has lost his head and disgraced the regiment, Clarence turned his eyes on the Doctor. Guilt wrapped round him like a stocking. He imagined Autumn's defenceless body rotting from a punitive Western plague, ditched into a furnace by the Chinese authorities.

"Well, be sensible," said Wally. "No good waiting till the horse bolts."

They passed from the courtyard to a shaded marble corridor that led to a little garden. A few students were squatting on the rocks under a pavilion watching the water run in ornamental channels under their feet as they smoked and chatted. One, who looked up, had tufty hair and heavy glasses, his open shirt baring his belly and tight shorts. He seemed to squat precariously in his high sandals, and seized on the two foreigners with such intense recognition that he almost toppled over. It was Philosopher Horse, who was holding court with his comrades.

They stood and shook hands politely, Philosopher Horse acting the keen go-between. He explained that they had come to inspect the imperial court, and had been discussing the overthrow of empires in Chinese history. Each time the pattern repeated. The words of the wise went unheeded, and those honest men who criticized were cast out, only to return in the form of implacable opposition, the nemesis. The doors and windows of the palace were always blocked. Empire was a blindness that the Chinese people revered. They surrendered their eyes. They were made to feel so gloriously small that no blame would ever light on them, and so grand because of the great shadow under which they lived. It was the dragon's disorder.

Philosopher Horse expounded to the Doctor as if to one of his disciples who, Wally noticed, all had similar X-shaped scabs on their forearms.

"Our blood brotherhood," declared Philosopher Horse while the others stared with grim loyalty. "We are training in *qigong* together, the breathing power. We've got people coming up from the South, not ordinary people but powerful people. Our *qigong* master from Guizhou will come. We are in touch with powerful forces. You foreigners don't know anything about it."

"Are you organized?" asked Wally.

But Philosopher Horse would not answer questions. He was whispering now. "We have connections. We are in communication. Something will happen, you will see, Doctor. It can change."

He made a silent gesture of pressure with his hands, pressing down until the pressure was too great, when his hands opened into an opposing gesture of explosion, like a blessing, or like fireworks going off, his lips mouthing the bang.

CHAPTER TEN

Travelers Among Mountains and Streams

1

The Doctor's summer was passing in days of sleeping and swimming and he lacked all stamina. China's fine net had ensnared him. His goals came no nearer and he could pursue no direction other than his aimless laps of the International Club swimming pool. Then everything changed with explosive suddenness. Emeritus Professor Wu at the Academy revealed to Ralph, who passed it on at once, that Professor Hsu was connected with the Hangzhou Chinese Medicine Factory—another wild-goose chase, perhaps, but a clue that must be followed. Then a flyer came in the mail with a scribbled message from Azalea about a Peking opera festival to be held—in Hangzhou. All roads led south. After a brief consultation with Song, who was still being vague about Jin Juan's whereabouts, Wally confronted Mrs. Gu about tickets and hotel bookings.

She bustled benignly to arrange the Doctor's holiday, worried only that he was traveling alone. Wally explained that he preferred to travel alone. He planned to rest his body and spirit beside the serene waters of China's most famous beauty spot, a proposal that met with Mrs. Gu's favor.

Rocking him to sleep as it sped southwards, the train made him think of the woman. Which woman? When he put himself to the test he could not specify whether his thoughts turned to Jin Juan or Azalea. They were physically similar, but their personalities and the nature of his encounters with each were quite different; mute intimacy with Azalea, wiry idiomatic exchanges with Jin Juan. As his eyelids grew heavy in the stuffy compartment, and his face turned an embarrassing red, he analyzed the phenomenon whereby Jin Juan and Azalea merged in his desire. Even as he tried to recollect the body he had held, his imagination became abstract: softness, slenderness, silkiness, neckness, a child's breasts with a woman's hard nipples, a face that yielded no inner life, a being whose lack of human particulars allowed the enactment of a *yin-yang* fantasy, female passivity and male activeness, mysterious Eastern surrender to determined Western penetration. Such was the distasteful deep structure of his sensual confounding of Jin Juan and Azalea. In all sex there was perhaps an element of attraction to otherness. But Wally's analysis found in his attitudes a residue of his native Australian racism. As long as he was confined to speechlessness with Azalea, he would feel uncomfortable about the ardor that had him clackety-clacking southwards. If only the two cousins could be combined. For the moment, Azalea would have to suffice. He admired the silent, lucid way she had sent her instructions. If there was potentially an element of distortion, of exploitation, in the excitement his big loose-skinned middle-aged body found in embracing the supple girl-form, the way to deal with it, he justified himself, was by plowing on. He was *yang*. Was it the same *yang* character as the animal in which Australia abounded? The sheep? Or the goat?

2

Wally set out, with no great determination, to explore one of the places on China's list of tourist clichés where enchantment was still possible. He strolled past dragon boats, touting photographers, ice-cream vendors, resort hotels painted up like sideshow alley, through a street of red-latticed houses to a park of magnolias and sweet osmanthus that gave again onto a shore where "both wavelets and willows listen to birdsong." The scene had the same romantic prettiness as the Italian Lakes through which he had driven, how long ago, with Bets, en route to Tuscany. The memory, struck like a tuning fork, set tender reverberations rippling. The West Lake receded into the misty embrace of mountains in a series of landscaped spurs and inlets. The horizon was a dike devised by a constructive poet-governor-sage and engineer of ancient times. A string of six bridges and walkways undulated across wide water that reflected like photographic paper. To that distant causeway the lakeside path led indirectly, past picture-book villas and sanatoria poking out of russet woods. By the time dusk was blurring the gardens, he had reached the first of those bridges that curved less than a bird's wing. As a pink twilight invested the scene, Wally was captivated by a moment that seemed to be his own precious fortune—as it had to thousands of others; as if, on buying a Willow Pattern plate, one believed it to be the original.

When he returned to the Hangzhou Hotel, that stood as splendidly functional above the lake as in a revolutionary painting a hydro-electric power station stands among the mountains

193

and streams of tradition, Wally found that he had missed a caller. Two tickets had been left at the desk for a performance of Peking opera on the following evening. Song had informed: his whereabouts were known.

Wally wondered what to do with the spare ticket. In the event, he went alone. The program consisted of three pieces. The first was acrobatic; a ruthless general goes crazy with remorse and kills himself. The second was a comic second-time-around love story in which a widow and widower who have renounced marriage fall head over heels in love when a matchmaking nun brings them together. The third was the spectacularly tragic finale from *Snow in Summer* that Wally had seen in Peking. Once again the self-betraying heroine was acted by Jin Juan's cousin, with the sinewy body that Wally knew, and the fine, leached voice.

At the curtain the smiling performers duly clapped the audience. Wally tripped over the crutches of an old man beside him and hurried backstage. Azalea was alone in the stark, drafty dressing room when he knocked. The lustrous costume had been replaced by a cotton robe, the braided coiffure was still in position, and the thick make-up was the shocking pink of peonies. Azalea was fiddling with pins around the hairline, and clenched a couple between her teeth. She had not turned when he knocked. Wally came close and laid his hands on her shoulders with a tender squeeze. Azalea carefully lifted the hairpiece into the air, without turning to him, set it on a dummy, and revealed a scalp of short flattened black. Wally ran his fingers forward intimately. From among the hairpins between clenched teeth came a murmured, "What are you doing?," in a lower, flatter register than the singsong accent he remembered from the night Azalea had visited. Something was different. The body did not respond in the same way. He stared at the thick face paint, the wisps of hair pinned back behind the ears, the bumpy white throat. Tenderly but testingly he reached his hands forward, then pulled back. He stood to

194

one side uncomfortably to appraise Azalea, whose sexiness in the half done-up, half undone state gave him goosepimples. Azalea was not a woman.

In a man's voice the figure before the mirror turned with a budding smile to ask if he had problems.

"You—are—not," was as far as Wally's Chinese got. He didn't know what was happening. To his mortification he acknowledged that he must have mistaken one dolled-up Chinese for another, as if they all looked the same after all. But this one did have an ambivalent appearance, did look like—and seemed to have been expecting him.

Then Jin Juan herself walked through the door, in jeans and a t-shirt, plain and fresh, and without missing a beat said, "Hi!", as natural as anything, "so you did make it after all. Welcome to Hangzhou." She shook his hand.

"You!" he gaped.

She laughed a little bit. Azalea was grinning at Wally's expense, and in response to old friends reuniting. Wally was strangely happy, though entirely baffled.

"You know my cousin," Jin Juan went on.

"Your cousin?"

"He does *Snow in Summer* brilliantly, don't you think?"

"You saw it?"

"I was hoping to join you. I got held up. I thought I might find you backstage. I gather you wanted to meet him."

"Him."

"Unfortunately his English is no good. I'll have to interpret."

"Okay okay okay," said Wally. "I'm happy to see you. Where have you been hiding all this time?"

"I've been with my family."

"Song told you I was here, right?"

"It was convenient that I could be here too. Show you around."

"Quite a coincidence," said Wally skeptically. Azalea was

now wearing jeans and a light jacket. The mask was smeared off with cold cream, leaving his face greasy. He brushed his hair up to give it fashionable height. Without the trappings he was an ordinary-looking young man—but seeing him beside Jin Juan, the resemblance was nonetheless striking. What was beauty in her was oddness in him, a peculiar animation and plasticity of feature that could be transformed on stage.

"You're not brother and sister?" Wally asked.

"Cousins," corrected Jin Juan. "Double cousins. Our parents—two brothers married two sisters—a Chinese arrangement."

"They live here?"

"Dead—also a Chinese arrangement."

The young man nodded, bobbing several times as he ushered the Doctor out the door; and Wally, scrutinizing his shiny face and cocked fingers, was all at sea.

3

The track through the tea terraces led to Dragon Well, source of the choicest green tea tips. When the women from the temple tea house stirred their hands in the waters of the well, a twist of light, known as the Dragon, appeared. Wally and Jin Juan shook their hands dry and moved to the pavilion, to sip their steaming tea in the sun and split their teeth on melon seeds. Around the pavilion were great tiered camellia bushes and the light seemed to bubble and steam from their glossy leaves. The tea was topaz green.

Wally thought it best to admit his quandary. Maybe, maybe, he could elicit an explanation.

Jin Juan smiled a little, her long eyes full of intelligence.

"Cousin," she began. "Normally in English you distinguish between genders, such as 'actor' and 'actress,' whereas in

Chinese we don't. Family members are one exception. Your word 'cousin' can mean male or female whereas our words differentiate. You got confused in translation."

"But your cousin visited me in Peking."

Jin Juan bowed her head. If the visit were of that nature, she could not be expected to explain it away. "He visited as an impersonator, you mean? It's possible. They train in such tricks. Perhaps."

"It hardly seems likely," murmured Wally thoughtfully. Much remained unclear. Who was the creature that had come to his room in Peking? Better let it wait. "So tell me about your cousin," he said.

"He's a little older than me, my mother's elder sister's son. On my mother's side our family was very cultured, but had a bad class background—old landlords. My cousin inherited the love of old opera. On my father's side it was different. The brothers were Party. Two young scientists who went teaching in the army as part of the revolutionary work. They took their wives with them at first. Later things got nasty. The two wives were sent out West for re-education. The husbands didn't lift a finger. There were only two little children, and we went to my grandpa in Peking. Our mothers never came back. Then it turned out that grandpa was bad too, so my cousin's father took the kids away. The brothers had achieved a position in the Party by then. We were all in Peking. It was 1965. But it turned out that the brothers had played their cards wrongly after all. They were now the counter-revolutionaries. You could not get a worse family than mine. My father was murdered. My uncle was sent to the pen of cow spirits and snake demons. We kids made ritual denunciations. My cousin had got himself into the Peking Opera School on Uncle's influence. He denounced Uncle with sufficient vehemence to stay on at school. He came to perform all the Eight Model Operas during those later years. That was his training. One doesn't blame him. He's an artist. Madame Mao liked him. Well, you see, I've told you not only about my cousin, but all my family's sorry history. Apart from my cousin, there's only grandpa and me left. Anyway, what brought you here?"

"I think you know. Kang, the Director of the Medical College, gave me a pile of his papers. I've collated Kang's published work with Professor Hsu Chien Lung's unpublished work from the archives of the Traditional Medical Academy. Kang made his name using Hsu's material. Does that interest you?"

"Proletarian appropriation," commented Jin Juan drily, "applies also to intellectual property."

"Then you're not surprised?"

"That kind of plagiarism is not such a crime in China."

"Probably not, now," acknowledged Wally. "But how does your grandfather feel about it?"

"My grandfather?"

"He lives near here, doesn't he? How old is he now?"

"He's over eighty."

"Can I talk to him?"

"Well, he's retired now. In the end he wanted to be left alone, in peace. For a while they forced him to clean latrines, then to make amends they gave our old family house back, at the end of the Cultural Revolution."

"He's no longer working on cancer research then?" asked Wally, tackling another melon seed.

"You're very clever," said Jin Juan, smiling in affirmation.

"He's Hsu Chien Lung."

"He's no longer working on cancer research," she echoed.

"Does he mind meeting me?"

"It would be his honor. Your friend's colleague, old Wu, has kept us informed. Naturally we knew about Kang, but not in detail. The fact that you as an eminent outsider have so much knowledge makes it more interesting. We can take the train tomorrow."

198

4

Shaoxing was a water town sited at a crisscrossing of canals on a wet inland river plain. Deriving its mild prosperity from waterways and the plants and beasts that flourish with water, the town followed a watery pattern of curves, lanes and bridges, and a watery spectrum of cuttlefish whitewashed to pebbly gray for the walls, and blackwashed to grainy charcoal for the roofs, smudged with patches of "crow" as the locals call the peculiar faded sooty violet color of umbrellas, of awnings on the narrow barges, of the peaked wool caps that workers wore against the town's excessive portion of rain. Shaoxing floated between water pressing from below, water pattering from above, and water that soaked the air. Even the golden evening was thrown into relief by heavy morning and evening dewfall.

The house of Hsu Chien Lung derived its distinction from the watery aspect. Through a gate in a gray wall was an austere entrance chamber that gave onto a stony courtyard where the greenery was strictly in tubs. The living quarters followed, a few spacious rooms with pearly light and black wood supports that failed to raise the roof high enough to overcome the dim, dank, suppressed sheen of an old Chinese interior. At the windows were creepers, and beyond the living quarters a garden, not large, but suggestively wild, of purple bamboos, potted prickly exotics, and a carpet of mosses and water grass, like some giant sponge, through which stepping stones picked a way. One was wary of treading too heavily on the stones. There was a black rectangular pond which was below ground level and marked by a stone viewing parapet. Colors of olive, ruby, chocolate were suggested in the water, against basic black. Only three sides of the rectangular pond were visible. The water ran under the house, concealing a fourth edge. It was as if the house did not rest on solid ground but formed a kind of bridge, or cover, for the black water, making the rooms seem to float as in a house boat. The water, without boundary or bottom or color, was a mysterious image of nothingness.

Beside one corner of the pond grew a thick trunk greened with slime and lichen. The roots reached into black ooze, the branches separated above the sun line and ran across a trellis to become recognizable as tips of wisteria. Fronds had been trained around the exposed roof beams and twirled prettily about the window frames. The wisteria's arms prevented the house from floating away altogether. A leaf wafted pettishly from the eaves, a tiny golden feather to tickle the black skin below.

The honorific speech gestating in Wally's head aborted in the bustle when Professor Hsu met them at the station. They rode in a three-wheel "rickshaw," Hsu joking that the visitor was sure to enjoy a reminder of old China. They traveled through the autumn evening in appreciative silence. Wally wondered whether to speechify; he wanted to be adequately respectful. They jolted out of their seats beside a modest gate, and with shrieks and cries two women from the house came grabbing bags, shaking Jin Juan's hands, and scolding the old professor for some oversight. Wally was left out of histrionics that were perhaps for his benefit. Inside the house the light, once switched on, only confirmed the gloom. Hsu was grinning like a kid—he made the Doctor sit but couldn't sit himself for more than an instant before bobbing up on business. Jin Juan was making a bid to take over the household running from the two women. Wally attempted to stray beyond the front gate, to stretch his legs, and was immediately stopped by a hitherto-unseen chap who led him back to a privy within the walls. Such was the household.

Refreshments appeared: subtly American-style, pickles, peanuts, and, as an aperitif, Hsu explained, a small glass of the best Shaoxing yellow wine, which was "really rather like sherry. Cheers!" Wally remembered the sherry substitute from instructions in his *Chinese Cooking Simplified* book back home. He tilted his glass and began a speech. Once again Hsu overrode him with affable insistence: he must make himself "feel right at home."

The house and the living were shabby-genteel. The room suggested layer upon layer of experience, understanding and lateral displacement. A cabinet was stuffed with books, including old medical classics that Wally recognized; and the opportunity offered once again to introduce professional matters into the conversation.

Hsu, as if mind-reading, forestalled. "How'r the Red Sox doing?"

Wally imagined the lonely dedicated foreign PhD student whose strongest passion had been reserved for the democratic game of baseball. Where Jin Juan's English was idiomatically perfect with a synthetic accent, her grandfather's was fractured, with a period flavor; his genial bass was an immigrant's voice laced with 1930s Boston demotic alongside the Harvard drawl, a voice used for speaking with one and all. Hsu's mannerliness extended to not making a display of the language. Jin Juan was more flashy. But the roll of voice was enough to summon up a warm, wise and wily Cambridge parlor where Hsu had once been accepted, and which now seemed to surround Wally—so that he was as Hsu himself must once have been, a foreign newcomer visiting the distinguished professor at home. There was a subtle realigning of roles that suggested less the culmination of a quest than the beginnings of what both sides must hope would be a solid working relationship: master and student. There was all the time in the world, it seemed, and certainly enough for important matters to be deferred. So the first evening passed with pleasantry and potent yellow wine. Hsu got tipsy and relived each moment of a famous baseball game. He was a man in his eighties, agile, stooped, hair thin and downy, skin smooth and shiny, and only when he stretched the smooth pouch of flesh around his eyes were the myriad tiny wrinkles revealed. He wore modern, clear-plastic rimmed spectacles, and had good protruding teeth that were alternately bared in smiles or hidden behind pursed pensive lips. He was quietly jolly with no sense of urgency. Even when his deafness caused him to lose a remark, he glided on. At the end of the meal he leaped to his feet, seizing on his walking stick, to adopt his baseball hero's batting stance. Like other sages before him, he inhabited a zone where accumulated knowledge yields delightfully (and to one's great relief) to childishness.

Yet against the merry chortling of the stream, there was a back current. What did Wally register? Was the old man's batting posture shaped by old rheumaticky pains? A shadowy cold element was just out of sight.

In the dewy morning, when Wally woke, the old man was outside doing his slow eloquent exercises in the black pajamas of a prisoner or a monk. But when he passed the bed where Wally lay dozing, he seemed to be singing: "*Zippity-doo-dah* . . ." Over breakfast the old man's face was as delicate, as refreshed, as the skin of a plum.

The time would come, thought Wally—but the old man was reluctant. Was it a power play, an insistence on the rites? Very gentle, if so. In response to resistance, Wally's interest turned to Jin Juan, where there was more give.

Hsu took great pleasure, however, in recalling his Harvard days. Such was the face he readily turned outwards, the greater part of his life—in China—silently turned to the wall. He loved to tell over his old haunts, historical edifices and hamburger joints alike, and twinkled as Wally updated the memories with glimpses of a later Cambridge, Massachusetts.

Thus it was, at last, that Wally introduced into their nostalgic talk the subject of the papers Hsu had contributed to the *New England Journal of Medicine*. They were out walking. Hsu registered the mention and reverted to baseball. But on returning to the house Wally was able to riffle from his bag his copies of the articles. Exhibit One of good faith. He expected the sight to unlock a door.

Instead Hsu nodded with polite disinterest, and a touch of annoyance. He cherished the memories he chose to preserve, and did not wish to be reminded of his responsibility for the greater part of his past that he, not time, had willfully abandoned to oblivion.

Wally pushed on with his explanation, since the articles were important to him if not to Hsu, of how he had wanted to invite the professor to Australia as visiting fellow in his department, how his letters were never satisfactorily answered, how that had brought him to China in person, how his own research interests had taken a direction which made him, years after, remember back to the day during his post-doc at Harvard that his boss Harvey Heilmann slapped down Hsu's papers.

The old man scarcely bothered with the details of Wally's narrative. He nodded nervously, anticipatorily, as it unfurled, until he pressed his head against the hard-backed chair, straightening his spine uncomfortably, closed his eyes, and said:

"He passed away, I believe."

Wally didn't follow—then made the leap. "Yes, that's right. A great guy, Harvey."

The old man opened his watery eyes and directed them unwaveringly at Wally, but spoke as if to inside, with no trace of levity, as if a skin had been peeled away.

"We lost a lot after Liberation. They took my home. Later, more than once, I needed to retreat. I had no choice but to stick it out at the College in Peking. I had my granddaughter until the Cultural Revolution, when we were separated, degraded. I was unable to work. My aim was only to survive, in order to retreat, to retire. I confessed my crimes. What's in a word? At last, at the end of the years of chaos, I was able to put Peking behind me and return to my old home. My house was put to other uses, naturally, but I was able to insert myself in a corner. After the Gang of Four they began to restore property. I filed my claim with the authorities. I knew I must wait. One day the legal process was brought to an end. The old home was mine again. Later I found out it was Harvey Heilmann. He wrote letters. He asked they treat me fair. He was a big man. He wrote to the right person. I am lucky. Perhaps one in ten thousand had my luck. I am unworthy," he shrugged. "No God to thank. I thank Harvey Heilmann. Thank you his long memory."

"That must have been just before he died."

The old man nodded. He spoke not again. Wally had expected to bring surprise; he had not expected to be surprised himself.

The old man's life was a nimble and graceful kind of dance. He had a goldfinch in a cage that was his joy and around the clock he would exercise the bird, removing the cloth cover and swinging the cage as he pottered about the garden and walked out the gate and down the lane to a sunny corner where he could sit on a stone slab with the other old boys and compare the songs of the birds. How proud he was of his finch's lusty note. Or he would pay attention to his cactuses, and since it was autumn, tease out insects from the whorled buds of his potted chrysanthemums. He was a jolly, active man whose various concerns ran like diverse currents in one stream. He easily rode from one to another. So while exercising his bird he might notice a shoot on the wisteria that needed snipping, and, never forgetting, he would come in due course with the knife. He knew even the habits of the carp in the black pond beneath the house: invisible except in the rarest light conditions, when their murky forms could be admired.

He made no other contribution to their rearing. To admire was enough.

The book cabinet was never unlocked.

Jin Juan no more than Wally could sustain conversation with the old man, although their mutual accommodation and assistance in the household, and their ribbing small talk, suggested years of symbiotic closeness. But Jin Juan became a hard-edged modern Pekinger in this environment, rather than melting like an old-style Southerner. She folded her arms tight, turning a sharp nose towards the quaint old man in the mossy garden. The amahs shook their heads.

"What's up, doc?" the old man would say whenever he passed Wally in the room.

One afternoon Wally went walking with Jin Juan, just the two of them, two of a kind, on the same wavelength of the world. Such was the transformation Hsu had wrought, all difference seemed to have vanished.

They walked by the white-banked canal under a canopy of plane trees. Each house along the canal was open to reveal a table between two high-backed chairs beneath a gaudy poster of the Old Man Kitchen God, improvised domestic shrine. A lighter came down the water with two men fishing out bamboo husks and other debris. Women on the lower steps were pounding laundry in the vile water.

They visited the town's centerpiece, the museum to commemorate Lu Hsun, China's greatest twentieth-century writer. Moving through the hagiographical chambers arranged according to the most orthodox Marxist-Maoist historiographical myth, Wally was struck again by the despair in China's history, an evolution so slow and chancy as scarcely to deserve the name of progress, mutation rather, each wave of reform, enlightened, idealistic, suicidal, feeding straight back into the self-devouring maw of the organism. The museum showed touching photographs of the early advocates of democracy, a century ago, and later the martyred writers of *La Jeunesse* who had felt a new ardor heat their country; and in the last equivocating chambers the attempt made to establish an affinity that never existed between Lu Hsun and Mao Tse Tung's policy of art in harness to the revolution of the proletariat. It was a museum of sorry lies that made hope soggily impossible, Wally thought; yet had not Lu Hsun written "Hope is like a path in the countryside: originally there was no path—yet, as people are walking all the time in the same spot, a way appears"?

Afterwards they looked at the room where Lu Hsun slept, the room where Lu Hsun ate porridge, the vat where Lu Hsun pissed, and, out the back, the acre of profuse weeds where he escaped from the discipline of school.

Revisiting the past placed Jin Juan and Wally more squarely together in the present.

"You let me go running all over the country making a fool of myself," he said. "Why didn't you trust me?"

"I didn't know your motives. A foreigner arrives, a stranger; he is hell-bent on tracking down my grandfather. Just think. It was sheer chance that my friend Song was able to inform me of your intentions."

"Why has it taken you so long to tell? You didn't trust me, or you still don't?"

He no longer knew what his aims were or how things stood around him. Was there a further message behind Jin Juan's message?

"Do you find my grandfather eccentric?"

"He's unpredictable."

"He's had his ups and downs, but he's in pretty good shape all things considered. He's had a good innings, would you say?"

Wally laughed, throwing back his head and shoulders, his arms flying out with an Australian abandon, indifferent to Chinese niceties of space. His hand brushed Jin Juan's and

206

they found themselves sauntering down the canal hand in hand.

5

That night he sat up late with Hsu. Jin Juan had gone to sleep early, but the old man was alert and quietly talkative. Hours passed, over the steady sipping of diminutive glasses of yellow wine, and their laconic exchanges settled into serious conversation. The Doctor was cast in the role of disciple, and at first did not press or question, except when a tentative spur was required to nudge the conversation along. Hsu sat remarkably straight-backed, not stiff, throughout, his hands moving minimally between table and arm rest, his pale face screwed up so his eyes disappeared into wrinkled flesh. His glasses had been removed; Wally suspected he saw nothing, heard only his foreign interlocutor's voice. The room, in any case, was virtually dark.

Wally too was sleepy from the wine and from the exertions of the day; well-being smoothed away the nervous necessity to communicate and made things easier. Hsu talked at length of Chinese herbal medicine, and the high rare skill involved in its successful application—a dying art that had become commonly nine parts quackery and guesswork. It was often said, he smiled, that herbal medicine worked, although no one knew why. In reality, the practice was no less obscure than the theory. Most who claimed extraordinary successes in its application were liars. "I do not accuse. They are not deceivers, merely self-deceived." But there were recorded cases where the prolonged application of herbal medicine by a master coincided with remarkable cures—cures brought about by faith or accident perhaps, though in Hsu's analysis (the investigation of such cases in relation to cancers had been the foundation of his work) the connection was causal.

He spoke of a certain wizard who had operated from the mountains beyond Shaoxing before Liberation. The man was feared and revered, and carried forward the traditional techniques wrought to a high pitch. He was a kind of male witch, a witchdoctor or shaman whose medicine was inseparable from meditation, manipulation, breathing techniques and the wilder, anarchic fringes of popular Daoism. As a young man Hsu had witnessed some of the famous cures. There was no doubting the shaman's effectiveness, and from Hsu's materialist viewpoint he became convinced that the application of rare, complicated medicines was the key. That had led him into further case studies and analyses. He was puzzled that the chemical synthesizing of organic Chinese medicines failed to produce substances of comparable effectiveness. He was no Luddite or naturopath; maybe the technique was deficient; but it was clear that artificial materials failed to behave; hence failed to provide the results needed for further research.

The tragedy, he said, was that, after Liberation, Chinese medicine and Western medicine were severed from each other. What passed for Chinese medicine, though allegedly the great pride of the people, became an ignorant travesty; and what passed for Western medicine was often crude and behind the times, an application of technique without understanding. That had led to the present-day "reconciliation," where, for instance—he gave a bucktoothed grin—the common cold would be blindly treated with a huge shot of penicillin in the bum and a sack of dirty dandelion roots to be consumed as gallons of bitter tea!

His complaints were not against medicine in China. In many areas skill and progress were great; it was the larger failure, of the creative vision required to understand the wisdom that already was there in the culture and the people, that grieved Hsu. For however terrible China's history, however riddled with folly, one thing remained certain: the common people had powerful resources.

Wally asked at what level of abstraction or practice the Eastern and Western traditions might meet. He explained that Hsu's work in the States, which had seemed to keep its distance from the conventional research of the day, had curiously anticipated the directions that Western oncology had latterly taken.

Hsu became philosophical. East and West meet where they merge, he said, where they can no longer be separated. They meet on the common ground, he said, where all doctors meet, in the impossibility of their task. He yawned, rubbing his invisible eyes.

"You have been reading Director Kang's papers?"

Wally laughed. "They contain some excellent passages."

Hsu returned the laugh. "Indeed they do."

"Then you have known?"

"We know about Kang. But it was clever of you to discover." Wally's pride in his and Ralph the Rhino's cleverness for a moment made him forget the crime, to which he now averted with a vengeance. "You must be very angry."

"Oh? I have not anger for everything. The Director's publications list is, after all, quite a civilized form of contempt. You might say it shows respect. In any case I am grateful that my work has had an outlet. That might not have been so otherwise."

"You don't consider intellectual dishonesty a crime—as brazen as Kang's?"

"Before, no. But now you have given it a new name, now that you have discovered, then it becomes something. A minor international incident, perhaps. That brings no pleasure to me, however, unless of course the information can be used to help someone very dear to me—?"

"Jin Juan?"

The old man nodded.

After due pause, Wally returned to the question of whether Hsu felt cheated, whether at the end of his life he did not have a desire for his finest achievements to go down to posterity.

From the darkness came the old man's lucid voice. He had closed his books, locked up his cabinet of active ideas, research, exploration, invention. Those manifestations of the intellectual life had been discarded like an old skin. Maybe he had indeed been re-educated by swilling the latrines. Or maybe he had become that bane of old China, the empty Daoist boat floating on a sea of non-being. But he was joking. It was simply that, as he had been saying, the body had come to his rescue. Frail, brittle old man's body in need of warmth, empty of passion, it was nonetheless his friend, making him forget the intellectual struggles of his life. Happily, the old thing stopped him from achieving. That reconciled him to a doctor's failure; it was common; and now he cared not one way or the other whose name was attached to writings that pitifully scraped away at the laws of death.

His advice was simple: "Forget it."

"Do you not care that your work may be of value to others?"

"If the work is true, others will discover it for themselves."

"Do you not allow for a quantum leap of understanding?"

"I tell you something, son. You say that I, not Kang, was the creator of that work. I tell you. I am not the creator. I too am a thief, a plagiarist, as you say. I was told about the shaman of Heaven's Terrace by a young woman with whom I worked in Ningbo Hospital as a student long ago. She had grown up in an area where the shaman operated. A young woman with Western education, she was skeptical but impressed. It was she who had the idea of recording the cases. It was she who wrote the first papers. When, later, I had the opportunity to go abroad to study, and she, being a woman, had not this

210

opportunity, she told me I must take her work and develop it. Of course under her inspiration I too became interested, and for several years together we collected material for our case studies. I was in love with her, you see, and before I left for the States she became my wife. You are surprised? Those famous papers you mention are the result of my wife's work, based on her drafts, which I was able to re-express in the light of new attitudes I was learning at Harvard. It was for her sake that I returned to China. She had become very idealistic. She believed I should return and work for my country. It was she who brought up our two little daughters, while I was in the States. She was a reformer, a modernizer, with her feet on the ground. But in our two daughters something of old refinement came back, the hankering for the old culture. My wife had great faith, in me and in our country's future, but that could not protect her finally. My work took me to the capital when I returned to China. She stayed in the provincial hospital. Later she was made to answer for many crimes, most bitterly when she was accused of being unpatriotic for carrying out birth-control programs in the region. I was unable to help her. Who was to predict those years? We were blind perhaps. We had not the imagination to foresee that my granddaughter would be all that was left me of my family. I have no imagination now either. At last the lack of imagination is a blessing."

His voice cracked and he shuffled to his feet. He turned the dim lamp to an angle that illuminated a woman's photo-graph on the wall; large, black-and-white, grainy, indistinct.

He chortled. "Who is the source? Chicago gives Kang a medal for ideas he lifts from me. My ideas cannot exist without my wife. But she records the doings of a shaman. So perhaps he is the source. But he is just a mountain man, one of the masses."

The face in the photograph was like a mask, yet those woman's eyes with their patiently unveiling insights were what

Wally would see in future when he read the dog-eared pages from the *New England Journal*.

"Pei, my wife," said the old man, who belched, ready for sleep.

"Wait a minute," said Wally. "Can't we talk a little more?"

"I'm tired," said Hsu.

"You said your wife came from Heaven's Terrace, near Taizhou."

"You know it? It's not far from here."

"When was that? Were there foreigners there?"

"Oh, it's certain that there were foreigners, all through the province."

"Did you know my own father was born in Hangzhou?"

The old man raised his eyebrows. The visitor did not seem to have Chinese blood.

"Sit down, let me tell you the story." And the old man quietly sat again, the perfect host, to listen to another variant of the story he had heard so often, in the States and in China, of a family connection, all but random, that exerted its indirect tyrannical power to bring the younger generation back. It seemed less a question of individuals than a gravitational force, and Hsu failed to share Wally's boyish excitement in the story. He commented only "It's possible, it's possible," when Wally drew the lines of coincidence in tight.

"Don't go to bed," pleaded Wally. "I want to ask you about the targeting of the treatments. Take the liver, for example. Do you treat the tumor there, or other malfunctions?"

"Please—" the old man bent to Wally laying a hand on his shoulder, "—let me sleep. It's not important. It can wait, can't it?"

It could wait, thought the old man, for other people in another time and place.

6

Wally tossed and turned in broken sleep, and before first light he was up. He pulled out Retta's diary from his luggage and sat outside rereading the last pages in search of clues.

> It's the season of the river frogs. Peg insisted on an excursion. Lionel and Jerry were suitably decked out in galoshes and I carried nets. What a lark! We followed the river to a shallow lagoon and there in the rushes the frogs hopped into our hands. The boys were very merry, and very mucky. Waldemar would have feared for our sanity more than our health. What a treat we gave the peasants, most especially when Lionel, a budding linguist, cried out "Such fun!" in their own dialect. My boys looked like frogs and as I could not help fearing that the peasant men might have thought them fit to eat, so I can understand the terrible imaginings they have of our intentions towards their babies. One fancies witches and wizards all round. Peg led the expedition home, Jerry on her shoulders and a bucket of frogs heavy in her proud hand. She showed me how to cook them, in brown sauce; W. thought they were pieces of fowl. I smirked at his grace: "For what we are about to receive, may the Lord make us truly grateful."

> W. is perturbed. Peg also is perturbed and relays the news that the whole town is agitated. Seemingly the rains have not only brought the frogs but also a faith healer who has come down from the mountain and inspires great respect in the people. For some days Peg has been distracted, then she confesses that she has

213

been chided by a matron of Patriarch Lu's clan acting
under the instructions of this witchdoctor. She has not
sufficiently reverenced her mother. The healer demands
to know why he was not called to save the woman. Peg,
who has been skeptical herself, urges me not to scoff.
The man has knowledge, she says, mixed with power.
Peg is edgy. W. is edgy, noting a falling off in the usual
line of patients and petitioners. I long to see the fellow,
alas the chance is denied me.

We hear that a tug-of-war has taken place between
the Magistrate and the Patriarch, with victory to the latter. The healer has moved into the clan house. Lu has
declared himself afflicted with one of those Chinese illnesses that have no symptoms and in no way impair the
faculties but nevertheless demand cure. Peg says it's a
problem of balances. He's certainly obese. It's an old
man's malady, she explains patiently, to do with *yang*,
the masculine force, and requires the gruesomely appropriate application of snakes, bear's paws and the unmen-
tionable part of a bull. More important, says Peg, are the
healer's investigations of the surroundings through the
methods of geomancy. He has sworn success. Peg does
not distinguish between the Patriarch's physical condition and the state of his war with the Magistrate. Both
she describes as manifestations of "force." I cannot wean
her from these notions. How she snuggles to me as we
talk our nonsense.

I wake to a world washed of color and feeling. Waldemar administered laudanum. I was overwrought with
fatigue, having wept and not slept, and having shouted I
know not what terrible accusations at Waldemar, who is
blameless. The matron came from the Patriarch and announced that Peg was wanted. She allowed no time for

preparation. Peg's things were bundled up by a servant. Again it happened like a charade, and I disbelieving, except for Peg's air, that told me she had expected it. The clan was reclaiming her. The servant had not yet opened the gate when she dived into my body and clung there, shuddering with fervid spasms, and I gripped her, her hair falling down from its plait, and we clung with limbs like pincers, and fingers that left claw marks through our flesh. To inflict pain was the only recourse. I slapped the matron's face as she prised Peg away. Wrong, I know. I begged Waldemar until he made a visit to the Patriarch. He had a far frostier reception than in former co-operative times. There was no hope of my girl returning. She was betrothed in marriage to a clansman. The healer had declared it auspicious, necessary. W. did not see Peg. But he described the bony form of the fellow, his blackened bullet of a skull, his deep empty sockets of eyes, his dirty black tunic and trousers and voluminous brown coat, his blind man's walking stick and wriggling nose. Bracelets of gold. W. tells me he should properly be designated a shaman, a practitioner of the most ancient mischief and devil worship. I am frightened, and have not the conviction to pray.

Is it the odor of the ocean that invigorates, or its sheer space and constant inanimate life? We keep the boys in Chinese wicker hoops on the deck. They can stand up and move about, and I watch like a hawk all the same, lest . . . Jerry is content, but Lionel protests. W. demands they keep still as he experiments with his camera. I write to record, despite being in low spirits. The insomnia continues, and my nerves are torture to me. So, to be brief. We were woken from sleep by an almighty din. Waldemar ran down as he was and saw the great round hole gaping in the wall of our courtyard. It was not yet dawn, a clear night. The cannonball lodged where it had smashed a water jar. Brave W. stepped out through the gate, standing in his night-shirt, and began to remonstrate. The Patriarch's cannon had been moved outside our gate and the clan was lined up behind it to enjoy the sport. While W. stared, a second ball came whizzing through the air. "Good Lord," W. reported as his oath. The missile overflew the wall and landed square in the fork of our magnolia tree, splitting the wood in an outburst of flames. I had hurried to the boys, and from their window, hugging them, saw the burning tree. W., furious, strode across the parade ground, but Patriarch Lu led his contingent away. Demonstration over, W. was insulted with their backsides. The shaman had promised the Patriarch that his manhood would revive if the barbarians were exorcised.

Well, my husband is not one to retreat from difficulty. Indeed his principles are founded on strength of will. Yet as we took counsel in those small hours, something turned him round to a wiser resignation. It took us forty-eight hours to make preparations, before we could leave on our arduous cart ride over the mountains, whence we came via calls on Bishop Mowbray at Ningpo and the Professor of Anatomy at St. John's, Shanghai, to embark on our voyage home.

Only before departure I was permitted a visit to the Patriarch's house, where in full view I made my farewell to Peg. She was pale and puffy. I squeezed her hand. I made a presentation to her of our best books, dictionaries and text books. "Save you. Don't forget. I am always your friend." She showed no emotion. I understood from the toughness in her young face that she would hold on, she would defeat them, she would survive. Yet my heart aches, with each day the unconscionable burden weighs heavier on me, that she has been abandoned to her fate.

I take nothing from this land that I did not bring. My boys were born here, but they are not of here. My Wee One, my strength, my belief, dare I say my husband, my God, my Peg. What I take with me from this land are absences only.

W. strikes the board and declares he will go in for straightforward General Practice when we arrive in South Australia. He no longer holds himself so stiffly. He too has lost, or gained, a quality.

Mercy upon us. No more.

Added in another hand: "Retta Frith née Glee deceased Adelaide aged 32, of an undiagnosed 'exotic' condition."

Replacing the hand-written pages in their envelope did little to banish his grandmother from Wally's presence. From the unknown woman, whom he could visualize only according to the posed studio portraits in the family album, his thoughts glided to what he recalled of Nobodaddy Grandpa Frith, across a span of ninety years between the two Chinas, the two worlds, they had known, and back to Jin Juan and her grandfather, Professor Hsu, and the fuzzy photograph of Hsu's wife, Jin Juan's grandmother, who had once, probably, been Peg. But did it matter that he could not prove the connection? It would remain a hypothesis which even Hsu, if he knew and if Wally asked him pointblank, was not in a position to confirm or deny. The black pond that ran under the house returned no reflection, only darkness. Wally's disappointment was quite irrational. Hsu had spoken, at the last, clearly, openly, and no mystery remained. He spoke matter-of-fact, clarifying language, and perhaps there lay the problem: no mystery remained, yet no answer had been given. And if the wise old man's dry assumption was that no answer need be given, then surely the implication was that no question need be asked—which snubbed Wally's exploratory, inquiring urges. He felt hollow and anxious, his anger displaced, for where was there now to go? He was coldly amused by the deft way Hsu had disposed of Kang's perfidy, by disowning (and why not truthfully?) his own part, by removing one backdrop to expose another, and behind that another, in infinite regression. He stared blankly as a sheen of light began to glow on the pond. He wanted to talk practicalities with the Professor, believing that somewhere, just beyond the reach of them both, were things of great usefulness; pointers he could triumphantly place before doubting colleagues. But the old man resisted. Was the Professor muddleheaded, out of touch, pleading to be handled gently? Was Wally a fantasist? Was the greatest secret human ignorance? He had come up against not a brick wall but a rectangular stretch of black water that had no measurable depth and no visible boundary, showed no motion and offered no reflection. And where was there boiling water for shaving?

7

The white churned-up dust on the narrow mountain road clouded the bus and reduced visibility to zero. To the valley from which they had climbed was a sheer drop, but still the loutish driver in his mirror sunglasses continued to pass the timber and cement trucks, and the timber and cement trucks groaned after the bus in billowing dust clouds. The scrubby conifers had curious nibbled bundles of hay halfway up their trunks, and the laden orange trees were snow white with dust. Jin Juan, who had a seat, and Wally, who sat in the aisle, screwed up their eyes as much against their possible fate as against the

218

dust. With each jolting stretch of the ride from Shaoxing, each breakdown and cranking, their bodies became more cramped and knotted. At the top of the mountain was Heaven's Terrace, a ramshackle dust-fertilized town with Red Star 1950s buildings that looked as ornate as those from the Ching dynasty and the one formerly Christian hospital.

After Heaven's Terrace the road flattened and widened for the coastal run through orange groves that shone like enamel and well-watered rice paddies overseen at intervals by cozy villages of grand two-story houses with stepped roof decoration and eaves curling upwards like stretched toes. There was little to distinguish the oldest houses from those under construction. Sometimes a woman in scarlet satin smock, belly swelling, would stand on the balcony to watch the others march home across the fields. The peasant's dream was well on the way towards realization here: a house, a mate, a kid, a grandson. In their sleepy, deceptive prosperity, protected by high breaks of flowering black bamboo as they were protected by the mountains on one flank and the river that wound to the sea on the other, the villagers of the county were at once the most conservative and most radical of Chinese, simply regarding their own laborious livelihood.

After dark the bus reached the river town. It was the event of the day to judge by the hawkers and scouts who assailed the passengers. Jin Juan shooed them off, until one middle-aged woman came quietly forward to say that she ran a private inn.

They were received, through a door off a narrow alley, at an agreed price with no formalities. It was a farmhouse, really, but the man of the house, who had twenty years earlier served as an indentured laborer on a Chinese construction project in Africa, had shown enterprise by setting up a hand-turned printing press in an annex of the house, and began putting up his assistants in the loft. Where his wife was silent, if not demure, the man was coarse and sociable and shook Wally's hands with great enthusiasm—the Australian was the first white man he had seen in their town.

Asking no questions, he led them up a ladder to a room where they might sleep: in it were three wooden beds covered with tatami mats and bedding and draped with mosquito nets. There was a basin and a chamber pot, and a flask of water and mugs for tea. The floor was laid with smooth black boards, and air flowed from a window that looked to a modest mountain against the starry sky.

They were assured of no noise or disturbance, but the host first insisted on bundling them across the market square to a place where they might eat, by one bare bulb, the local river crabs and frogs fried with garlic.

The courtyard of the inn had a profuse bougainvillea and racks of flowering pots. The air, under the sparkling night sky, was fragrant and bracing. Wally stripped to the waist before an urn that was big enough to stew two men and ladled washing water into his basin. From a kettle simmering on the coal stove he added some hot, and rubbed the dust and grime from his skin, arching his neck to the heavens as the water trickled down his throat to his belly button and inside his belt. The pleasure of a camp was combined with the special virtue of cleanliness and the sense of having gone farther from his moorings than he had ever imagined. But because he was with Jin Juan, as a friend and as his true companion, he did not feel estranged. She brought him a human focus, and plenitude. He passed her by the ladder with her towel and toothbrush. She looked happy.

The host pointed to a round basket by the foot of the ladder. "Kee-kee kee-kee!" he imitated the rooster in the basket that would wake them before dawn. But they were warm and content in bed and slept through the rooster's crowing, and the market was in sunny mid-morning bustle when they first looked out.

220

Half-heartedly Wally returned to his quest. Was it not already an achievement to have come so far? Quest was simply a sluggish flow of the current. He had reached the town where his grandparents had built the mission hospital, where his father had been conceived and learned to toddle; the place that had been reconstituted in family lore and a young boy's myth of China. As a scientist, Wally had felt obliged to check for traces since the town was only a day's journey, however arduous, over the mountains from Shaoxing, and Jin Juan had been willing to accompany him. On the other hand he expected, in fact, to find nothing. Traces, like radiation, were more often than not a leftover poison.

In her high-heeled sandals Jin Juan stepped like a Sui princess through the streets of the undistinguished town to which the century had bequeathed its haphazard layers. The old at each stage remained, with the new grafted clumsily on in a wonderful palimpsest. Abutting a storehouse of functional Socialist Reconstruction ugliness (poverty's Bauhaus) was a minor Daoist shrine, like a rotten pulled tooth, standing askew but still standing, because no one got around to heeding the order of demolition.

Softened by plane trees, the grid of central planning was upset by asymmetries of nature near the surging coffee-colored river. At each point they inquired: "Was there an old hospital hereabouts? Was there a place where foreigners had lived long ago? Was there a Christian church?"

Every tongue, eye and hand pointed a different direction and they wandered in pleasant confusion from one perimeter to another and along the squelching river bank where a sow and piglets wallowed in the sun and ducks skittered across the mud to bob on the water in the shadows of low-bottomed boats. Across the river the bright fields stepped rapidly to high ragged mountains that were washed in sunlight to the color and texture of stone-scrubbed denim.

Coming on a weedy survival of the old city wall, and the

site of a stone ford, Wally's memories were stirred, and after interrogating a string of old pipe smokers who were helpful as far as dialect permitted, they came to a walled compound and a locked gate. Through a crack in the gate they saw an old crone dandling a baby's naked bum in the sunshine. They called and called. She was preoccupied or deaf. In the end Wally shinned up the wall.

Amidst a commotion that combined utter astonishment with utter acceptance, as if the Second Coming had occurred, Jin Juan was admitted and the two visitors were ushered to an upper room. At one end were wide open windows flooded with white light. The walls and low ceiling were white. Varnished wooden chairs were arranged in rows. A ceiling fan was motionless below the height of Wally's head. At the front was a large chest covered in a flower-embroidered cloth, on which stood two glass jars of plastic flowers. Beside this altar was a lectern at which a white-haired man was speaking inaudibly. As they moved closer, he did not register their presence, until they were right in front of his nose. There were two people listening to him, and for them too the words must have been almost inaudible. They stared from swarthy faces under mop hair, frightened.

The preacher hurried down to greet Wally and Jin Juan. From the film over his eyes one could guess at an immense age. The man spoke no English or standard Chinese, although the word "theology" seemed to emerge from his babble. With the greatest difficulty, at the top of her voice, Jin Juan tried to explain who they were and why they had come. With hand gestures the man communicated that his age was ninety-five. But they could get no sense from him. His hair was neatly combed, his clothing stained but correctly buttoned (unlike the tatters worn by his audience of two), in his face was a lambent, baby-like emptiness. Wally guessed that he was far gone into senility. This hypothesis was disturbed when the man began excitedly pointing at the other two, who were much younger though not young, indicating his brain and their brains. If Jin Juan understood aright he was explaining that they were crazy in the head and came to him for help. They were two black sheep and he was their ancient shepherd.

They trailed downstairs to a reception room, and here Wally noticed that the fittings of the building, the style and materials, were different from the upper story. The room was darker for a start. There were exposed beams and dark paneled doors and fittings. The doors were tall and wide, not built to Chinese proportions, and the broad lintels were elaborately grooved. They were, Wally guessed, the work of an amateur Victorian carpenter. Foreigners had assisted in the construction of the sturdy lower story, which had survived assault and refurbishment to this day.

His guess made him confident enough to ask questions. But the old man had reached a confusing stage of overexcitement. Tiny bubbles of spittle dribbled from his mouth and his watery eyes seemed painfully, pathetically empty as he struggled to grasp the visitor's questions. It was too hard.

In a desk where there might have been records was nothing but tatty committee pronouncements and the old man's few photographs of a family dispersed.

He wanted so much to help. To make it easier Jin Juan was reduced to putting the bluntest questions, and to all of them the old priest nodded enthusiastically, an obliging host. Yes, there were foreigners. Yes, there was a hospital. Yes, there was a man called Frith. Yes, there was a missus. Children and grandchildren. Oh yes, so long ago. His mother always remembered. Yes, there were so many foreign friends. Never forgotten.

They settled for a group photograph in the courtyard. It seemed better to extricate themselves. They lined up, the senile white-haired preacher, the two black-haired mentally disturbed ones, Jin Juan in her scarlet gauze scarf, Wally in his running shoes. Who was to take the shot?

As they made their farewells, a great big tear rolled down the old man's face. Such visitors had come in a dream. He seemed to remember a likeness, a ghost, so long ago in childhood. The contours of his pastoral work were obscure, concluded Wally; the heart was pure. Water again, not the grit of fact.

He thought of the creature who had lost his faculties in the sanatorium at Beidaihe, the wrong professor. How far he had come, questing. Had he found his trace?

Walking back they stopped on the bridge over the wide silty river, and Wally tenderly put his arm round Jin Juan's waist.

"Do you understand what I have been looking for today? Does it seem a waste of time to you?"

"Barking up the wrong tree? No, filial piety is our custom. I only hope the old-fashioned ritual does not leave you feeling empty."

But he was full of her.

"My grandparents probably walked here," he said. "Singly, perhaps not together. They were devoted, but not in love, and more cut off than they wanted to be."

A crowd was gathering at one end of the bridge to point with disapproval at the visitors, the foreign man and the Chinese woman who were carrying on like lovers.

"Do you think your grandmother might have walked here too?" asked Wally.

"Silly superstition! I don't care about that." She broke away.

That evening the host of the inn feasted them in his own quarters. He had a magnificent red and gold dragon-and-phoenix carved double bed, an ancient heirloom. When he sat on its edge to take food from the little table, he grew full with well-being. Across the courtyard his young daughter worked the bellows to make the furnaces roar and the wok so hot that the crabs, fish, clams and soy beans cooked as soon as they were plunged in. The table was constantly replenished, and they got drunk on toasts of yellow wine and fervid white spirits.

Wally went out the back and perched, somewhat precariously, his head reeling from drink, on the edge of the great earthenware vat. He hung there in the fetid darkness communing tipsily with the sky above his head. His fuzzy thoughts seemed an expression of satisfaction not so different from the snuffling of the two big pigs in the adjacent pen. He smelled them and they smelled him, and a few wide-awake chooks came pecking at the trousers around his ankles. From a mound in the center of the yard grew a magnolia tree, higher than the inn, past flower, in full leaf. Through the fingers of the leaves were the stars. He contemplated the movement of the planet, and the prankish, unpredictable, unguessable laws—beyond race, creed, nation—that had brought him there and held him perched there, the poor, bare, forked, drunk, and, for that moment, unwarrantably happy creature.

The bus left early the next morning. The host's wife was squatting in the courtyard to pluck bean pods from the picked branches and the host was bleary eyed. Jin Juan and Wally splashed their faces awake, and said farewell.

At the last farewell with Hsu Chien Lung in Shaoxing the old man wryly apologized for not answering the Doctor's questions. It was an offence to a guest who had traveled so far. Hsu brought out a stack of papers, some English, some Chinese, offprints, notes, unpublished articles. "If you and your colleagues work through these and find anything of value, you have my thanks. I suspect it's as long and stinking as the proverbial old lady's foot bandages." He chuckled, and it was time for the train.

In the sleeper back to Peking Wally considered how little he had discovered on the trip, how few of his questions had been answered, how few even of the old questions remained intact. Yet his brain was sparking with new questions and devising new experiments to follow up when he got back. He repudiated Professor Hsu's fatalism and felt a new determination take hold. He had ascertained one thing. He knew who the woman was who had visited his residence in Peking. There was only one woman, Jin Juan, who had no substitute. As the train rocked north he mulled over the predicament his various feelings placed him in, knowing that the action he had decided on could be accounted for in more ways than one. He was in love with her and loved being with her. It was not only desire but delight in her presence, in her sharpness and strength. Yet the pleasure of her was also an addiction that he couldn't see beyond. He couldn't tell how much she might reciprocate his feelings, or for what purpose. He assumed that she, of all people, would want to leave China. She had suffered, and her talents continued to be wasted. She had the English, and other qualities that would allow her to succeed abroad, to find and fulfil herself. If the result of his visit proved nothing more than to have placed him in her path, then he should do the right thing and help her, squarely setting the end against the means. Should he offer to marry her on that basis, as the most useful thing he could do for her? And if they should come actually to live together as lovers, why not? If the condition of helping her out of the country was to marry, he could afford to risk their feelings for such a cause. Or was he seeking means to justify a blind holiday romance, an infatuation with Chinese skin and eyes and fatalism? The thought discredited Jin Juan who was cautious, balanced. She could live in one of his empty rooms. She would be there, solid. What else did he have? He would marry her, if she would have him.

CHAPTER ELEVEN

Encountering Trouble

1

The band was on stage. Behind the curtains the poets plotted and planned in factions. Out front their friends and hangers-on crammed the front rows while the rest of the auditorium filled up with students who had managed to procure tickets. It was a fine late-autumn evening, and permission had been given for the reading to be held in the mock-Oxbridge hall of Peking University.

A lighting and sound system had been installed to render the presentations more dramatic. Shafted with a red spot, a broad-shouldered poet in black recited his "Old Summer Palace Drunk" like a pop singer, his shadow doing a tango against the scrim. The obese editor of *China Youth News* sat on the boards with his back to the audience mumbling his words into a mike. By the time it was Build-the-Country's turn to recite, the band was in place. A twang of guitar chords accompanied each over-emotional phrase.

The theme of their poetry was I: isolated, having no past, no future, not believing in the present, a wraith haunting a

227

great ruined culture, consolable neither in body nor spirit. The poems were blackly sentimental, and to the packed audience of contemporaries, the audacious inflection of their language was like a drug; the poets were heroes. The monkey-faced one read an epic of the rough sensuality he had saved from the regime's attempts to iron him flat. The editor of the pro-democracy magazine quashed five years earlier read a tribute to his comrade-in-arms who had turned schizoid in prison. The lean and hungry proclaimed their slogan: I—DO—NOT—BELIEVE.

It was poetry of walls and extinction in search of a cadence with which to hymn a cruel society. They wore drainpipe jeans, boots and bodgie sweaters. When the music pounded, they moved on stage like stiff robots, stamping with their heels and hammering with their heads. There was no room for dancing so the audience stood on the spot in the narrow rows of seats and stamped and swayed with grimacing faces, hands beating their sides like pistons, releasing a fraction of the hot, rank energy a hard power had pressed down into them.

Backstage a university official was talking to a representative of the poets. It was the official who gave the orders. He had turned a blind eye when the unauthorized band appeared on stage, but he was perturbed by the mass dancing, which was strictly forbidden. There was danger of a riot, however, if hundreds of students were too quickly checked in their defiance. The poets were conciliatory. The music slowed, quietened, and the students gradually resumed their seats until the music stopped altogether, leaving the rumbling of discontent and disappointment as a thousand cigarettes were lit up.

Among the lesser writers saved for the end was Philosopher Horse. Although his name had begun to be whispered around, he was unfamiliar to the Peking crowd. He looked like any kid from the South with pimply skin, thick glasses and cropped hair, but for his expression of obsessional conviction. He wore unfashionable gray worker's clothes and his delivery began

228

flatly as he read a piece of reportage. Really he was explaining himself. A boy from a rough, weird province in the South (they laughed at his accent), he had been a student in a provincial college until expelled for skipping classes and exams. Then he walked away from an ill-paid, boring factory job, and remained unemployed. It was an ordinary case history in which all could recognize themselves. Only from Philosopher Horse's aimlessness had grown his extraordinary intensity.

He used to spend his days at his elder sister's house, with his sister and her kid. His brother-in-law worked at a unit three hours' journey outside the town and only returned at weekends. His sister worked on the far side of town, an hour's journey away. Their child was left to get to school, to buy a midday meal, to play in the afternoon, by himself. Philosopher Horse spent many hours hanging round with the kid as there were no other family members. Their parents were still in the country village from which first his sister and then the boy himself had moved away. His sister had an old friend, also from their village, who was thirty-five and unmarried. He was known as Lao Men, which meant Old Gate. He would often call in to play with the kid, or chat with Philosopher Horse, or share in the meal when sister came home. Old Gate was tough and dismissive of unnecessary refinements, yet exceptionally courteous, even chivalrous. He appreciated what he got of family life in the household. Fortune had not shone on him. He worked in a chemical factory and lived in a dormitory. One of his legs was twisted from polio, but he was stronger than any other man in the factory. He was happiest when sister's husband, his special mate, was home at the weekend. The two men shared rough and ready opinions, a taste for strong wine, a love of chess, and a code of honor that included torturing hard work. By contrast, Philosopher Horse had views a little too abstract, but on nights when his mate was away Old Gate could also enjoy a debate with the younger boy, whom he had known since childhood.

Philosopher Horse told the ordinary story in direct, un-mannered language. The audience listened. Its very plainness was unusual. At the time of the crime crackdown in 1983 a girl was raped in the town. Old Gate was rounded up. There was no evidence for or against. As usual on the night in question he had been drinking at sister's house, and slowly meandered home. No one had seen for sure what time he returned to his dormitory. He was, anyway, too old to be unmarried; a man with insufficient ties, not a true member of society. On the street everyone spoke well of him. But he was from a peasant village, not from the town. The appearance in court was, in any case, a closed affair. Within three days of his arrest he was sentenced. He was paraded through the town with a truck full of other alleged criminals, their misdoings proclaimed on yokes round their necks. At one point Old Gate yelled out his innocence, to no one in particular. In the stadium along with the others he was shot in the back of the head. A large quota of executions was required that month.

"After that," Philosopher Horse concluded, "I understood."

He had finished.

He held a fist in the air and cried out, "Defend the People!"

He cried out that phrase once only, bowed quickly and left the stage.

Some mouthed the words in silence. Defend the People! No one dared to shout them aloud. Transfixed by recognition, the audience burst into roaring applause.

2

The concert petered out and Clarence marched to his motor-bike. He got a nice shot of the kid with his fist raised. "Something is happening here, and you don't know what it is, do you, Mr.—" he howled to himself as he rode south through the night. The New Age Bar would still be open via the back door and he would tank up.

"Black Chinaman?" quipped Young Bi, who looked consumptive. Bad types had taken over the bar. The glamorous people, except for Clarence, had stopped coming, and without them Bi's dreams took a battering. The hours of work were long, conditions were poor, and his practiced servility was wasted on ruffians. Bi was solicitous, without knowing the wound in the Englishman's heart.

One night Clarence had brought the Han dynasty pot that Autumn dug up. He showed it to Foreign Trader. Foreign Trader asked to take the piece away for expert examination and, to prove his honorable intentions, offered to take Clarence along too, but Clarence accepted the man's honesty. Foreign Trader was rich enough from his fake Tang horses not to be a blatant thief. Clarence was not in the smuggling business himself but hoped that Foreign Trader could dispose of the pot through his Hong Kong network and return the proceeds to Autumn.

Foreign Trader was in the bar with his friend Party Greenhorn. They were laughing over Irish coffees, and Clarence thought it best to wait. In the end Foreign Trader came over, offered a cigarette, and announced his price for the pot. It was not low enough for the piece to be a fake, and therefore was too low. Foreign Trader asked Clarence how much he would accept. "Much more," said Clarence, upping the amount ten times. Foreign Trader laughed. Clarence said he was reluctant to sell. "Okay," said Foreign Trader, compromising, "don't sell." The pot was worth the price Clarence had named, more, but there were difficulties. Foreign Trader sauntered to his seat and returned with the pot carefully wrapped in old towels, as Clarence had presented it. The failed transaction was somewhat graceless. To gain face Foreign Trader asked Clarence if he was interested in conveying some substances to Hong Kong . . . Clarence gave a blunt refusal, and Foreign

231

Trader lumbered back to his cold Irish coffee where his friend Party Greenhorn quizzed him.

Clarence ordered another drink. He had not sold the pot for the available offer because Autumn was not around to profit. For some weeks he had not seen or heard from him; he was worried and had no one in whom to confide. A bilious hacking cough was his body's response to the Chinese vodka in the cocktail. He shouldn't drink it; he'd be wrecked again in the morning, but what matter? His health was wretched. He had ignored the Doctor's advice. He could not bring himself to go to Hong Kong.

He roved over every grim possibility for Autumn—sickness, detention, worse—and kicked himself for every time he and Autumn had let down their guard of discretion. The boy had vanished without trace.

Clarence had gone looking at the No. 3 Vehicle Plant. He had gone during daylight hours and inquired of the management, which drew suspicion, and he went again at night to ask the workmen dossing down in the dorms if they knew anything. Then he remembered Autumn's sister, who lived south of the city. He knew that Autumn had occasionally visited his sister's house where, if not exactly welcome, he was at least taken in. Clarence remembered the name of the bus stop and the sister's work unit. He knew the visit would implicate more people, but he had no other lead.

It took him the better part of a day's questioning in workshop after workshop to find people from the Shandong countryside where Autumn's family originated. Clarence felt sure there would be some kind of local network. People were curious enough; they crossed the road to hear him put his questions, and they paid him back in questions tenfold. But no information came out. He grew angry and suspected concealment. Yet they told the truth. For all their love of gossip, their scope was narrow. They had learned that the people in the next lane, the family across the street, those girls from out of town, that foreigner with his fluent mangling of the language—those things were safest ignored. "I seldom go out the door," was the common reply. They meant it. Clarence could only repeat his questions until the odds brought him up against someone who might know.

Word had got round and suddenly a woman came running up to him. Suspecting that the foreigner might be connected with her, she came alone. She was Autumn's sister, and she ushered Clarence furtively to her house.

She poured tea and was hospitable. Neither side was patient, yet neither asked outright. The sister tried unsubtly to investigate the nature of Clarence's relationship with her brother, and Clarence, not knowing what the sister had been told, was wary. Foreigners brought unlimited possibilities for boon and bane and, since sister had never been so close to one before, she was confused, as Clarence explained that he wished to find her brother.

She volunteered the information that Autumn was not there. She did not know when he would be back. He had not been there yesterday either. Or the day before. At last the woman admitted that she had not seen her brother for nearly two months. She had not worried, thinking him to be at work. They had no fixed arrangement, he was under no obligation to visit, yet—she had thought it a little strange and started to worry. Autumn had mentioned once that he had a foreign friend. She imagined, perhaps, that Autumn had left the country with the foreign friend. Or perhaps the foreign friend had brought trouble upon his head.

Clarence grew pale at the sister's news. He said quietly that he had not seen Autumn himself for two months. She sat down and bowed her head. Her round, weathered face turned red and she started to cry, imperceptibly at first, then in heaves. Clarence didn't know what to do. She called out piteously that perhaps he had gone home to the mountains. When Clarence laid a hand on hers to comfort her, she pulled away convulsively. His own tears had dried up.

Then she stood and paced the room violently. "Maybe it's you who's brought him trouble. Certainly it's you foreigner who's brought him trouble."

"Possibly," said Clarence, chastened by what he recognized as a real possibility, insensitive to the woman's emotional fit.

She screamed. "Where is my brother? What have you done to my brother? How could it happen? What am I going to do, my mother, my father?" She was rooted to the spot, cursing and shrieking. "You—go! Go! Never come back."

Clarence pushed out through the door, the neighbors, threw his pale head in the air and strode across the puddles in the muddy alley. He was afraid not of the woman but of the scenarios—her fears were hysterical and unfounded, yet she knew her society, she recognized the disruption of the normal: Clarence's fears were specific. If there had been some kind of suspicion? If Autumn had been called in? A final twist of the knife was the likelihood that he would never know anything. Vanish! Non-being! Puff! The gritty wind in his eyes as he rode the motorbike gave him an excuse to scream and bleed.

3

At boiling point Jumbo approached Dulcia's apartment in the Friendship Hotel. He had not been stopped at the gate, but the fat little spy at the bottom of her stairway called to him, "Where are you from?" (meaning: what is your official status?).

As Jumbo had passed the man almost nightly for the last six months, he merely grunted in reply.

"Hey," the spy yelled, "which unit do you belong to? Where are you going? What's your relationship with that person?"

Jumbo shouted in a blather, "I belong nowhere. I come from nowhere. I am going nowhere. I am no one." Then he turned and skipped up the stairs.

The spy decided to leave it for the present, and made notes in his file.

Dulcia was in a flap. Her cat was off color. She couldn't get her aerobics routine to work. She'd poured herself a drink and, when Jumbo came in, she glided into his arms and led him a dance.

But he was a heavy weight.

"What's up?"

He had come from the Public Security Bureau, Passport Section. On previous visits he had been fobbed off. He'd been told to wait. This time he went early in the morning and waited all day. Each time he demanded to see a higher official. At last he reached the wall, an official who told him point blank that his application for a passport to America had been refused and the decision was final. Jumbo stayed his ground. He knew that if he did not demand an explanation for the decision he could never again apply for a passport. It was essential to find out the reason. He was told to wait, for hours, and at last he was brought to the office of the highest official of those who manned the barricades to protect the entirely inaccessible, real decision-makers. The rosy-cheeked young man, a football fan who accepted a foreign cigarette from Jumbo, put it clearly. Jumbo had been placed in the Fifth Category, consisting of those people who might bring the motherland into disrepute if they were allowed out. It was a category reserved for counter-revolutionaries, doubters—and especially young artists whose work was insufficiently "patriotic." The ruling could not be overturned. Never. There was no point reapplying. He would never be given a passport. Smoking Jumbo's cigarette in the most appreciative fashion, the young Public Security officer said in a spirit of friendly advice that Jumbo should have thought more carefully beforehand.

When Dulcia heard the news, she started to shout. She ranted. She hurled cushions at the sick cat and laughed weirdly. She could not register the fact; she had no training for a reality that failed to square with her wishes. From Jumbo's contained anger, his determination to maintain good-humored decent behavior in the face of evil fate, she recognized that for him this was the bedrock. They were utterly powerless. Nothing could be done.

They did not make love as they had most other days. The whole contour of Jumbo's relationship with Dulcia was changed by this fact. Not that he had been using her, but he had been swimming with her in a current that flowed towards a future; and even their complicated lovemaking was a training in that direction. For Dulcia their relationship was a thing of romance and salvation; in some future world it might dive into tragedy, but that would be their own doing, an expression of the logic of two individual personalities. It would never be imposed by the State.

"Why? Why? Why?" she shouted. "Just because they don't understand your paintings? Just because you have a foreign lover?"

"There's more," he said. "I never told you. I couldn't. Now what does it matter? They came to me, months ago, after we first started seeing each other."

"They?"

"They. They knew about you. Your friends—the journalists—the diplomats. They wanted information. What you did. What you thought. Who you knew."

"What were they trying to find out?"

"They just want to understand."

"There's nothing to understand."

"That makes them suspicious. I told them I had no infor-

236

mation to give. They were unhappy. Then they contacted my mother in Xian. She's an old woman, a simple woman who cares about my father and my sister and doesn't think outside the family. Once she was different, but her experiences taught her to be simple, unthinking. They came to her and told her that her son must help them, help China, for the good of the family. How could she refuse? She begged me. I could not say no. So I went to them. I gave some information. Very little. I reported some conversations. About art and culture. Nothing important. Nothing they would even understand. They were unhappy with me. They could make no sense of my information. They accused me of lying and concealing. Of course I did conceal, but they could not have understood anyway. They were unhappy with me. They finished with me. That was when Central TV decided they could not sponsor my study in the States. If I went, I would have to pay for myself. That was their doing. And now this is their final revenge. The Fifth Category. There is no way out."

Dulcia beat him on the chest. "Why didn't you tell me before?" She felt betrayed.

"I wanted less trouble. I thought I could handle it."

"No one can do that." She moaned, "Oh Jumbo. The bastards! The blackmailing rats! Your poor mother! All because of me, because I was nobody and they'd blown their cover for the sake of nothing. What can we do?"

"Nothing."

"That's impossible. Are you safe?"

"While you're still here."

"I'll stay, I'll stay," she declared. But she knew she had not enough love for Jumbo in her heart to stay in China with him for the rest of her life. Not enough love, not enough constancy. Right now, however, she had passion. She looked at him and said: "I'm not gonna take this lying down. You've heard of pulling strings? Well, I'm gonna yank the fucking ropes!"

"There's no way," said Jumbo with quiet firmness, and he picked up the wine glass and bowed his nose to it like a child.

4

Celery and shallots spilled out on the table. Wally chopped while Jin Juan kneaded the dough, laughing at his clumsiness. She had come to him as soon as she returned to Peking. She knew the place, she reminded him, from her visit as Azalea.

"Now why did you do that?" he asked.

"Did you enjoy it?"

He shrugged. "Certainly."

"It was no more than a practical joke. I suppose I was testing you, and protecting myself."

"It could have backfired."

"It almost did." She laughed again, not revealing her true motive, that had to do with Zhang. Coming to the foreigner had been a trial by ordeal. How could he understand her coldly irrational behavior? She had been abandoned and had forced herself to act the whore. She had also come for revenge.

It was chilly outside and the plain warm flat offered Wally and Jin Juan the luxury of a private, peaceful space. She rolled the dumplings with nimble fingers, pinching them tight, and made him copy. But his fell open in the boiling water. The dumplings steamed in a large dish between them, and they had a saucer each of vinegar and a glass of cognac to sip. They played question and answer about China, Wally's sense of the positive things encircling Jin Juan's negatives as in a game of Go. Wally had already made backdoor inquiries about her possible job transfer to the Medical College.

Those days were happy. Her alliance with the Doctor was noted by the College authorities and protected her. He was drawing her into the circle of privilege. She could come and go as she pleased, and, although she wasn't indiscreet, she stayed with him when he wanted her. He had arrived somewhere at the end of his haphazard quest, and threw himself into work with his colleagues, his satisfaction made headier by the approach of departure. What he had arrived at was Jin Juan, the feel of her intelligence, her body, her attentiveness, her Sui dynasty aloofness, head arched away. He saw a future.

They were replete with dumplings. The curtains were drawn and dusk closing in. As they sprawled disheveled on the bed he began talking, as he had several times, of the practical problems of taking her to Australia with him. He wanted to plan the strategy move by move. Implicit in the plan was his proposal of marriage, the firmness of which Jin Juan recognized. The future for him was now a logical line. For her such a line, like the ruler at school, spoke of coercion, a willed dream. But not interrupting, she curled against him like a cat, her face golden in the dim light, her sharp chin tilted upwards, her curving eyes glittering.

She had tested him and he had proved steadfast, to her and her grandfather. And there was their joy together. Director Kang, to safeguard himself against discovery, had for years now kept her out of the Medical College. Kang feared Hsu Chien Lung's granddaughter. Knowing her involvement with young Zhang, Kang could also do his part to prevent her alliance with so powerful a family by keeping her out of a respectable job. Kang knew from discussions with Zhang's father, his patient, that the family would look down on a middle-school teacher with no connections. So Kang's motives had been several in blocking Jin Juan's way; and in a similar way, Jin Juan recognized, her motives in coming to the foreigner were mixed.

On this winter's day she left Wally before the gates closed, took the bus, and walked the last stretch of slippery track that led to her dormitory. The duck's-down hood was tight around her glowing cheeks. A car was parked outside. Zhang was waiting for her.

"When did you get back? You haven't been in touch." He tried to look concerned, but his irritation showed.

"Come in," she said energetically. "I've been busy since I came back. There is some business to do with my grandfather."

"Is that all?" He examined her suspiciously.

"I'm planning to change my job to become an interpreter at the Medical College."

"You don't look much different. There are no problems, I trust."

She weighed him up in return as they went into the dormitory. As he had grown older and more successful, he had become more bound, an agent of Party attitudes, or feudal attitudes. His self-interest no longer chafed against orthodoxy. What was right, what maintained the system of power, was right for him. So he had come to her like an investigator.

"I hear you've been hanging round with the foreigner. What's that all about?"

"Does it matter?"

Her color rose, not from shame but anger.

"What's your relationship with him?"

"Actually I think he wants to marry me."

Zhang snorted. "They're always looking for our women."

"He's quite serious."

"Well, maybe it's a good opportunity, but you couldn't come at that, could you?" He was so cool Jin Juan could have scratched him. He took her hand. "Even if there wasn't our situation. Are you all right? How's the little problem?"

She pulled her hand away. "It's never been your problem."

Across his smooth, smug face passed a quiver of perplexity.

"I got rid of it," she said.

"What!"

"It might not have been your problem," she repeated.

At once he saw her meaning, in a grotesque vision of violation, alien blood mixing with his seed in a witch's crucible, producing a monster. He slapped her viciously and she fell back on the bed, covering her head. "Go!" she ordered.

He stood, legs apart, and put his nose in the air. "I don't want your stinking cunt. Marry the foreigner, get your passport and leave."

She sat straight up. Her head was aching and her cheeks smarted. She rose to her feet, shaking as she faced him, and said, "I don't have to listen to you any more."

5

Wally got a polite pressing invitation from Mother Lin explaining what had happened and urging him to visit. He had not seen Eagle since the summer and was embarrassed that his own affairs had come to preoccupy him so entirely. Eagle was one of the brightest, most uncomplicated people he had met in China. Wally was distressed to hear that things were as bad as the letter suggested. He had not known of the injury. As soon as he was free, he jumped on his bike and rode the short distance to the house near the station. As on previous visits Mother Lin spied him first from the tiny kitchen.

"He's come! He's come!"

She led the Doctor inside. There was Eagle, who blinked and grinned in surprise. He was lying on his side under a quilt on the platform bed, in a crimson sporting shirt. But he had not been exercising. He was thin and sallow, his eyes sunken, his hair flat and lusterless. When he smiled to the visitor, he gave off that air of panicky impatient exhaustion that comes with sickness.

Mother Lin was babbling about her son's condition.

"You tell me yourself," said Wally to the boy. "What's the matter?"

"I can't walk." He was apologetic. "I had an accident playing basketball. The doctor said I should rest and it would heal. Now I can't walk at all."

"Let's have a look."

Eagle wore several layers of loose pajamas under the quilt. The pajamas were damp with perspiration and the bedclothes were smelly. He had lain there many weeks.

The leg in question was swollen around the knee. It was years since Wally had carried out such a physical examination. Eagle winced when the Doctor pressed the knee, and couldn't oblige when he was asked to move it. The leg was unable to bend.

When Wally made him stand, Eagle's face screwed up in pain. He managed to laugh as he hopped about the room on his good leg. But the difficulty was too great when he tried to walk normally.

Mother Lin produced her usual excessive meal, fussing over Wally while Eagle picked without interest. He was thoroughly deflated. The Doctor's visit had lifted his spirits a little but for stretches he reverted to those hollow inward starings. He felt victimized. He had fought his difficulties courageously, taking an active, determined role, using self-discipline and a disgust for self-pity as means to his ends. He had regained his place on the team. He had re-established his understanding with Pearl, on track again in the task of getting a decent flat for his old and ailing mother. And now the misfortune of his injury was compounded by its incurability. He had rested, he had eaten the good food his mother slaved to prepare, he had taken the expensive medicines his brother had bought. But the situation was hopeless. The Sports Institute denied him its superior medical attention. Pearl had taken the accident as a well-timed omen. And now Eagle's strength was draining out of him. More than once he had discussed with his mother the idea of calling the Doctor, but he had always dismissed it as something not right, as if he should bear his fate alone. It was his mother who acted, since her duty was to use any connection that might help her beloved son. Wally was thankful she had done so. He would help if it lay in his power.

"You'll have to go to hospital," he concluded, "for further examination. My guess is that the knee will have to be opened up. A tricky business."

Mother Lin panted, her hand on her heart. The obstacles that lay in the way were beyond explaining to the foreigner. Eagle reverted to his dull stare.

"The doctors say I should rest here," said Eagle flatly. "They say I do not need further treatment."

"Rubbish."

"I'm not eligible."

Wally saw what his part was to be. The operation—the reshaping of the knee, the resetting of the bones, the process of cartilage healing—was long, complicated and expensive. In China medical treatment of a high quality was in short supply. Access was a privilege. The underpaid medical profession was compensated, to an extent, by its power over the distribution of the privilege. He had been in China long enough now to have a crude understanding of how the system worked. He had his trump card. Immediately an appointment should be made with Mrs. Gu, and through her a meeting requested with Director Kang.

He rubbed Eagle's shoulder warmly and shook Mother Lin's hands, giving his word that he would return.

So it was that two days later a car sent from the College arrived at the entrance to the narrow *hutong* and Eagle was laid carefully on the back seat.

Mrs. Gu, recognizing the Doctor's determination, had wasted no time in setting up a meeting with Director Kang. Wally had so far kept his discoveries secret from the College, though he assumed that Song knew, and that through her some information would leak out, which would not hinder his purpose. He need do no more than allude subtly to his bargaining point.

The meeting with Kang was amiably circuitous, the easy manner helped by the Director's muting of his habitual excessive humor. There were compliments, inquiries after health, regrets that they had not seen more of each other, expressions of unavoidable commitments and healthy reports from both sides on the state of research, and a profession of sadness from the Director, polishing his brow, that the Professor Doctor must soon be leaving their College. Director Kang insisted that if the Professor Doctor, a man of such wide experience, had any suggestions for improvements in the running of the College, then he must be frank. And if there was anything, anything, that the Director could do to assist . . .

The offer appeared to play too close to Wally's ulterior motives, so he substituted a lesser request.

"As a matter of fact—" and went on to explain how in his opinion the College suffered not from any deficiency in medical expertise but from being a little under par linguistically. To put it bluntly, there was no one with adequate capacities as technical translator and interpreter. The matter was essential if the College was to keep abreast of outside research and if its own attainments were to be truly recognized by the medical fraternity at large. In short, the authorities should appoint a person with sufficient English-language ability and if possible a medical background, preferably someone young and energetic, with a commitment to the work of the College. This should not be regarded as a low priority, but of prime importance, and the College should endeavor to find someone of high ability by offering suitable enticements.

That was Wally's bid.

Not understanding what he was getting at, the Director nodded with a practiced combination of general approval and specific disengagement. It was possible, after all, that the foreigner was making a disinterested suggestion that could safely be ignored, sensible idea though it was.

Talk of translation allowed Wally to introduce the topic of rewarding medical reading, how enormously he had profited from studying Kang's papers—congratulations—and how even those in Chinese had been illuminating once a translation was made by a linguist friend who happened to be researching at the Traditional Medicine Academy—and by a further happy chance the archives of the Academy had proved to house fascinating unpublished papers by the same Professor Hsu Chien Lung whom Wally had been seeking.

"As a matter of fact," said Wally, "I finally did track down the old Professor over the summer."

"You visited him?" Kang laughed. "Ho-ho-ho! I didn't know."

"He sends his regards. Anyway—" and with an abrupt change of subject, so the connection would be clear, Wally made his higher bid. He wanted a room for Eagle in the best part of the hospital, where the high cadres go, and he wanted the best orthopedic surgeon in Peking in attendance as soon as possible.

It was perhaps a more difficult request than Wally realized, and Kang became more thoughtful as Wally described Eagle as "his friend"—who proved to be an unemployed worker with no status at all, a person the Doctor should never have known. But it was too late now.

"I vouch entirely for the genuineness of the person and the case," said Wally, "and I will regard your help as a personal favor to me."

Kang looked unhappy as he promised to make inquiries immediately.

"I hope you'll be successful, and quickly," concluded Wally, who made as if to stand, then sat again for his last statement.

"By the way, I learned less from old Professor Hsu than I had hoped. He's quite lucid. But when I leave China and write up the results of my medical experience here, I suppose I won't have anything to say on that score—a pity—since all over the world, at every conference, people are asking about what goes on in Chinese medicine. Anyhow, I mustn't keep you. You've got phone calls to make. Let's get together again soon. Oh, will you let me know through Mrs. Gu as soon as possible—about my friend?"

6

In the autumn of the year a disparate chorus of voices was raised for democracy. The workers were complaining about price rises. The reforms had loosened a few screws in the economy and income had not kept up with inflation, nor spending money with rising expectations. In Shanghai a chemicals factory burned to the ground while the workers passively watched. They recognized the new face of exploitation. Middlemen grumbled that the Reforms were not moving fast enough and that bureaucratism strangled opportunity. Each day China seemed to slip further from its grandiose goals. But hope persisted. Let a hundred flowers bloom! Let a hundred schools of thought contend! appealed the Party, enticing people to speak their blueprints for the future. Blinking like tortoises, they stuck their necks out.

In an environment of optimism the students nurtured hopes as dazzling as the grand propaganda dreams of their parents' generation. They grew their hair and pirated videos of "We Are The World, We Are The Children." They experimented with new notions of romance, sexuality, psychoanalysis, existentialism and democracy. They planned to get rich by doing Chinese computer programs for IBM. Either they must change their country or it would change them. If the curve of hope continued upwards, they would be the generation to make China open-minded, scientific, modern. They would put the Chinese in space. They had a slogan, "Break out of Asia, advance on the world." And in the autumn of that year, it might almost have been possible.

On Saturday afternoons throughout the city, salons for democracy were held. Items on the agenda included: modern management techniques; cybernetics and systems theory; artistic individualism; an independent press; the separation of Party and government. People talked their heads off.

At one salon Philosopher Horse was invited to speak. Transformed, as his fame had gone before him, he gave a rousing address which had a packed crowd of Peking Teachers College students clapping and chanting. He argued against Marx and for Nietzsche, asserting the power of individual will to recast the world. Nietzsche's texts were a new bible, the other path.

Bizarrely they chanted. "What do we want? Nietzsche! What do we need? Nietzsche!"

At the end of his speech Philosopher Horse produced a thick bundle of mimeographed sheets. He announced that he had formed his own political organization. The document laid down some basic principles. It appealed to the spirit of Wei Jingsheng who was still imprisoned for demanding the Fifth Modernization, Democracy, without which the Four Technological Modernizations could never be achieved. *"Let us try to discover by ourselves what is to be done,"* quoted Philosopher Horse.

The leaflets were eagerly grabbed. And as he left the seat, he called out the name of his invented party:

"Defend the People!"

The phrase raced around the salon.

"Defend the People!"

In early December in Shanghai tens of thousands of students and workers assembled in the People's Square. There had been nothing like it for a decade.

247

7

Clarence joined the Peking press in the rush to Shanghai. In the afternoon, as he was running to catch the taxi, a letter from Autumn arrived at the office.

Dear Clarence,

It is already two months since I left Peking. I have recently passed my twenty-first birthday. According to the regulations it is permissible to volunteer for the army between the ages of eighteen and twenty-one. I have decided to become a soldier. It is a good opportunity. Shoveling coal at the Vehicle Plant is too hard and the pay is too little. The army will give me the opportunity to study and to see other places. I am also happy to help the motherland. The fitness training is already over. Soon we move, and I will learn to use a typewriter and to drive a car. It's real fun.

After I left Peking I needed to return to my village to get approval to enlist. I had a health check, then joined the army in the county town. I had no opportunity to return to Peking to farewell you. Excuse me.

We two have different nations, different languages, different backgrounds. Our friendship has left a deep impression on me. You have treated me with respect and kindness. There is genuine love between us and I miss you ardently. But I do not think you can take me with you to your country. It is an impossible dream. We two must travel our separate roads. For this reason I have decided to join the army. In the barracks I dream of you. I imagine you by my side. In the future perhaps we will meet again.

I hope your health is good. I hope your life goes smoothly. I wish all things may go as your heart desires.

Your friend,

Autumn

The press corps clubbed together in the Peace Hotel, but Clarence deserted for a back alley place where a chuckling old lady was glad to pour Scotch into him. He saw Autumn's skull shaved of its permed curls, a brown belt several times encircling his slender waist, khaki billowing, his pocked complexion growing pasty on mess food. Television paraded the legless and blind veterans, of twenty and twenty-one, who came back from the nasty border war with Vietnam. What of the others? All China's borders were in conflict. There was a saying that military boots required iron nails. But the boy was right. Clarence's fantasy of taking him to London in his suitcase, lugging it from the cab, opening it on the porch of his mother's Nash terrace, would never have eventuated. The Englishman's stomach twisted. Fuck! The boy was gone. Nothing ever lasted. It was better to feel nothing. But he would be taunted by the memory. The boy at least—the letter said nothing to the contrary—was alive, and well out of it. Clarence stumbled from the bar, took a wrong turn in the alley, spat and blindly wended forward. The air was opaque with a putrid mist, not exactly rain, that descended slowly from the obscured sky. Shanghai was sodden with water seeping up from the spongy ground and subterranean net of canals into which the city was said to be sinking, like Venice. Clarence wandered towards Suzhou Creek for the hell of it, the moored barges reminding him of patients in a stinking ward. As he crossed the humped bridge he sang in a throaty theatrical imitation of Marlene Dietrich, *Johnny's gone for a soldier, Johnny's gone for a soldier*. He could only remember one line. A bundle in the gutter reared its head.

He made a wrong turning, revolved, retreated, and found

flagstones under his feet, with obscure yet familiar inscriptions that demanded attention. Tombstones. Humphrey Stenhouse Waterman, d. 1919. Juliet Jane Keswick, d. 1922. Marcel Hubert Villeneuve, aetat. 27. The road was paved with slabs removed from the foreigners' cemetery. Clarence's feet passed over their memory as if he were a ghost with them. Then he sang his despairing line again. Then he emptied his guts good and proper, and found his way. With sham dignity he disturbed the night porter of his hotel, and took the lift seven flights to his room. Watercolor was rising from the river, juices excreted according to the body rhythms of the monster city of solvents: liquid and money.

The morning began with crowds of demonstrators invading the Mayor's office. They were young, curious and passionate. In the afternoon a car was manhandled, overturned and set ablaze. It was a sign that things were getting out of hand. Mao said it takes only a spark to light a prairie fire. Clarence took the shot that was used worldwide by the Western press.

At midnight, returning to his hotel with his camera, he was prevented from crossing Nanjing Road by a mass of people moving towards the Bund. Like a mighty water dragon, the crowd followed the river front and pressed up against the blockaded portals of the Municipal Building, the headquarters of the city authorities. They carried bread rolls in their hands, hundreds of bread rolls that were hurled at the iron grille.

8

It froze early that year. Against a classic winterscape of broomstick trees, russet pavilions on exposed hills muted by draperies of mist, and the veiny rumpled ice leading to treacherous patches where water was visible beneath a glass membrane, Wally and Jin Juan ventured out onto the ice at the

Summer Palace. Wally, who had not skated since New England, trod cautious as an old fox. His feet shuddered painfully on the high blades. Wistfully he watched Jin Juan describing loops around him, swift as a vixen. He attempted a figure of eight and, hearing the ice crack behind him, just managed to reach the safe, thick part. Then Jin Juan came up behind and pushed him down, and stood there laughing at his long struggle to right himself.

As the year was turning towards Christmas it seemed, for Wally, to be closing in. His thoughts turned homewards—to his querulous son Jerome who had written only one letter. The first snows had come in Peking, and the diplomats were flying to sunnier zones. A hybrid Old Kitchen God-cum-Santa Claus had been set up in the courtyard of the Medical College. Wally could no longer postpone booking his flight home if he was to be on deck in Sydney at the end of an Australian summer.

"Dad," Jerome had clipped, in a cockatoo monotone, when Wally put the call through. Dad or dead? "Geez, we've deleted your file. You're coming back? Good stuff. How is it? Going along. Country's joined the Third World. No change. Jasmine's crook at me. Things are pretty stagnant. Great news! Send us your details and we'll see you in the VIP lounge."

Wally had said nothing about Jin Juan. How could he?

After skating they walked arm in arm around the frozen lake. A decision had to be made. He wanted the woman to know that his offer stood. He was willing to escort her, on his passport, to the so-called free world.

"I am in debt to you," she said. "I owe you. Most women would grab at what you offer, and I have obligation, gratitude, on top of that. But—for me, it's not right. I can't go. What you propose can't be. I have my grandfather. I have—thanks to you—my job. I have, shall we say, unfinished business here. Forgive me, please. I'm not free to follow you."

251

Wally had not expected her answer. He frowned, his eyes prickled in the cold.

"I'm not imposing anything on you," he said.

"That doesn't make it easier. It's a completely free choice such as I'm not used to making. If you imposed the authority of our love—"

"I want you."

"It's not necessary."

Her response to his rational, magnanimous gesture made him realize suddenly how much he feared going back, to emptiness empty-handed. He was grasping at Jin Juan, on her shoulders erecting the scaffolding he had devised, and now the dream was disappearing into mist.

"If you didn't want to go through with this, why did you come that first night?"

"I was never looking for a passport. I was acting like a ghost, perhaps, on a caprice. But you desired me, didn't you, and I came to you, fascinated by the path you were on. You welcomed me, and we traveled together, with our own private story. But that doesn't amount to anything, does it? My life is here. Look, sorry, they're closing the gates."

Despite her resolve, Jin Juan continued to visit him, and together they visited Eagle who was set up in a salubrious ward with his elephantine leg swinging from a contraption above his bed. He scowled, cracked gags, was patient. He was putting on weight. All the hospital staff knew he was the foreigner's friend. Sometimes, when Wally was working, Jin Juan sat with Eagle and bantered in Peking slang. Because Wally had taken responsibility for his relationship with Eagle, elder brother to younger brother, Jin Juan could take him seriously as she could never have done otherwise, since their backgrounds were different. They came to know and respect each other, sharing their complex stories. Each day Eagle offered Jin Juan one of the delicious treats his mother had made him.

CHAPTER TWELVE
Thorough Democracy

1

Big feathers of snow fell all night and continued in the muffled daylight, piling on black branches and rooftops and reducing traffic to a crawl. Wally started early, arguing and haggling for a taxi. The drivers were either staying home or out to make a killing. At last he commandeered a minibus that snailed to the journalists' compound where Clarence was waiting and on to Peking Station where hordes of quarrelsome travelers were fearing havoc from the snow. Under falling snow all rugged-up bodies looked the same, until Clarence's photographer's eye caught a woman swigging wildly from a bottle. It was Dulcia. With hoots and hugs Wally and Clarence joined her huddle, passing the cognac as they shuffled in the snow in greatcoats and walking boots. When Wally had last seen Dulcia, some weeks earlier, she was a jumpy, chain-smoking, slush-gray figure who'd had no sleep for days. She had exhausted her power, done everything at her command, pitted all her faith in individualism, and in herself, against the system, and everyone said the cause was hopeless. Through friends from the aerobics session she led at the United States Embassy she had pushed through to a meeting with the person in charge of scientific and educational exchanges. At Happy Hour she had collared the World Bank representative who monitored educational aid funds. She had even wangled five sympathetic minutes with the Ambassador. Then she locked her case into place with an imminent visit by the President of UC Berkeley, to whom she had a line as a friend of his daughter. She used what she had down to the last dime. The President was the key figure in the exchange program. He was the man who could lay his hands on the funds and who understood the technology that the Chinese Academy of Science wanted so badly. The agreements were all but signed, and the President was flying to Peking to be ushered by the Ambassador into high presences in order finally to set his seal on this expensive, strategic act of friendly cooperation. And the Ambassador, being in a mood to make suggestions on the morning of the signing, was prompted to raise a certain matter during his off-the-record banter with the Chinese Minister. The President of the University of California would be particularly gratified if a young Chinese artist could visit his school, and he placed the name as if it were an arrowhead. The game was chancy: fifty-fifty. Too much American interest in one suspect painter could have him sent to a labor camp. But two mornings later a valid passport arrived special delivery for Jumbo at Central TV. "That guy has all the luck," said Dulcia, playing down her own part. She was still laughing as they hopped in the snow in a celebratory hopi dance around the cognac bottle and the stuffed suitcases.

Body to body the masses squeezed through the turnstiles, shoved through the doors, stumbled up the alarming, unfamiliar moving stairways. Burdens of luggage caught, pressed, bashed; sewn sacks, leatherette cases on wheels that came adrift, motors slung from poles, bags, bundles, bedrolls, apples, pears and cartons of cola; old people, businessmen, ba-

254

bies, and others in a range of military and civilian uniforms banged, kicked, spilled forwards into great waiting rooms where giant unruly queues formed against the final barrier. The system that kept Chinese trains more or less on time was cast-iron in its regulation of the never-ending torrent of people. All of China was pressing forward, as if driven by a metaphor, a siren call: progress; the Long March; the Red Guards rampaging during the Cultural Revolution; troops and dissidents on one-way journeys to the border regions, and now the pressure on every crack in the door to the outside world. All of China, and the drive and futility of Chinese history, moved through Peking Station.

Dulcia and Jumbo were settled in a soft compartment. The heavy suitcases of books and scrolls—the Chinese culture he carried outside his skin—were stowed, and Dulcia's backpack. Their friends waited on the platform as they leaned out of the window arm in arm, two heads, differently grinning: Dulcia in triumphant relief, Jumbo with a clown's black grin as he prepared, disbelieving, for the last shunting out. They were taking the train to Canton. They would walk across the border at the Special Economic Zone of Shenzhen. They would see Hong Kong, multi-faceted glass jewel; then they would fly direct to San Francisco. "My Golden Gate," Jumbo repeatedly quipped. Dulcia hoped to share the miraculous experience with her lover. But Jumbo's dreams, and judgments, would be as silent as a child's, as subtle and mean.

Clarence's camera kept clicking. Face after face: which would bear the true expression of flight, emigration, exile? Beyond the platform snow was blizzarding, the obscurity into which the train would burrow. Hot white steam was rising, swirling with cold white snow. The train began to glide, slowly, as smooth as ice. Kisses, hugs, tears, clicks. It was history.

As Clarence and Wally walked down the platform with Jumbo's Chinese mates, who were suddenly glum, wondering what their odds were, Wally said, "He made it by the skin of his teeth. To get off the blacklist and get out. A hundred thousand to one?"

"A million to one," bet Clarence. "Anyway, getting out is no solution to the problem."

"Save yourself," grinned one of the fellow artists in contradiction.

2

Snow fell, and when the sky cleared for a spell the city became magnificent, its blood reds and mortar purples glowing like velvet against the intense white. Yet as the skies cleared, the temperature dropped and the ground froze even harder.

Outside in the snow, as Wally crossed from the administration building to the residential block, the room attendants were pelting each other with snowballs, leaping and landing like ruffled crows. A snowball hit Wally in the back and he whirled like a dervish, grabbed a mitt full of snow, and roared after the boy he knew best, who looked after his room. Usually the room attendant sat sullenly at his post. He was teaching himself English without making much progress. In the blank space left in the textbook for constructing sentences, Wally once saw, he had neatly demonstrated his command of Subject-Verb-Object structure with *I am nobody. I am nothing*.

A few days late for Christmas, Ralph the Rhino paid a call to drink the Doctor's health. His red, peaked beanie made him the closest thing to Santa Claus. Like old comrades, they talked through Wally's time in China, the revelations that had turned into nothing, the nothings that had become revelations. They toasted their minor victory over Director Kang.

Ralph was working through the Chinese part of Hsu's papers that Wally had brought back from Shaoxing. It was a huge job. Wally had read the English sections and hoped that he and Ralph would collaborate back home in putting together a festschrift, for Wally was still chewing over the implications of Hsu's research. He didn't plan to let up. There were materials, ideas and hypotheses to be investigated, and he was the only person in a position to do so. His intellectual energies had been recharged, not by the prospect of answers but by new nagging questions. There was a path to be taken that no one but he could take.

"There's gold there," declared Ralph. "The quest continues." He yawned heartily. "Santa brings you a tidbit of news for Christmas." He had marched through the snow all night, fifteen kilometers from the Old Summer Palace to Tiananmen Square, from midnight to dawn, with thousands of jubilant students who sang and chanted "Freedom! Democracy!" as their cloth-shod feet defied the cold. The mood had been good, the police restrained. But at Tiananmen Square the police had provided buses to ferry the students back to their residences and warned them not to be silly. A second rally was planned.

"We'll meet again," declared Ralph as he pulled on his boots in readiness for the snow. "Under a spreading avocado tree down under, eh? Ho ho ho!" That was his parting shot. "Be on standby, Doc. New Year's Day. Ho ho ho!"

3

The authorities acted swiftly. Ten regulations were brought in to prevent unofficial demonstrations. Certain places were expressly forbidden. Heading the list was Tiananmen Square, the vast space thrown open to the people when the heroic Communists demolished the clutter of the old walled city.

At the turning of the old year, according to the solar calendar, in the small hours of night, the square was flooded with water in the name of hosing away the snow. The water set hard. The square became an ice rink, hard and smooth as stone. No matter how the crowds surged they would never make headway across that stony, glassy ice. Besides, a railing was erected around the perimeter of the square, and along the railing were stationed uniformed members of the Public Security Bureau in numbers almost as great as their plain-clothes counterparts who idled on the strip of road and pavement that surrounded the square. From early morning, however, people began to gather, in straggling groups along the edges and congregating a little at the corners of the square.

The snow was light, drifting in the wind. The day was bitterly cold, and the figures were so wrapped in clothing as not to be easily recognizable. Students could hardly be distinguished from onlookers and tourists, though perhaps the distinction was unimportant because they shared a common, concealed motive. Only the students might be a little more overt than workers who were vulnerable to greater penalties. At the top of the square the great red wall of the Forbidden City was almost luminous. Above the Gate of Heavenly Peace Mao Tse Tung's rejuvenated, rouged portrait beamed down from beneath a crest of snow. Behind the wall the snow-laden, green-gold-tiled pavilions of the Palace lay like moored battleships.

In the square people stood alone. Wally watched, his balaclava pulled down over his brow and his scarf up round his mouth and nose. In his standard-issue greatcoat he could have been anyone. He moved among the crowd, avoiding people. Two joined in conversation would halt as a third came near. The crowd continued to mill slowly around the four sides of the square, round and round, back and forth, as the energy of frustration and expectation grew. The numbers were not large, some thousands excluding the police. Most had sensibly been frightened off by arrests, detentions and ceaseless denunciations from the media, from professors and parents, from friends. The diehards remained, their grievances overflowing, but forbidden to assemble, to speak, to shout, to sing, to hold banners, to step on their square. They paced restlessly. Here and there would be a scuffle. A few kids would link arms and flow forward against the cordon of security, then ebb back as if rebounding from elastic. A knot of voices would grow loud. A lunge, a dash, and a fellow was drawn into concentric circles of police, always just out of eyeshot, and quickly dragged to a van—shouting, mouthing, cheered by the crowd. Doors closed before others could run to see. The arrested ones, officially described as workers, were students. There were foreign press in the crowd. The secret police were thick with videocameras from which there was no point ducking. Two, three hours passed edgily, and no one succeeded in trespassing on the ice.

Wally was an observer, but as he moved among them he was drawn closer into their midst. The crowd was tightening, and their suppressed passion became palpable. Their bravery stirred him, all helpless, naive and hopeless, but at the core fearless and full of hope. He was on their side but, recalling his own neglected revolutionary ardor, feared that power and history were not. Was he ashamed of his skeptical apostasy? His eyes prickled under the woolen overhang of his balaclava. If they were powerless to change things, nothing would ever be changed if the powerless did not try.

Then it happened. Some friends linked arms, others pushed against them, girls held tight to boys, waists, belts, arms were grabbed, and they became, like cells metastasizing, a concentration of force. There was a direction in the crowd that pulled people from all sides of the square. They shoved forward, and the police, who had been waiting for the inevitable moment, followed their strategy to force the crowd back. And then, as if in an act of collective intelligence, the organism turned tail on itself. The unguarded rear became the point of advance and the demonstrators turned away from the ice rink to swarm in apparent retreat along the Avenue of Eternal Peace, and as they did so, no longer straggling and gaggling but racing in a fluid parade, they had their target. They were singing in unison. Banners unfolded to stretch over their heads. Democracy! they shouted. Freedom! Down with the Secret Darkness of Our Society! They were charging towards the headquarters of the Public Security Bureau, spilling out onto the road where limousines slewed sideways and lurching buses stalled while hydra heads of passengers popped out in awe. The little police vans screaming to the fore got snarled in the chaos. For this brief moment, playing cat and mouse with the security forces, the demonstrators were calling the tune, and the mob shouted angrily at the Public Security Bureau that provided the foundation of their society's control through fear. But they knew better than to linger. As the police rushed to the head of this most slippery and dangerous organism, its tail became its head again. The crowd sprinted. Everyone ran together across the slushy ground, oblivious of crackling megaphones or isolated policemen. They were across the barrier. They were inside the forbidden space. They had made their way onto the ice.

Wally ran with them. His walking boots gripped the ice. He was running with arms open to grasp something that he knew must be there because its absence hurt so much. Charging forward to grab at its hem before it vanished, Wally was like all the crowd who had the conviction stronger than any dream that what they demanded was real and necessary and kept from them by a curtain only. He cried tears of rage. He no more wanted an illusion than the students did. As the students rushed across the ice, the alien wintry shade of their protest was transformed into a hot human mass.

Then the forces came from behind in a pincer movement and had them in their net.

People skidded and turned. Wally slipped. Two sets of hands pinioned him from behind and dragged him to his feet.

Squirming, he twisted to face his assailants, two smooth-skinned boy policemen whose grip slackened as soon as they saw his long nose and tear-filled round eyes. It was an internal matter only; it did not concern foreigners. Wally, who had fancied himself a participant, was left with his two long arms free and flailing against thin air.

Lenses chased the police who chased the students. A kid with glasses jumped from the crowd and stood his ground defiantly on a patch of ice, yelling out as his arms circled in an invocation of the breathing power. He was Philosopher Horse, instigator. As he was surrounded, thumped and rough-handled out of sight, Clarence, from the sidelines, got the shot.

4

Wally's friends met in a small privately run restaurant to farewell. The doorway was hung with black matting to keep out the cold; inside it was hot and noisy, and "Wind of My Homeland, Clouds of My Homeland" blared from the tape-recorder. At the next table a slick chap in a Western suit presided over a lavish banquet while a fat waitress from the countryside teetered back and forth with piles of plates.

Eagle proposed a toast—to Wally, his brother.

"We're all mates," replied Wally, "and we'll meet again soon."

They laughed. It was up to Wally to return to their world.

"Ganbei!"

A man at the next table had his back rubbing against Jin Juan's. He turned to excuse himself, checking the group with a sharp grin. "How about it? What's her price?" he whispered to Eagle. His weight pressed against Jin Juan's shoulder.

"Cut it out," said Eagle.

261

Neither old nor young, the man had a pock-marked face and lank receding hair. He had a flat bony chest and his eyes were swimming with drunkenness. Putting his cigarette butt to his lips, he arched his body across the table of dishes to his companion in the Western suit and declared, "That pimp's selling our Chinese women!"

Eagle leapt up and glowered, "Say that again!"

"Be careful of your leg," said Jin Juan, tugging him to sit down.

The insults continued. Why wouldn't the pimp sell his woman to real Chinese men if he was prepared to sell her to the foreigner? Because the Chinese had no U.S. dollars, that was why the pimp had come to like the foreigner's smell.

By now Wally had understood enough to be offended on everyone's behalf and rose to his feet. He was the tallest man in the restaurant and began to tell them off in comical elementary Chinese. The man in the Western suit stood and jeered in the foreigner's face, his own face red with affront and hostility. Through sleazy business in the provinces he had made stacks of money and was vain of his sophisticated ways. To be undermined while throwing his cash around in a cozy restaurant made him explode.

"Throw the foreigner out," he ordered the boss. "We don't want foreigners with our women. We are China. My father was skewered to death trying to keep the little Japanese out of our town. My uncle joined the Red Army to throw off foreign oppression. My grandfather was a Boxer for the Emperor. Am I not a Chinese man? Kill the foreigners!"

He had a babyish, well-fed face and nothing would stop him. People gaped nervously, their sympathies washing back and forth in confusion. A crowd was gathering. Eagle insisted on a fight and Mother Lin hissed at him. David tried to make Song leave. Everyone was laying down the law, and punchy arguments sparked around the room. Wally made fists with his hands as the big mouth continued to rave.

Then the wily boss calmly ushered the waitress forward to the man's table. At its center was a huge fish in a sea of sauce, ancient symbol of fortune and prosperity and the meal's crowning piece of ostentation. The diners had been too full of drink and of themselves to touch it. The waitress picked up the dish and, from a height, overturned it and dropped it onto the table. Steadily she took the other dishes and smashed them down one by one, with whatever food remained, against the upside-down fish plate, until the table was a mess of shards and slops. In the awed silence the boss led the man outside, the crowd mildly making way. When the boss returned the place was tidy again.

"Someone from out of town," he said to Wally. "Please accept my apologies."

"It's nothing," said Wally weightily.

"What an idiot!" people began to murmur, "What a jumped-up fool!" Yet they were obscurely impressed.

"I'm lucky to be alive," said Wally to Jin Juan when they were alone at the end of the night. "That same craziness. You understand that's why I want to give you a way out."

"That's why I'm staying. Do you understand?"

"Because you're Chinese?" At this last moment he could no longer maintain his philosophical acceptance. "No, I don't understand. Is it me you reject, or my culture, my shape—what is it?" He held her and kissed her closed eyes, and she responded soothingly, with tenderness born of affection.

When she was asleep, he lay thinking in the darkness. He would take the plane alone and fly to the other hemisphere. He was always restless and perplexed before long-distance flights, as if part of him had already lifted off. He thought of his dead wife and wondered how her existence in any other world might compare with the life she had led with him. He had come grieving to China, and through all its layers—his searching for a treatment, a past, a lost old man, a lover—had been his quest for Bets, for a body to wear her shadow. What

263

Jin Juan had done was to refuse his offer. She had profited from his kindness only so far as suited her independence and dignity. He felt cold and lonely, and tossed over onto his stomach in a spasm of rage. The woman sleeping beside him did not stir. There were political struggles and human struggles and a compulsive groping for sense. People were running forward with their arms open. But like the supernatural visitor of old legend, Jin Juan was gone. He screwed up his eyes. It was Bets who had gone, and all of China could not take her place. Jin Juan was there, outside his personal equation, and China was there, part of the great world in and for which he must continue to work and strive. And slowly his grief would be turned to loving memory. How he looked forward to landing back on the solid routine of work and science, as the plane pointed for home.

At the airport Director Kang and Mrs. Gu, Jin Juan and Eagle managed a united front. The Doctor promised to return, shook all their hands and passed through the barrier. Later, when the plane was flying, he put the headset on. *You must dance for two instead of one.* The music surprised him. It was no longer ghostly, just a song. He would go on dancing for two, with China's bony arm hooked round his.

Director Kang and Mrs. Gu had use of an official car for the ride back from the airport. With her new position and her new flat at the Medical College, Jin Juan was also entitled to the privilege. She chose, instead, to accompany Eagle in a taxi they would have to pay for. He had to be careful of his leg, deprived of the Doctor's protection. He was no one's responsibility but his own now. Jin Juan helped Eagle into the car, and held his hand on the long ride into town, for miles, approaching the capital down the straight bare avenue of flashing trees.

5

The world's feathers were scarcely ruffled when, two weeks later, in the wake of the demonstrations, a foreign news photographer, Clarence Codrington, was deported at twenty-four hours' notice on a trumped-up charge of "activities incompatible with his status as a journalist." He was found to be in possession of a proscribed cultural relic, a Han dynasty vase. In the wake of the incident a young and over-rich trader in fake Tang horses was investigated for corruption, along with the management of the New Age Bar. Egregious Party Greenhorn was commended for doing his duty in drawing the matter to the authorities' attention and the bar was demolished. The world was also unaware that an impassioned young man called Philosopher Horse, who had been detained without trial until the fun died down, was branded a counter-revolutionary and locked up for fifteen years, along with his democratic dreams. In Tiananmen Square the crowds continued to tramp across the frozen moat, under the red arch and the dead leader's portrait, and video cameras installed by the security forces, to visit the Forbidden City.

Afterword:
The Peking Massacre

After completing the manuscript of *Avenue of Eternal Peace* in 1987, I stayed on in China. As time elapsed, I watched in reality the extraordinary, and finally hideous, development of what had been fictional possibilities when I wrote the book.

The student demonstrations that took place in many cities in late 1986 and early 1987 were suppressed. Party secretary-general Hu Yaobang, a moderate, became the scapegoat and fell from power. A hardline campaign against "bourgeois liberalization" was initiated, but its full excesses were curbed by power-broking among the leadership that resulted in the shaky compromise of late 1987: economic reform would continue, at the expense of political reform and with increased vigilance against liberalizing tendencies. Li Peng became Premier, with Zhao Ziyang as General Secretary.

The uneasy balance was maintained through 1988 against growing economic, political and social confusion, and rampant official corruption. As the government became paralyzed by the challenges it faced, power reverted to the "emperor," Deng Xiaoping and other elders.

Early in 1989 democracy advocate, Fang Lizhi, who had called for an amnesty on political prisoners, was forcibly barred from accepting George Bush's invitation to dinner during the presidential visit. Young dissident Chen Jun was expelled. Martial law was imposed to suppress the independence movement in Tibet.

A day of reckoning was approaching for the regime in the seventieth anniversary of the May 4th Movement for democracy, science and the revitalization of Chinese culture. On May 4, 1989 the state of the nation would be judged, and found wanting, against the ideals that had driven China's long revolution.

Swelled by millions of itinerants from the countryside, the urban population was nervous, depressed, and angry at rising prices. Young people, including students, were generally disillusioned and cynical. On April 15, Hu Yaobang died, allegedly of anger, during a high-level meeting. Hu's funeral on April 22 presented an occasion for huge crowds to fill the square: "The one who should live has died, those who should die are still alive," was their slogan.

Mourning the one uncorrupt minister implied criticism of the government as demonstrations spread. Apparently unconnected rioting and looting in two provincial cities provided a pretext for the *People's Daily* editorial of April 26 that thundered Deng Xiaoping's and the party's line—that a tiny minority of lawless elements was conspiring to bring China to chaos.

In response, on April 27 tens of thousands of students marched jubilantly through the capital, with mass support, breaking peacefully through lines of police, asking "Are we really a tiny minority?" They sought "dialogue" with the leadership and recognition that their concerns were patriotic.

When the authorities ignored their requests, the students, on May 13, began a hunger strike around the Martyrs' Memorial in Tiananmen Square. As the hunger strikers weakened, the citizenry grew outraged at the leaders' callous indifference to the plight of China's bravest children. The slogans sharpened: "Down with Deng Xiaoping!"

As the foreign press flocked to Peking to cover the first Sino-Soviet summit in thirty years, the demonstrators found themselves at the center of the world stage. To prevent him seeing the crowds in the square, the Chinese authorities had to usher Mikhail Gorbachov in through the side door of the Great Hall of the People. Zhao Ziyang, strangely, explained to Gorbachov that all decisions were taken by Deng Xiaoping. Outside, the demonstrators swelled to one and a half million and there were three days of press freedom in China. Inside the party conclave, Zhao argued for dialogue with the students and was voted out.

At dawn on May 19 Zhao came weeping into the square, too late. Troops surrounded the city and, towards midnight, Li Peng and army chief President Yang Shangkun announced that the square would be cleared, by force if necessary. On May 20 martial law was declared in Peking. The people of Peking poured on to the streets and erected barricades across main roads to stop the army entering the city. Nearly half a million heavily armed troops had been brought in from around China. Every effort was made to persuade soldiers who were ignorant of the true situation to go back. On May 21 a million unarmed people maintained an all-night vigil in Tiananmen Square preparing to meet the military's might with confidence that the people's army would not fire on the people.

For several days and nights a war of nerves ensued as the army appeared to advance no further. There were rumors of feuding among political and military leaders, and students and citizens went home to recuperate after their provisional victory. The martial law orders had not been implemented.

Some students advocated continued occupation of the square, their bargaining point and a humiliation to the regime.

But many were prepared to leave. The movement may have been petering out when a thirty-feet high styrofoam and papier mâché statue of the Goddess of Democracy was erected in the square, outfacing the portrait of Chairman Mao across the Avenue of Eternal Peace. On the summery evening of May 30, grandparents, their grandchildren, and tens of thousands of others came out to view the new arrival.

On June 2 the military moved closer to the square, and then seemed to be stopped again. Thousands of troops were reported to be hidden in the Forbidden City and other surrounding buildings.

The final military crackdown came in the small hours of June 4 when armed troops, backed by tanks, entered the square. At the last minute, the students negotiated with the military leaders a safe departure for those caught in the square. But before the students could move completely away, the troops advanced and opened fire on them. Bayonet and club attacks followed. Then the bodies of the dead and dying were crushed to pulp by the tanks. Thousands throughout the city were wounded and slain.

A purge was commenced to eliminate the regime's opponents. House searches, arrests and executions were accompanied by an unremitting propaganda campaign to maintain the "big lie" that, in putting down the "counter-revolutionary plot of a tiny minority" and clearing the square, the heroic troops had not killed one student. Within a few days the blood-stained and mutilated square was resurfaced. On June 25 Zhao Ziyang was officially removed from office.

A corrupt regime that had betrayed the people and the country, and the hopes of young China, had maintained its hold on power by the only means at its disposal—violence and lies.

Author's Note

Perhaps it is impossible to write a book about China. I prefer to think of China as the element in which my work is plunged. Everything in the novel is fictional, but I could not have written it without the many people who helped me make sense of my experience of China. I owe a special debt to my first teachers of Chinese, especially Con Kiriloff and Nancy Lee, who got me hooked. Other friends provided help and advice over the years, including Jocelyn Chey, Sue Dewar and Bruce Doar, Linda Jaivin, Geremie Barme, and Madeleine O'Dea, who was with me in China. I must also acknowledge those many Chinese friends who cannot be mentioned here, especially those to whom the book is dedicated. The book could not have been written without a grant from the Australia-China Council, the Literature Board of the Australia Council and the Australian Department of Foreign Affairs, making possible an extended period of teaching and research in China in 1986–87. Jane Hall, Rosemary Creswell, Bruce Sims and Sarah Brenan helped bring the book to life.

The lines from Lao Tzu are translated by Witter Bynner; from Yang Lian by John Minford; from the *Book of Odes* by Yang Xianyi, Gladys Yang and Hu Shiguang; from Lu Hsun by Simon Leys (Pierre Ryckmans). Clarence's guidebook is *Peking* by Juliet Bredon. The line quoted on p. 157 is from "A Poem for October" by Mang Ke, translated by Susette Cooke and David Goodman; the lines quoted on p. 162 are from "The Old Summer Palace Drunk" by Hei Dachun, translated by myself; the line quoted on pp. 227–28 is from "The Answer" by Bei Dao, translated by Bonnie S. McDougall; the lines quoted on p. 247 are from "The Fifth Modernization: Democracy" by Wei Jingsheng, translated by Simon Leys. The Chinese title of Chapter XII is Qiu Xiaolong's translation of T. S. Eliot's "In my end is my beginning." The passage from *The Castle* by Franz Kafka, translated by Edwin and Willa Muir, is quoted by kind permission of Penguin Books. The seal calligraphy is by Jia Yong.

Official *Hanyu pinyin* is used for the romanization of Chinese words except when an alternative form is already established, such as "Peking," or for names, such as in Retta's diary, that predate 1949.